DEAD OF SPRING

DEAD OF SPRING

o

COLETTE RHODES

A HADES AND PERSEPHONE RETELLING

COVER DESIGN BY: COLETTE
FRONT COVER IMAGE:
© MARIE-LAN NGUYEN / WIKIMEDIA COMMONS
MAP DESIGN:
@CARTOGRAPHYBIRD
ISBN: 978-1-99-117320-1

"Go to heaven
for the climate
and hell for the
company."
Benjamin
Franklin Wade

THE KNOWN LANDS OF
THE UNDERWORLD

CHAPTER 1

SOME YEARS PRIOR

No one was better acquainted with wasted potential than me.

I was King of the Underworld, God of the Dead. Every day, scores of souls entered my realm, most of whom had never reached their full potential. Perhaps because of the interference of more vengeful gods than me, or perhaps due to poverty, or ill-health, or laziness. Whatever the case, very few souls arrived at the Port of Charon having achieved everything they could have achieved. Everything they *wanted* to achieve.

It irritated me.

Watching through the clear waters of Lake Pergusa as Kore—'the Maiden' as she was so infuriatingly known—took her daily walk along its shores, and my irritation ebbed and flowed through me, moving as the waters did. Kore was not living up to her potential. She had never been given the chance. She loved her mother too much, a love that was reciprocated, to break free of the invisible shackles that Demeter had confined her in.

Yet, I could never be truly irritated looking upon Kore, distorted as the view was through the water and distance that separated us. Seeing her face—bronzed, heart-shaped and glowing with life—thawed the ice that lived under my skin, even if just for a moment.

Wasted potential.

I was going to do something about it.

I was going to give her everything she needed to be the bright and brilliant goddess she was meant to be.

What was the point in being king of my own realm otherwise?

Kore tipped her face to the sun, smiling as the rays warmed her, and I swallowed thickly at the vision of *life* she made. I couldn't give her that. I couldn't give Kore sunlight on her skin, or the cool lake breeze whipping at her long chiton.

But I could give her power. A title. A crown.

I could leave my heart to her keeping, and hope she didn't destroy it.

I would make Kore my wife and queen, and demand that my realm and every other worship at her feet.

Lounging upon a sofa, not a stitch of clothing in sight, lay Zeus, the King of the Gods. Fortunately, his lap was covered by a man's head, his curled hair not quite long enough to hide what he was doing underneath. His curls bounced frantically as he moved up and down, pleasuring a relaxed-looking Zeus. I wished to be anywhere else.

This was why I never visited Olympus. Not once since I'd drawn the underworld as my lot to rule.

Well, this was one of the reasons.

There was no spouse, mortal or immortal, less faithful to their partner than Zeus. It was an embarrassment, the number of mortals that entered my realm because Hera had punished them for her husband's transgressions with their lives. I was certain that if I ever visited Olympus again—unlikely—I'd find Hera sitting on his throne, having successfully figured out a way to imprison her philandering husband for good.

Ganymede, I recalled, watching the man's muscular back ripple with each movement. A Trojan prince so beautiful that Zeus had brought him to the heavens to serve as cupbearer.

Among other things, apparently.

"Hades!" Zeus boomed once he finally noticed me, never one to moderate his tone. "What an unexpected surprise to see you out of the underworld."

I raised a questioning eyebrow at Ganymede, who had stiffened slightly at the news of my presence, though he continued his ministrations, regardless. It was impressive in a way, I supposed. I couldn't fault his dedication.

"We should throw a celebration while you're here. I'll send for the others. Except for Hera—she's visiting her sanctuary at Mount Euboea," Zeus said with an unapologetic grin, gesturing at Ganymede's bobbing head.

"How fortunate for you," I replied wryly, appalled at the very concept of a party in my honor. Especially *here*. "There's no need for a celebration, I can't stay. But speaking of wives, that is the reason for my visit."

Zeus' eyes flashed silver, the raw power of the storms he could wield rising within him. "Has my wife been behaving herself? What have you heard?"

Pointing out his hypocrisy was a fruitless endeavor, but if Hera ever managed to successfully overthrow her husband, I wasn't going to do a thing to stop it.

I would never treat my wife with the disrespect that Zeus treated his.

"I'm not here about your wife, Zeus. I'm here about mine."

Zeus roughly pushed Ganymede off his cock with a palm to his face, effectively dismissing him. And that was one of the lovers he *liked*. Ganymede scrambled away without a word, closing the door silently behind him while Zeus lazily sat upright, stretching an arm over the back of his chair and making no attempt to cover his nudity.

"I have been saying for years that you should take a wife."

"You have," I agreed. Hermes mentioned it every time he brought a new soul to the underworld.

"You had no interest," Zeus pointed out, raising an eyebrow, a small smile making his beard twitch.

"No one had interested me."

"Is it a mortal?" Zeus sighed, glancing at the closed door the once mortal Ganymede had gone through. "Not the end of the world if so, but it's more work."

He reached for the goblet on the table, regarding the nectar within as he swirled the cup.

"She's a goddess," I replied curtly, watching his face as he mentally considered which unmarried goddesses hadn't sworn an oath of perpetual virginity. "Kore. Demeter's daughter."

Zeus' eyes lit up in delight. "Ah, Kore! Yes, of course. She's my daughter too, did you know? Not that Demeter lets me spend any time with her. Beautiful, is she not?"

Only my practiced self-control stopped my features from betraying my protective rage. Thank the Fates that Demeter kept Kore away from Olympus and her father. Hera was not known for her sympathy to Zeus' illegitimate progeny. I suspected it was only Demeter's formidable power that had protected Kore thus far.

"But Demeter…" he continued, mostly to himself. "She has been very careful to keep Kore away from the gods. Her palace on Olympus has been empty ever since Kore was born because she won't bring Kore anywhere near us. Both Hermes and Apollo have made Kore offers of marriage, and they were turned down."

They'd proposed to Kore?

Did she love one of them? Both of them? How could I have missed this?

They weren't kings, but I wasn't blind to the fact that they were both Olympians, and had traits I supposed could be considered desirable. Hermes as the messenger god was welcome everywhere—no palace was barred to him, not even mine. For Kore, who'd never left Demeter's court in Henna, that may hold some appeal.

And Apollo… Frankly, I thought even less of him than I thought of Hermes, but perhaps Kore would like a husband who could write her poetry and devote ballads to her beauty.

How could I make her love me more than them? There had to be a way. A method.

"I just can't see Demeter rejoicing at the idea of Kore marrying *you*. No offense meant, of course," Zeus added.

Well, I was offended, so that point was moot.

He stroked his beard, brow furrowed, and my patience grew thin. Kore was the ideal wife for me, anyone could see that. Demeter may not *like* it, but it wasn't Demeter's decision to make.

It wasn't Zeus' either. This meeting had only been a courtesy gesture.

It would be *Kore's* choice to marry me or not.

"I have absolute faith in you to convince her," I told him, unnecessarily boosting his ego. If it got me what I wanted, I was willing to play his game.

For now.

"As you should," Zeus replied, puffing out his chest before deflating slightly again. "But I cannot give you my approval to wed until I'm sure Demeter will accept it. She's protective of her children—especially Kore, for some reason—and powerful enough to make life very difficult for us."

I pressed my lips together, not satisfied with that solution at all. Why should I be forced to wait any longer to accommodate Demeter's feelings? I was one of the three kings of the gods, something Zeus had seemingly forgotten since I never demanded anything. Perhaps that was the problem. Perhaps I'd made myself too scarce all these years, not giving the Olympians enough reminders that I, too, was sufficiently powerful to make life difficult for them.

"Just give it some time," Zeus said evenly, watching me warily. Good. Let him sense my displeasure with his noncommittal response. "Once Demeter is made to see the advantages that marriage will provide for Kore's future, then we'll warm her up to the idea of marriage to *you*. What's the rush, Hades? We have nothing but time, and I'm sure you can find some willing nymph to heat your bed in the meantime. Take one of mine," he offered magnanimously.

"I'll have Kore in my bed or no one," I replied flatly.

Zeus gaped. "*No one* else?"

"I understand that is probably a foreign concept for you."

He shrugged, unoffended. "What is the point of being an all-powerful deity, if not enjoying the perks?"

That didn't *sound* like a question that required an answer, so I said nothing. I had no time to enjoy the perks that came with being an all-powerful deity, I was too busy managing the *responsibilities* that came with being one. Especially in a realm where gods were thin on the ground, unlike up here. Then again, I preferred being busy to whatever it was Zeus did all day.

"Well," Zeus said stiffly, eyes darting around in that way people seemed to do whenever I assumed incorrectly that they hadn't required a response from me. "While I've got you here, I wonder if you could trouble yourself to collect someone for me."

I raised an eyebrow at him. I wasn't in the business of collecting mortals. They died, then Thanatos would fetch them and drag them to the underworld. If they'd lived a particularly lauded life, Hermes would do the honors instead.

I stayed in the underworld where I belonged.

"Or send Thanatos. You know what I mean," Zeus continued, flicking his hand dismissively, not bothering to feign interest in how the underworld functioned. "His name is Sisyphus, son of Aeolus. He's flagrantly insulted both myself and the gods. It cannot be borne."

"What did he do?"

"Well, he frequently violates *xenia*, turning guests away from his palace in order to prove his own ruthlessness, or some other nonsense," Zeus grumbled. I nodded, accepting that would be a legitimate affront to the gods, and to Zeus in particular, who was the patron of hospitality. "And when I took a sweet nymph to lavish her with my affections, that rogue Sisyphus reported her whereabouts to her father."

I chose again to say nothing, because Zeus was looking at me like he expected me to be as outraged as he was by this news, and I couldn't understand why.

It seemed fairly reasonable to me.

Either way, I wasn't about to turn away another soul. The existence of my realm depended on them, and I'd take as many as I could get.

"Fine, I'll send Thanatos to collect Sisyphus, son of Aeolus. As for the other matter, I will give you *some* time, but I won't wait forever."

I'd *been* waiting, and it had felt like forever. Waiting and watching, hoping for some kind of sign that Kore was ready. Ready for marriage, ready to leave her family behind, ready to be the queen she was always meant to be. Ready to no longer be the Maiden.

"No, of course not," Zeus agreed, frowning to himself. It had probably been a while since anyone had troubled him with a task he had to actually expend effort on. I was doing us all a favor, but my patience was finite.

I had gone through the proper channels, done what was expected of me, shown appropriate deference to the King of the Gods. It would do them all well to remember that I was a king in my own right, and I wouldn't wait forever for my queen. Not when she needed me, even if she didn't realize it yet.

CHAPTER 2

I buried myself under my blankets, holding still for a moment and straining my ears to make sure I was truly alone. I was almost *never* truly alone, but Mother had been called away on urgent business to Olympus, and the nymphs who usually crowded me at her request were more relaxed than usual.

I wanted to feel relaxed too.

Confident I had relative privacy, I closed my eyes and let myself sink into the fantasy of my memories. Years ago, when I'd been more rebellious than I was now, Mother had left me in my older sister's charge while she attended a festival held in her honor.

"Come on, Kore. It's fine. I'm supervising you," Despoina urged.

"You're meant to supervise me here at Henna, not... wherever it is we're going. Where are we going?"

"You'll see," Despoina sang, her grip on my hand unyielding as she dragged me through the forest. I hoped Mother was distracted enough with the festival to not be watching us through the trees.

"What's that noise?" I whispered. "It sounds like something is dying."

Despoina snorted, not bothering to keep quiet. "Someone is very much living. Perhaps even making a new life."

She shot me a sly grin, and I blushed golden, probably illuminating the surrounding woods with my embarrassment. I wasn't totally naïve—I'd seen copulating animals before. I understood the mechanics of the act, even if I'd never seen humans or immortals engaged in it.

From the way the nymphs complained about the aches and pains the next day, I wasn't sure I had any interest in learning more about it. In that respect, swearing to a life of eternal virginity didn't seem like such a terrible idea.

Despoina pulled me down behind a fallen tree, still giggling to herself. Probably laughing at whatever look she saw on my face as I took in the scene in front of me.

There were copulating mortals everywhere. Lying out in the grass underneath the stars, entirely lost to pleasure.

The woman closest to us moaned loudly, the sound muffled by the male organ in her mouth while yet another thrust roughly into her womanhood. I could admit that I'd never seen one female with two males when animals copulated.

"Is she... Is that enjoyable?" I asked Despoina. The man thrusting into her had pushed the woman's knees up to her shoulders, exposing her entirely, while the other man was positioned over her head, hands braced on the ground above her as he rhythmically moved his hips, his own head thrown back in ecstasy.

"Oh, yes." Despoina sighed, staring longingly at the woman. Not in a jealous way, I didn't think—I'd caught Despoina giving the nymphs looks that seemed more than friendly in the past.

It was the man thrusting his organ into the moaning woman's mouth that had my attention. He was strong and defined everywhere, with thick arms and trunk-like legs, and the muscles of his backside flexed as he moved in a way I was surprised I found so appealing. A dense, black beard covered the lower half of his face, and I vaguely wondered what it would feel like against my skin...

I pushed the fabric of my heavy, woolen chiton aside and slid a finger into my already wet heat with ease, sighing at the sensation I so rarely got to enjoy. My mind easily conjured up the image of the dark-haired man with the rough beard, and the corded muscles that rippled with each movement he made. I dragged my finger up to my sensitive nerves, circling them as I imagined the man climbing over *my* body. Imagined that beard tickling at the delicate skin of my neck, my breasts.

In my fantasies, he roughly pushed my knees up next to my shoulders, pinning me in place as he took his pleasure. It was my greatest shame—the idea of letting a man use me for his own pleasure. The pleasure that idea gave *me*.

The faceless man in my imagination pinned me to the bed, his manhood filling me in a more satisfying way than my fingers ever could in one thrust, and I circled my nerves roughly, breathing heavily as I found my release, biting down hard on my lower lip to stop myself crying out.

For a moment, there was only pure bliss. My body was languid and relaxed, and a pleasant hum filled my mind. There was no pressure of the future, no walls closing in on me, forcing me to fit into a narrow space where I felt like I didn't belong. There was only satisfaction in its most base form.

But nothing good could last.

The high faded, and in its place I was left with sticky thighs and the lingering shame of how depraved and un-goddess-like my fantasies actually were.

What kind of goddess craved being a vessel for someone *else's* pleasure? It was just a fantasy—even if I was allowed to marry, I'd never trust anyone to be with me like the man in my dreams was. But the fantasy itself still brought me shame.

It was probably a good thing that I so rarely got to indulge in it, since Mother always sent a companion to sleep in my bed to safeguard my virtue from any gods that might try to steal me away in the middle of the night.

"Kore!" Despoina called from the corridor. "Are you in here?"

I shoved my chiton into place and scrambled out from under the covers, stumbling over to the basin of water in the corner to freshen myself up.

"Here," I croaked, clearing my throat so I sounded slightly less guilty. Not that Despoina would judge me, but I didn't need my sister to know I'd been pleasuring myself.

If anything, it would make her feel sorry for me. Kore the Maiden. Kore who Mother won't let get married. Kore the perpetual romantic. Kore who craves a challenge. Kore who's meant to swear an oath of virginity on Olympus and sit at Mother's feet for the rest of eternity.

Poor Kore. It wasn't any less than what I heard the nymphs around the palace whispering most days. They were drawn here, seeking Demeter's protection and influence. Leimoniads from the meadows, oreiades from the mountains, dryads from the forests, oceanids from the water and more all resided at the court of Demeter. Beautiful, vain, and pitying.

If only I loved my family a little less, I'd run away. I'd finally use the gifts I kept suppressed, and grow into a fearsome goddess in my own right. But I couldn't do that to my mother. It would break her heart.

"I brought you wine, since you're hiding in here instead of joining the fun in the grove," she announced as she entered my room, thrusting a goblet into my hand, uncaring as some liquid sloshed over the side. "The nymphs are getting outrageously drunk in Mother's absence, and I *know* something big is happening on Olympus, but they won't say what. It's infuriating."

"You're such a gossip. Mother won't let them tell us anything, especially you. You'll get ideas," I laughed.

Despoina smirked, throwing her dark brown curls over her shoulder and taking a generous swig of her own wine. We couldn't be more different in both looks and temperament. Despoina hadn't inherited any particular gifts except immortality, despite being a daughter of Poseidon. It meant that she was free to do whatever she liked so long as she stuck close to the palace, because Mother was confident no god would ever take an interest in her.

I wasn't so sure that I agreed. Despoina may not have been magically gifted, but she was beautiful and brave. Well, brave or foolish. The line that separated the two was thin.

"I'm not giving up that easily, Kore," Despoina replied, shooting me a triumphant look that absolutely meant trouble. "Something *big* is happening, and we *must* investigate. Why else would Mother refuse to hold court for days? Usually, when she's called to Olympus, she still comes back to Henna regularly to make sure you're not getting any ideas about... well, anything."

Truthfully, I hadn't questioned Mother's absence because I'd been enjoying the reprieve too much. I loved her, but it had been so nice to have fewer eyes on me for just a little while.

"Come on, let's go explore. Mother will return from Olympus later. There's a delegation of priestesses arriving from Priene and she won't ignore them. We have to go *now*," Despoina pressed.

"We really don't," I sighed. I missed the adventures we used to go on when we were younger, but where Despoina had just gotten an exasperated word from Mother, I'd been given long, guilt-inducing lectures that stuck in my head until this day. The adventures stopped being worth it. "Go on your own. Mother won't get angry with you."

Despoina scoffed. "She will, but not as angry as she'll get with you, I grant. I can't go alone, I need you close by if something goes wrong."

I gave her a sharp look over the top of my drink. "There's only one possible reason you could need *me* close by, and it's forbidden. What exactly are you planning on doing?"

"It's only forbidden if Mother finds out, and she'll be too distracted on Olympus to notice," Despoina replied, tipping up the bottom of my goblet so I was forced to drink or let the wine spill all over my chin. I gulped it down as quickly as I could, setting the cup aside and letting her pull me to my feet.

"Even if Mother doesn't find out, I might not know what to do," I protested, following behind Despoina with her hand still clamped firmly on my wrist. "Despoina, you can't rely on my—"

"It'll be fine," she called over her shoulder, stomping through the corridor. There was no way to avoid being seen—the palace was all marble columns with leafy vines weaving between, a tree canopy overhead making up the roof. There were no walls here, no doors, no privacy. It was only fear of Demeter's wrath that kept her rooms semi private, and all of her children's quarters were intentionally accessible, the nymphs encouraged to sleep nearby to watch over us.

I stumbled after Despoina as she dragged me out of the palace, avoiding the grove with the dais and Mother's throne, instead veering right into the undergrowth to the tree that Mother secured her prisoners to. A man was there already, a stream of curse words escaping him as he struggled, his hands bound above his head with vines.

The only males in my mother's court were my younger twin brothers, barely more than infants. I could admit that I stared more than a little when a fully grown *man* was in our presence. He was handsome, I supposed—dark hair peppered with gray, a strong jaw and prominent nose, broad shoulders. He was dripping in lavish jewels, and the expensive blood red cloak that had probably once been magnificent was now dirty and torn. It wasn't often we saw men with this kind of wealth here.

Wealthy men didn't pray to goddesses of grain unless they *had* to. They prayed to gods of war and glory.

"Hello, we're Demeter's daughters," Despoina announced cheerfully. The man perked up, ceasing his struggling.

"Are you here to free me?"

"Oh no. I'm here to kill you."

"Despoina!" I gasped, yanking my hand free of her grip. "Have you lost your mind? You can't kill someone. And I can't bring someone back from the dead."

Could I? A lifetime of suppressing any hint of my gift meant I wasn't exactly sure. Despoina looked over her shoulder at me, throwing me a very non-reassuring wink, before pulling out an adamantine sword forged by Hephaestus himself from a bush where it was most definitely *not* meant to be. That sword had been gifted to Mother and stayed in her rooms at all times. Despoina had planned this entire disaster, and I had no idea how to stop it.

"Despoina!" I shouted, lunging for her, but it was too late. With a clean sweep, she sliced the blade clean across the man's neck. His head fell to the ground with a thump, and my stomach turned in revulsion.

And then he screamed.

His *head*, unattached to his still flailing body, screamed.

"By the Fates, Despoina. What have you done?" I asked, staring down at the disturbing sight in horror.

"Yes! What have you done?!" the *head* asked, eyes swiveling to land on a *fascinated* Despoina.

"So it's true," she murmured, looking far too excited for my comfort. "I'd heard that there was some problem with mortals dying and *look!* He's not dead!"

She tossed the bloody blade aside without a second glance, stooping to pick up the shrieking head by its hair and *handing* it back to the body to hold.

"Despoina, this is an abomination," I whispered. My magic was rising within me instinctually. Every time I'd accidentally slipped and used my gift, it had been when someone I cared about was hurt and I'd wanted to help them. I didn't care at all for this mortal, but I was so revolted and uncomfortable with what I saw that I couldn't *not* do something.

"He's not dead. You can fix him," Despoina encouraged gleefully. "This is amazing, isn't it, Kore? You're always complaining about how boring it is around here," she added with a pointed look, like I was being ungrateful for not rejoicing about the existence of a talking decapitated man.

"Please just heal me," the head sobbed. "I'll do whatever you want."

"If you don't mention this little experiment to Demeter, my sister will reattach your head," Despoina said confidently. "Even if Mother finds out, we punished the prisoner. She'll be grateful," she whispered for my benefit.

"That is a bald-faced lie," I muttered. "Put his head back on his neck."

Despoina moved to follow my instructions, but the man got to it before her, hoisting his own head up and glaring at my sister like he was in any position to defend himself from her if she took another swing of that sword.

My stomach roiled as I placed my hands where the severance had occurred, closing my eyes and trying to ignore the butchered flesh and the blood that was now coating me. I didn't know how it worked, but I focused on life because that's what had always felt natural to me. Life was cyclical, rejuvenating, bright, and new. It was beginnings and potential and hope. I fed all those feelings, all those dreams and aspirations through my gift, my palms burning hotter than they ever had before.

The man gasped in a desperate gulp of air as the skin around his throat knitted itself back together, and I yanked my hands away guiltily, shoving my magic as deep down inside of me as it could go, pretending it didn't exist.

"Amazing," Despoina breathed. My heart thudded erratically in my chest, my palms tingling with the residual effects of my gift.

"Despoina, that was too much," I whispered, panic making my throat tighten and my words come out strained. "I used too much. Someone is going to notice."

She scoffed, giving me an exasperated eye roll. "Kore, I decapitated that man and he didn't die. I think there are more important things going on right now than you using a little bit of the gift that you *should* be allowed to use whenever you like."

True. That was true. That man had been holding his own head. I looked back at him, finding him hale and whole as he bent forward as much as the binds would allow and retched, his bowels leaking down his legs.

"Okay. Okay. We'll just return to the grove now before Mother gets back, and hopefully no one noticed," I agreed without a shred of certainty in my voice, nodding my head.

"Exactly." Despoina picked up the blade, and I briefly panicked that she was about to cut the man's head off for a second experiment, but instead she threw it back in the bushes where she'd stored it earlier. "Mother wouldn't have gone to Olympus unless The Twelve had convened. All the powerful gods are busy, stop looking so stressed, you're making me feel stressed."

I rolled my eyes, my sister's inability to care about anything except her own entertainment breaking me out of my panic. I didn't blame Despoina for being a little self-centered though—the moment it had become clear that I'd inherited gifts from my parents, her life had revolved around watching over me, keeping me safe from any god that might wish to steal me away. Despoina did her best not to take her resentment out on me, and that was all I could ask for.

It was no coincidence that any time I'd slipped up had been in her presence.

Some of the strain between us had eased in recent years, when it became clear that the twins hadn't inherited Mother's gifts either. *I* was the odd one out amongst our siblings, not her, and Despoina found comfort in that, even when she didn't want to admit it out loud. While their lives too often revolved around mine, Mother didn't suffocate them with her concern the way she suffocated me.

It seemed Despoina now realized that she was the lucky sister.

"The blood," she groaned, gesturing at my hands. "Come, let's wash it in the river. Human blood is so… obvious."

I wrinkled my nose at the crimson stain on my skin. The ichor in my veins was a luminous gold, and far thicker than mortal blood. I held my arms away from my body, hoping I didn't get a drop on my dark green chiton.

"Wait! You're just leaving me?!" the man shouted as we made our way to the lake, my favorite place at my mother's palace.

"Remember not to say anything to our mother, or I'll decapitate you again!" Despoina called cheerfully over her shoulder.

"He's definitely going to say something," I mumbled, following behind Despoina. She ignored me, too engrossed in the mystery of what we'd just witnessed. If Mother really wanted to keep Despoina out of trouble, she'd give my sister something productive to do with her time.

"So?" Despoina asked as we arrived at the edge of Lake Pergusa and I kneeled forward to sink my arms in to my elbows. The water was delightfully cool, helping to soothe away the last of my jittery nerves. "Why? Why didn't he die?"

I watched the calm surface of the lake, as still as it invariably was. Every day I expected it to ripple, or for some fearsome beast to emerge from its depths. The nymphs and my siblings always told me I had an overactive imagination, but the lake felt somehow *alive* to me.

"Perhaps the underworld is full?" I suggested, wiping my arms. Despoina gave me a scathing look.

"The underworld can't get *full*. That's not how it works. Hades needs new souls to draw his strength from like Mother needs prayers and offerings. He's hardly going to turn them away."

I glanced around, worried we would be overheard talking about things we absolutely shouldn't be discussing. The underworld and the gods who ruled it were to be revered, respected, but ultimately *feared*.

"Okay, so it's not full," I conceded. "Maybe one of the Olympians—"

A ripple of magic ran through the air, and I yanked my hands out of the water, hiding them guiltily behind me as my mother stepped out of a tree at the water's edge, eyeing us both coolly.

"Daughters," Mother greeted us, her voice deceptively calm.

CHAPTER 3

Even Despoina had the good sense to look sheepish.

"I thought you'd be at the grove, waiting for court to begin. The priestesses from Priene are visiting today, had you forgotten?" Mother asked. In many ways, seeing her was like seeing my reflection—the same bronzed skin and wheat-colored hair, the same heart-shaped face and ample curves. Where Mother's eyes were as green as the trees she loved so much, mine were golden, inherited from my father.

"We're just freshening up," Despoina croaked. My stomach churned nervously, the wine I'd drunk earlier suddenly heavy in my gut. "We'll go to the grove now."

Mother nodded, and a small bubble of hope formed that maybe she didn't know. Despoina must have thought the same thing, quickly grabbing my arm and pulling me to my feet. We each sketched a hasty bow, already retreating toward the safety of the palace when Mother spoke again.

"Kore." I froze, knowing whatever was about to come out of her mouth didn't bode well for me. Despoina shot me a quick, guilty look. "I spoke to Artemis before I came. After Hermes' visit, I will take you to Delos to live with her priestesses."

No.

"Mother—"

"The trees told me everything."

"Mother—" Despoina began, but a hard look from Mother silenced her.

"I trusted you with your sister's protection, and you deliberately put her at risk. Had the other gods not been so distracted with this Thanatos issue, they would have almost certainly noticed the amount of energy Kore expended, and then what? Which one would have arrived here the fastest to drag her to their palace? To their bed against her will?"

Despoina swallowed thickly, dropping her gaze to the ground. My heart pounded in my chest, that familiar fear rising in me at the hypothetical danger Mother had drilled into my head from the moment my gifts emerged.

Don't use it. Don't tell anyone. Don't draw attention to yourself.

If they know, they'll come for you.

"Kore will stay at Artemis' temple until she is ready to swear the oath of virginity in front of all the Olympians. Despoina, it's time you find a husband."

"Mother!" Despoina gasped in horror, grabbing my hand for support.

"You're bored, and when you're bored you seek out trouble—"

"The solution for that isn't *marriage*," I snapped, forgetting to be quiet and respectful, too enraged on my sister's behalf and my own. I *wanted* to fall in love and marry someday, and the opportunity was being denied to me. Despoina had never wanted to marry a male, and it was being forced on her.

"Enough," Mother hissed, her face strained. "I am your mother. Your safety is *my* responsibility, and my decisions are final. Despoina, go back to the palace. Hermes is due to visit later to deliver news from Olympus. I'll speak to him about suitable choices of husband for you then."

All my sister's bluster left her in an instant. She sprinted back towards the palace, sobbing the entire way, while I glared at Mother, who couldn't quite suppress the guilt she was feeling.

It wasn't enough to soothe my own rage.

Mother had never married *or* sworn the oath of virginity. And while I knew she'd suffered, she'd still had choices. She'd chosen to fall in love, despite everything she'd been through. Where was my choice? Where was Despoina's choice?

"Kore," Mother sighed, falling into step beside me as I strode through the field of flowers to the palace, wiping hard at the tears of frustration I couldn't quite hold back. "Kore, stop. Sit with me."

She moved to a wooden bench seat with poppies flowering over the arms and back and patted the spot next to her. I wanted to scream at her, to rage and fight and refuse. But I didn't.

I loved my mother, but I knew my place.

With my jaw clenched tight to keep in all the things I wanted to say, I stiffly took my seat. Mother gave me a soft, almost apologetic smile that cooled my ire a little, despite my best intentions to stay angry. When she wasn't furious, Demeter shone brighter than Helios, with a radiance that drew in both mortals and immortals alike. I held myself still as Mother smoothed my hair away from my face, eyes brimming with sympathy.

"I know what I'm asking you to give up, Kore. But you can still have a life filled with joy and excitement after you take the oath. *More* joy and excitement than you experience now, while you haven't declared your intentions and are still at risk."

"They're not my intentions though, Mother. They're yours," I reminded her. She was the one who had given me a name meaning 'the Maiden.' She was the one who'd decided from birth that I would swear an oath of virginity when I came of age, that I'd never marry.

It wasn't a bad path. While I'd never been permitted to meet them, I knew that Hestia, Artemis, and Athena had all chosen it.

But I *hadn't*.

"You're too much of a prize, my Kore," Mother said, thumbs stroking my cheeks. "You're beautiful and good, and even with your gifts suppressed, it's still clear to anyone who meets you that you're strong. That you're the daughter of two Olympians, and could bear powerful children. You'll only attract the worst kind of attention from the most ruthless gods, and they don't make for good husbands, my darling."

"I could marry a lesser god—"

"They won't stand for it," Mother interjected, draping an arm over my shoulders and pulling me close. "The Olympians are already circling you, and there's only so long I can keep them at bay. You know I don't like to speak about what happened to the twins' father..."

Her voice hitched, and I immediately moved to comfort her, wrapping my arms around her waist and resting my head on her shoulder. "You don't have to talk about it, Mother. It's okay."

Iasion had been Mother's one great love, and he'd died before my younger brothers, Ploutos and Philomelos, were born, but that was all I knew of him.

Despoina had been conceived against Mother's will after Poseidon hunted her down. A relentless pursuit by Zeus himself had resulted in my conception, also against my mother's wishes. Sometimes I wondered how she was able to *look* at us, let alone love us.

She never spoke of our fathers.

"Iasion and I met at a wedding," she said dreamily, resting her cheek against the top of my head. "The wedding of Cadmus and Harmonia—it was quite the event. All the immortals were in attendance. My eyes met Iasion's from the other side of the grove and there was this *jolt*, this feeling of rightness in my chest, and I just knew."

I listened carefully, not willing to risk interrupting when I was hearing this story that I wasn't sure she'd ever shared, not even with Ploutos and Philomelos themselves, though they were still too young to really appreciate it. I hadn't been there that night—kept home from the wedding and away from the gods as always, under the sort-of watchful eye of Despoina and the *very* watchful eyes of the nymphs to make sure I didn't slip up and use my magic.

"We watched the ceremony, hovering a few feet apart, exchanging coy smiles and flirtatious looks." I could hear the fondness in her voice as she spoke, and I couldn't help but smile myself, even knowing that this story didn't have a happy ending. "Once everyone was feasting and celebrating, we snuck away, disappeared into a field, and that is when your younger brothers were conceived. It was magical, Kore. The best moment of my life. But there was dirt all over us. It was clear to the rest of the guests what we'd been doing the minute we returned."

Mother went quiet for a moment, and I didn't press. I may not have been at the wedding, but I remembered clearly the state of despair she'd been in when she came home.

"Zeus was angry that Iasion, a mere demigod, dared to touch me, one of The Twelve. Zeus struck him down with a thunderbolt right in the middle of the wedding feast. He died in my arms at the edge of the field as your brothers formed in my womb."

"Mother..." I whispered, tightening my embrace.

"So you see, it doesn't matter whether you find a lowly immortal to marry, one who'll treat you well, or even if you have meaningless dalliances with humans. It will cause offense to those more powerful who believe they *deserve* you, purely because of who you are and the capabilities you have. I've never been more grateful to the Fates as when Despoina manifested no exceptional gifts. I've never been more enraged at them than when you did."

I swallowed thickly, my gift rising to the surface as if it knew we were speaking about it before I shoved it back down again. It never got any easier to deny such a fundamental part of myself, as much as I feared it.

"Take the oath, Kore," Mother murmured, a plea in her voice that she would never let any but her children hear. "Give me the word and we'll travel to Olympus tomorrow for you to stand up in front of the gods and declare that you will never marry, that you are and forever will remain a maiden goddess. Perhaps we can relax some rules once you have made your position clear. Start using your gifts, a little at a time."

She meant well, dangling that temptation in front of me, but that was all it would ever be. Temptation, just out of reach. Little drips of magic, never so much as to draw attention to myself. I wouldn't be *free* of my cage, it would just be made infinitesimally larger.

"I know you're asking me to do this from a place of love and concern, but eternity is a long time to commit to, Mother."

An eternity of a fate I already knew I didn't want. Besides, it wasn't as though the oath would make me immune to lecherous gods or mortals who couldn't take no for an answer. It merely gave me just cause to punish them for it.

Mother sniffled slightly. "It breaks my heart to send you away, Kore, but if you won't swear the oath, then you'll be safer at Artemis' temple. She is the Goddess of Virginity, she will guard yours closely. Terrible things happen to the men who cross Artemis," Mother added with a somewhat bloodthirsty smile.

A shiver ran down my spine. How long would it take me to break down and swear the oath if I was confined in Artemis' temple of chastity? No one visited there. I doubted even Despoina could visit. It would be a true prison—I'd be completely without allies, and trapped there until I conceded to Mother's will.

You're immortal, I reminded myself. *You have nothing but time. You can be stubborn.*

I'd just wait Mother out. Call her bluff. I could do it. Eventually, she'd miss me enough to call me home and agree that it was time for me to look for a husband.

I wanted to fall in love. I wanted to experience desire *with* someone. I wanted to marry and be the center of someone's entire world.

I wanted to *choose* all of those things for myself.

"I suppose we'll see how you like it at the temple," Mother said with another sympathetic smile. It was genuine, but so was the underlying threat in her words. "Come on then. Let's not keep the court waiting."

"Demeter, o Great Mother," the head priestess from Priene said, eyes trained on the steps that led up to where Mother sat on her elaborate throne of vines and branches that had sprouted from the earth. Vibrant red poppies blanketed the entire thing and the surrounding dais, tickling incessantly at my skin from my spot on a cushion at my mother's feet.

This might be the last time I ever have to sit here, I realized glumly. I never thought I'd miss it, but I was confident I would when I was cooped up at the temple.

Mother's leg nudged my arm, and I straightened my spine, forcing myself to pay attention to the delegation of priestesses who had journeyed here to Henna to give offerings and ask for blessings for a barren couple who'd traveled with them. Many made the journey here, appealing to my mother as a goddess of fertility, and while most Olympians would not be so willing to hear the plight of mortals, my mother had never held herself as far above them as other gods did.

"Nikeso. You have traveled so far, and are such a faithful priestess of mine. You are very welcome," Mother said benevolently, earning herself dramatic bows from the priests and admiring coos from the members of the court. They lounged around, dressed much less modestly than I would *ever* be permitted to dress, gossiping and giggling while always keeping one ear out for any information they could use.

"You honor me," Nikeso said, her upper lip trembling, eyes shining with excitement. "We have brought you a swine in offering."

The pig squealed in indignation, and my attention wandered again as Nikeso began talking about the married couple and their struggles to conceive, how devoted they'd always been to Demeter, how they respected the crops they grew and so forth. It was nothing I hadn't heard a million times before, and I knew how it would end. Most of the time, Mother was a kind and generous goddess and wouldn't like to see anyone suffer. She'd bless them all, and they'd leave filled with awe and appreciation for her generosity.

Sometimes, I wondered if that was why Mother struggled so much with me and my sister. We didn't offer her the same blind gratitude as her faithful followers, nor the flagrant disrespect of those who railed against her. We loved her, but didn't always agree with her. We respected her, but didn't truly fear her wrath.

Demeter was a good mother, but she was a better goddess.

The Cretan priestesses started backing away, bowing and effusively thanking my mother, and I winced internally that I'd missed an entire part of their conversation. Mother usually expected praise for her benevolence and would absolutely notice if I wasn't specific enough in my acclaim.

Fortunately, before she could ask, a new mortal appeared, wrapped in vines and struggling in the grip of the bloodthirsty-looking priestesses who were dragging him towards the dais.

Oh no.

"Ah, Erysichthon, son of Tropias." I straightened, the coolness in Mother's voice bringing the entire court to attention. The surrounding priestesses bowed low, yanking their prisoner into a pose of submission with them. "How good to see you with your head attached. You owe my daughter a great debt."

Erysichthon turned his hateful, defiant gaze on me, and my cheeks were so warm that I knew my face was tinged with a golden glow. He knew as well as I did that were it not for my sister, he'd have never been headless in the first place.

"Why do you think you are here, Erysichthon, son of Tropias?" Mother asked, her voice disconcertingly casual, as though she didn't already know the answer. "A King of Thessaly, are you not? I'm sure you have places you'd rather be."

He held his chin up defiantly, surveying his surroundings with all the imperiousness of a monarch, and I watched in fascination. Mortals were just so interesting to me. The hand of the Fates was ever present, their shears closing slowly over a mortal's life thread, but humans lived like they didn't know the end was coming. Or perhaps that they didn't *care*. It was a difficult concept to grasp.

"For the crime of expanding my palace, so that my court had room to move about comfortably."

Fascinating.

I imagined I'd be more circumspect with my words when nearly every poisonous animal or plant I encountered could best me. The man had already been beheaded once today. Maybe his brush with death had made him bolder.

Mother scoffed, unimpressed. "Do you have anything to say in your defense?"

"I stand by my actions," Erysichthon said defiantly, his gaze sliding to me. "And I've been punished enough. The gods have dominion over *everything*. Why could you not spare one tree so I could expand my palace?"

Oh dear. If he'd deliberately harmed any tree sacred to Demeter, then Erysichthon would soon learn the true meaning of regret. I straightened a little on my cushion, paying rapt attention now, as did all the nymphs sitting around the edges of the dais.

"You knowingly attacked a tree in my sacred grove. You were warned, given the chance to stop, and yet you did not. Perhaps you don't respect my authority." My mother tapped her nails lightly on the arm of her throne, letting that statement hang in the air. The nymphs and courtiers leaned in closer, blatantly watching the spectacle unfolding before them. "You seem like the kind of man who saves his prayers for Ares and Zeus, perhaps for Poseidon when your ships need to sail safely. And yet for me? The goddess who keeps you *fed* and alive? Nothing but brazen disrespect."

Erysichthon had lost some of his bluster, shrinking in on himself. Perhaps it had sunk in who he was dealing with, what he'd taken for granted.

Food was a daunting prospect to live without.

"My gifts, my generosity, have sustained you your entire life. Not just you—though you are selfish, and likely do not care—but everyone you love, every person in your kingdom, every servant who keeps your abomination of a palace running. None of those people exist without *my* gift, because you fragile mortals cannot *survive* without food."

A few of the more bloodthirsty nymphs tittered amongst themselves, pointing openly at the beads of sweat that were slowly dripping down Erysichthon's face.

I carefully leaned away from Mother's throne a moment before the vicious thorns that sprouted from the vines when she was angry appeared. The grove around us responded to her rage, the trees contorting, reaching menacingly towards Erysichthon. Not that he noticed when his terrified gaze was so firmly fixed on the goddess before him.

The whole thing made me nauseous—I didn't disagree with Mother's words, but I didn't glory in this mortal's suffering either. I'd never had much of a stomach for punishment. Mortality seemed like punishment enough—it wouldn't be long before Erysichthon would be in the underworld, along with the souls of every other human he'd undoubtedly offended in his life of wickedness.

"You will continue to enjoy my gifts, Erysichthon, son of Tropias. Eat the food of this earth that I gift to mankind, eat and eat and eat some more. Eat as much as you can." Mother flicked her hand dismissively. "But you will never feel satisfied. For the rest of your days in this realm, no matter how much you consume, your hunger, your *starvation*, will be insatiable."

A small ripple of her power shifted the air around us, and then Erysichthon was doubled over, clenching his gut as though he were in agony. His body seemed to shrink before our eyes, his cheeks grew hollow and protruding bones replaced taut muscle.

Were it not for his fine jewels, he'd be unrecognizable.

A pang of sympathy hit me as he stumbled on his feet, a once proud king being pushed around by priestesses half his size, not even bothering with the vines that had held him anymore.

"Remove him," Mother commanded the priestesses. "He is not welcome to share food at my table."

"Of course, goddess," they agreed, bowing as they dragged the groaning man back through the grove to whatever fate awaited him back home in Thessaly, if he even made it that far.

In instances like these, I thought death would be a kindness, but the Olympians didn't willingly give up souls. Here in the upperworld, mortals could still be convinced—perhaps by force—to worship the gods and goddesses and sustain them with their offerings.

Killing them sent them straight to the underworld, where mortal souls sustained those shadowy deities the Olympians preferred not to think about. Or so I'd been told, I'd never met any of them. The best I'd managed was seeing Hermes from a distance once, before Mother had hidden me away in a tree.

I supposed I'd be meeting Artemis soon.

Mother's hands found my hair, softly shifting the pieces that had fallen free of the ribbon it had been secured in—her favored style for me—the gentle touch at odds with the severe edict she'd just given.

"You have a kind heart, Kore," she murmured, her voice quiet enough that only the two of us sitting on the dais could hear. "I can feel the pity for him rolling off you in waves."

"I don't like to see anyone suffer."

Mother sighed, smoothing a hand over my hair. "I know, darling. You're not cut out for a court of your own. That's why I have to protect you. That's why I get so angry when you use your gifts. Sometimes I have to do terrible things to punish those mortals who disrespect me, but at least it's infrequent, and I take no pleasure in it. You wouldn't like to make the decisions that I have to make."

Another weakness. Another flaw that meant I was better off sitting here on this exact cushion for the rest of eternity, having sworn the oath of virginity and accepted my mother's plans for my life.

I was immortal. I didn't need food to sustain me, I needed *life*. Experience. Purpose.

I didn't need food, but my mother was starving me as thoroughly as she'd starved Erysichthon.

CHAPTER 4

I shoved a hand through my hair as I stomped away from the palace, the flames of the River Phlegethon parting just long enough to let me pass through unscathed as I approached Asphodel Meadows to break up yet another fight. Two of the six factions of souls had grown bolder while I'd been busy sorting out Thanatos' mistake, taking advantage of my lack of presence to try and subsume a smaller faction each.

The balance was too tenuous as it was, I couldn't let any of the groups grow stronger. I should have cracked down on them sooner, but as soon as Thanatos had been returned to me by an irate Ares, annoyed that the soldiers in the battles he started weren't dying, there'd been a sudden influx of souls. The souls that *should* have been arriving, but couldn't, because Death himself had been tricked by a mortal into demonstrating how the soul chain worked and found himself bound in Sisyphus' closet for days.

Humiliating.

Mostly for Thanatos, but I supposed he was a reflection of me. What a disaster.

"Hades! Hades is here!" the souls called, not for my benefit, but to warn the squabblers to separate. Perhaps I was too lenient with them—eternity was long, and many of those who joined the factions were relatively new to this life. However, I couldn't afford to be lax with those who'd explicitly taken advantage of my distractedness to make a play for more power. That went beyond a youthful indiscretion.

I sincerely hoped Thanatos wouldn't get in the habit of being tricked into temporary imprisonment. It was a bureaucratic nightmare.

"Bring me Onesimos," I commanded distractedly, standing in the center of the clearing that had formed around me. I didn't need sleep, but I was exhausted. With the rush of new souls, I'd been forced to assist the Judges of the Dead in determining which area of the underworld each soul went to, on top of the day-to-day running of the realm. The Judges were perhaps more furious at Thanatos than I was. Maybe.

What inconvenienced me the most was that the dearth and then sudden influx of residents had kept me from Kore. It had been too long since I'd laid eyes on her, and my mood was foul because of it.

Instead of being treated to a view of the beautiful maiden, I got Onesimos—a soul who looked to be a middle-aged man—stumbling nervously toward me while the other souls gave him a wide berth. He'd been dead a hundred years, but he'd never taken particularly well to the underworld, and was an incessant source of irritation for me.

"Did you attempt to throw Heron, an opposing faction leader, into the flames of the Phlegethon? A simple yes or no will be sufficient."

"Well, yes, but—"

"But nothing." I pulled the chain off my plain leather belt, wrapping it quickly and efficiently around Onesimos' wrists, binding him whilst leaving a long enough slack for me to pull him along behind me. *Like Thanatos should have done to Sisyphus*, I thought bitterly. That failure—mostly my failure to notice just how long Thanatos had been gone—was going to hurt my pride for centuries to come.

"Please, Hades," Onesimos begged, stumbling along in my wake. "I didn't mean it. I regret my actions."

I scoffed. As though *regret* meant anything when he'd nearly permanently incinerated a soul. Regret wouldn't have brought Heron back if he'd been successful. No—Onesimos' efforts had been deliberate and calculated, and the punishment had to be severe enough to dissuade anyone else from following in his footsteps.

The jeering crowd had fallen eerily silent as they parted to let us through. Even those from the factions who opposed Onesimos, who hated him, were quiet, keeping their eyes averted lest they be the next to attract my attention.

As gray and dull as the Asphodel Meadows could sometimes be, it was paradise compared to the endless, suffocating darkness that was Tartarus. A fact the souls seemed to forget, right until they were on their way to the pit to see that nightmare for themselves. It didn't happen often—the Judges of the Dead decided who went where when each soul arrived, and I did my best not to undermine their decisions.

But actions had consequences.

"Hades, *please*," Onesimos begged, openly sobbing. It wasn't a dignified way for anyone to make an exit.

"You have been here for a hundred years, Onesimos," I replied evenly. "You have had plenty of warnings. You acted in deliberate bad faith during my absence, and you will answer for those actions in Tartarus."

I whistled for my chariot, the piercing sound making Onesimos tremble harder.

"I'm sorry!" he wailed, but it was too late.

My golden chariot approached, and the crowds grew thin, creating space for the enormous black steeds who pulled it. I stepped onto the back and took the reins with one hand, flicking them slightly to instruct the horses to take us into the sky while Onesimos dangled below, only my grip on the chain keeping him airborne. I had my own entrance to Tartarus, one where I'd negotiate with its king, one ruler to another. That wasn't the entrance we'd be using today, though.

Today, we'd be using the pit.

Onesimos tucked his legs up beneath his body as the Phlegethon spat fire upward while we flew over it, following the river of fire to the chasm of darkness. A waterfall of flames poured into it, the river's end, but they quickly disappeared into nothingness. No light survived in Tartarus, unless Tartarus himself wanted it to be there.

The moment we were over the yawning great pit, I silently instructed the chain to release him. With an echoing scream, Onesimos fell into the darkness. I tugged the reins for a moment, doing a swooping arc over the gateway, both making sure that Onesimos didn't somehow crawl out again, but also to make a statement to the souls watching from the Meadow.

I grew busier by the day, and perhaps I wouldn't always respond to infractions the moment they occurred, but I *would* respond. There would be no clemency for those who broke the rules.

Satisfied the factions were suitably cowed for the time being, I guided my chariot back over the mountain ranges, my field of cattle, bypassing the palace completely to visit the forest where on clear days, I could occasionally see Kore near her mother's home.

Only occasionally. Never often enough.

Never enough recently.

The moment the chariot landed, I sent the steeds to graze in the mountains that cast a shadow over this flat plain, securing the soul chain to my belt as I made my way to the exact spot where I could see up through the clouds to the lake where Kore sometimes visited.

There was a flash of wheat-colored hair and I sucked in a breath, hardly believing my luck. She was there.

She was miserable.

I'd watched Kore for years. Sometimes she smiled—usually when she was with one of her siblings—but mostly she looked wistful, like her mind was elsewhere. Envisioning a more interesting life where she was treated with the respect she deserved was what I liked to think.

But not today. Today she sat at the lake's edge and *wept*. She'd tucked her knees up to her chest, hugging them with her arms as tears streamed unchecked down her face.

Why was Kore crying?

Who'd *dared* to make Kore cry?

The chain at my waist rattled with my disgruntled movements, reminding me that I could restrain whoever was responsible for those tears and drag them down to Tartarus for daring.

As I watched, Kore quickly pulled herself together, rubbing away the evidence on her cheeks with the heel of her hand before reaching into the lake to splash cool water on her face. I reached up instinctively, like I always did, like the Fates might be so gracious as to shrink the seemingly impossible space between us and let me pull Kore into my realm where she belonged.

I'd told Zeus I'd give him time, and I had. Many sunsets had come and gone while deities, both upper and lower, had worked to find Thanatos and fix the issues his absence had caused. I knew the Olympians had convened more than once in recent days, trying to work out why mortals suddenly weren't dying.

That meant he'd seen Demeter.

That meant he'd had an opportunity to speak to her about my intentions—possibly more than one opportunity—and yet Kore was no closer to being my wife.

Zeus had probably forgotten. Found himself enamored with some poor human who was trying to go about their day and was now being hounded by a randy god who wouldn't leave them alone.

A randy god who was shirking his responsibilities, like arranging my marriage. I couldn't even imagine being such an irresponsible ruler. I doubted Zeus knew what it was to be overworked.

Already, that familiar ache at the base of my skull was forming, the one that urged me to get back to work, to stop indulging in anything that wasn't running my realm. I'd been standing here too long, stewing in my impatience.

Just a little longer.

Kore stood, staring up at the sky, and I admired the profile of her form. The generous curve of her hips and breasts, the graceful dip at her waist, the long line of her neck. Everything about her called to me—body, soul, power, all of it. But the frustration she was trying valiantly to hide called to me more than anything. I understood what it was to feel trapped and frustrated, but at least I had the benefit of my position to force people to respect my decisions.

Kore didn't have that. She never would living in her mother's court, constantly watched and unable to live up to her full potential.

I'd had enough. Enough waiting. Enough watching. Enough *craving* from afar.

No more. I paced back and forth, knowing that there would be consequences to my actions, but unable to continue watching her spirit wither away with each day that passed, her life an unending sea of sameness. *No more.*

With a determined whistle, I summoned the horses back to me.

An emotion I wasn't familiar with stirred in my chest. Something akin to *uncertainty*. Since Zeus, Poseidon, and I had divided the duties of ruling among the three of us, I had left the underworld only once. There were always new souls arriving. Unlike the other kings, my role was a hands-on one.

Besides that, I'd been informed many times before that I was too brash, that I interpreted things wrong.

What if I was wrong about this?

But what if I was right?

My stallions materialized, whinnying furiously as I leaped onto the chariot and they swerved upward in one smooth motion. *Too late to back out now.* I took hold of the reins and directed them skyward, keeping my eyes on the distant figure of my future bride through the lake.

Now.

Kore leaned forward to pluck another yellow narcissus from the ground, and I briefly dropped the reins to raise my hands above my head, clasping them together before bringing them apart, the earth moving at my command. It wasn't a power I'd used before, but somehow I knew it would work. I knew that there was nothing in any of the three realms that could keep me from Kore. Without verbal instruction, my horses flew up through the gap, dragging my chariot toward the upperworld that was so foreign to me.

I felt Helios' blinding sunlight on my face a moment before the breath was stolen from my lungs. By the Fates, a more beautiful woman had surely never existed. Golden eyes shining with terror, hair the same color and secured with a dark green ribbon, full lips parted in shock.

Forgive me.

Before she could open her mouth to scream, my arm was around her waist, pulling her into the chariot against me, and my horses arched gracefully into the air before diving into the depths of the underworld, my future queen securely in my embrace.

Her head only came to my shoulder, and she was so *soft*, lush curves contrasting with my solid muscles.

"Let me go!" she gasped, twisting back and reaching up toward the sky as the chasm above us closed. My arm tightened around her as she squirmed in my grip, ensuring that she didn't fall from the airborne chariot in her bid for freedom. "Who are you? Let me go!" she demanded, hitting and clawing my forearms.

Had anyone ever treated me this way? Below ground, my word was law. Above, I was feared even by The Twelve. Perversely, I hoped she would continue to rage at me even when she realized who it was she was digging her nails into.

"You are safe, Kore," I assured her. "No harm will come to you here."

"You *stole* me! That is plenty harmful!" she shouted, squirming against me. If I wasn't so concerned that she'd injure herself, I'd be struggling to keep my cock in check. It had been *so* long—no other lover had appealed to me since I'd first set eyes on Kore. "Let me go!"

I secured her in my grip, my arm banding around her ribs. She gasped in outrage as I unintentionally brushed against the underside of her breasts, and I did my best to discreetly move my arm to a more respectable position so as not to enrage her further.

It would have been easier if she'd stop trying to escape.

"Who are you?!" Kore bit out, shaking with what I hoped was fury rather than fear.

"Look around, Kore." The horses were drawing the chariot over the River Styx, its black waters shining ominously below. My eyes had adjusted immediately to the darkness, but her eyes may have taken longer after a lifetime spent in the light. "I'm sure you know who I am."

My Kore smelled like lavender and sunshine, and I hoped she would keep that bright scent even in this dark realm.

"You're Hades. You're the King of the Underworld."

The words were quiet, resigned.

"Yes."

There seemed little point in apologizing for that unfortunate fact.

We were approaching the ferry where Charon deposited new arrivals, but the horses would take us directly to the courtyard of my palace. I had no idea how my court would respond to my guest—I'd never brought one back before.

Perhaps I should have warned them. I'd asked Orphne to prepare Kore's rooms after I'd returned from visiting Olympus, but she wouldn't have spread that news around. Orphne was the only nymph at my court who seemed to prefer keeping secrets rather than sharing them.

"I want to go home." My Kore sniffled. Her tears felt like a sword directly to my chest, twisting and digging, causing me an acute kind of misery that would leave permanent scars. "Why? Why did you take me? What do you want?"

Ah, a simple question. One I was glad to answer.

"I wish to marry you and make you my queen."

CHAPTER 5

This couldn't be happening. It was a nightmare. Any moment, I would wake up safe in the shelter of the ash trees in my mother's garden, with Despoina affectionately teasing me for my laziness and the nymphs giggling at me behind their hands.

I would take their catty whispers and thinly veiled jibes happily. Anything would be preferable to being trapped in the arms of the most fearsome of all the gods as he stole me away to his mysterious underworld lair.

To marry me.

Don't faint, I told myself sternly, alarmed at the way my head was spinning.

"My mother will never stand for this," I whispered, the horror of what he was suggesting dawning on me. This was the exact reason Mother had hounded me every day of my life to swear that oath. If he'd arrived just a few hours later, I'd already be cloistered away in Artemis' temple, held hostage until I was *forced* to do it.

To think I'd been crying about that. Now my situation was significantly more precarious.

Hades—*Hades*—stiffened slightly against me, his hand obnoxiously high up around my ribs flexing. In truth, I was glad for his secure grip, since we were in a flying chariot pulled by the four most frightening beasts I'd ever seen. Not being able to see Hades' face may have also been a blessing.

It was easier to imagine him as a monster when I couldn't see him, but logically I knew that very few gods were less than perfect looking.

I hoped he looked like the Erymanthian boar. He definitely had the manners of one.

"You will be very happy here," Hades said decisively, ignoring my statement about my mother completely. "Much happier than you were in the upperworld."

"You know nothing about my life or my happiness in the upperworld," I hissed, clinging to his stupid thick forearm as the chariot dipped. "How dare you."

"You will be much happier here," he repeated stubbornly, though his rich, low voice was still irritatingly soothing. If I was being charitable, I'd say he sounded a little uncertain of himself. "You will be a queen. You'll have more power and freedom than almost any goddess in existence."

I swallowed down the dangerous part of me that found that offer incredibly tempting. It was nonsense, just words meant to seduce me into doing his bidding.

"One of the most powerful goddesses in existence is my mother," I said primly. "And I know you didn't get her permission to marry me."

My mother would *never* approve of Hades as a husband for me. She would never approve of *anyone* as a husband for me. My life had been destined for eternal maidenhood since the moment I'd been conceived against her will.

Hades' silence confirmed my assumption.

"I'm to swear an oath of virginity," I told him haughtily, forcing more fire into my voice than I felt.

"But you haven't. You've had decades."

"And apparently you've been paying attention," I replied through gritted teeth. *How?* It was well known that he almost never left the underworld. He must have a spy at Henna, reporting back on my mother's court.

Why hadn't I just sworn that cursed oath the first time my mother asked me to?

Because you didn't want to. Because it had never been your idea, your plan for your life. Because you hoped against all odds that you could find someone to marry. Someone who could make you feel as good as the fantasies you could never quite let go of.

Hades smelled of cypress and narcissus, strangely bright and lively scents considering the dreary surroundings. It wasn't unpleasant, and I resented him immensely for it.

"You have to take me back," I murmured. "It's not too late. Just turn the chariot around and deposit me by the lake. I won't tell anyone."

Of course, he'd come when I was all alone. When I'd briefly shaken off the nymphs that were meant to be watching me so I could go sob by the water in peace before Mother dragged me to the temple.

"No."

"*No?*" I repeated. "You can't think to keep me here, it's... it's... ridiculous! Nonsensical. My mother will never stop searching for me. She'll figure out where I am, and she'll come for me."

"She's more than welcome to visit after we're married," he said flatly.

"I'm not going to marry you," I replied, another slightly hysterical laugh escaping me before I could stop it. Hades was silent, but his hold on me didn't tighten. There was no sign of anger from him at my pronouncement. Odd.

"Will you *force* me to marry you?" I pressed.

At that, Hades stiffened slightly. "I would never force you to do anything."

He spoke again before I could point out the hypocrisy of that statement, considering how it was I'd ended up in this terrifying realm at all.

"We're approaching the palace," Hades said calmly, those nerves in his voice I'd heard earlier so thoroughly gone that I wondered if I'd imagined them. "Your arrival will be a pleasant surprise to those in my court."

A surprise.

Despite the dire situation, another laugh burst out of me at the absurdity of his statement. All the self-control I held on to so carefully so as not to upset my mother or further inconvenience my family seemed to disappear down here in this home of death.

"Oh yes. A pleasant surprise, I'm sure. If they don't know I'm coming, then you are about to have some furious lovers on your hands. Not that they have anything to worry about, they can keep you."

You probably shouldn't laugh at the god of the underworld, I chastised silently. If he threw me into Tartarus for my disrespect, then my mother would never find me.

I waited, my body tense, half expecting Hades to throw me off the chariot into the Styx and save himself the effort of imprisoning me, but his only response was another light flexing of his fingers against my ribcage and a huff of hot breath at my ear.

"Your arrival is a surprise. A *welcome* one," he reiterated.

Perhaps he was a little dense.

I'd been so busy staring at the horse-like creatures in front of me and the faintly purple sky above that I hadn't paid nearly enough attention to my surroundings below. A sprawling marble palace emerged from the surrounding darkness, a stark white against the gray fields of flowers and blackened trees. There was a marshland above the palace, enormous pools of water either side, and a river of fire below it, plus a rugged mountain range in the distance, capped with snowy peaks that stopped me seeing any further.

Bleak. It was all so bleak.

I attempted to twist behind me to see where it was we'd come from so I could find my way out, but Hades' grip on me was unyielding. Regardless, it didn't look like there was an *easy* way out. Not when nearly every inch of space surrounding the palace was crawling with souls. The souls of *dead* mortals.

I was in the realm of the dead. Of course there were dead everywhere. I didn't know why I found it so jarring.

Perhaps because it was so large, the land sprawling as far as I could see in every direction. Or perhaps because I'd always been surrounded by life. Because if I'd ever been permitted to really use my gift, I imagined I'd grow into some kind of life-giving goddess like my mother.

How could Hades possibly think I'd be a suitable queen of the *dead*?

The chariot dipped closer to the palace, and it was obvious even from here that the front steps were busy—not only filled with souls but with the immortal residents of the underworld too. Perhaps it was always like this, or more likely they'd seen their king leave and were outside hoping to find out the gossip before anyone else.

We were descending, and I was in a state of increasing panic. I knew nothing about this court, but I understood *life* at court.

I would be carrion to these vultures in the condition I was in. They were here for his favor, not mine, and they wouldn't show me any more regard than they had to.

I wasn't an Olympian, but I was close enough to the twelve thrones that I assumed Hades had *some* respect for me and my reputation. Abduction and bizarre claims about marrying me aside.

"I need a moment," I said stiffly, hating asking him for anything, for showing any sign of vulnerability.

"Of course."

His hand twitched the reins again, and the horses climbed back toward the dull lilac "sky," detouring in a swooping circle around the palace.

Hades' easy acquiescence destabilized me, but I tried not to let it show. I discreetly used the loose fabric of my dark green chiton to wipe the evidence of tears off my face, and tightened my gold braid belt, trying to ignore the way my hands brushed against Hades' forearm as I moved.

In all the times I'd imagined myself in a man's embrace, it hadn't been like this. Those scenarios had always been heated and passionate, slick skin making it difficult for us to hold on to each other.

Still, this had been an educational experience, I could admit begrudgingly. Hades was a real man, not some faceless fantasy I'd made up. The hair on his arms made his skin coarser to the touch than anything I'd ever envisioned. His body was hard in places that I was soft, and the contrasts between us would have been pleasing in any other circumstances.

I smoothed any stray hairs back into the ribbon wrapped thrice around my head, glad it had mostly stayed in place. Had I known I was going to be the *guest* of a king, perhaps I would have requested some elegant braids this morning, or charcoal to emphasize the gold of my eyes. Aside from the brooches that secured my chiton at each shoulder and some golden bangles at my wrists, I looked barely more impressive than a common mortal.

"You look perfect, Kore," Hades murmured in my ear as the horses began their descent again.

"I know that," I snapped. I'd never thought of myself as a particularly great beauty, since I was surrounded by seductive nymphs all day, but I was an immortal goddess of Olympian parentage. I was pretty enough.

I didn't want him to think I was pretty anyway. He was my kidnapper.

A nice smelling kidnapper, who gave me compliments, but a kidnapper nonetheless.

There was that huff of breath over my ear again, and I almost thought he was laughing at me, but I didn't have time to examine it as the ground rapidly loomed closer, the upturned faces of Hades' courtiers unabashedly gaping at us.

And I thought this day couldn't get any worse.

For enormous, feral-looking horse beasts, Hades' stallions landed with surprising lightness on the smooth marble outside the entrance to the palace. The crowd moved back, forming an almost perfect circle as Hades stepped off the chariot, all but hauling me with him, his arm still securely around my waist like it had any right to be there.

As subtly as I could, I twisted back into his body, staring at his full, dark beard rather than risking looking into his eyes. "Are you bringing me here as your bride or your prisoner? Let *go*."

To my surprise, he listened, slowly releasing his hold on my body before moving so close to my side that his arm pressed entirely against mine.

His very thick, solid arm. I swallowed, turning my attention to the crowd rather than the impressively muscular deity beside me. *I just wasn't used to being around males, that was all.* They were much larger than I was accustomed to. Even the glimpse I'd gotten of Hermes once couldn't have prepared me for the immense height and breadth of the King of the Underworld.

"This is Kore," Hades announced, not bothering to raise his voice. He didn't need to—the palace steps were completely silent. "She is to be Queen of the Underworld, and you will treat her with the respect that the title confers."

The resounding silence was oppressive. I tried to think what would happen if my mother had brought home a god and announced she was going to marry him with no notice. The courtiers would have cheered, welcomed him enthusiastically, I was certain of it. We'd all gone into mourning when Iasion had died, and most of us had never met him.

This court was nothing like my mother's. Their disapproval of me was palpable, and they were making no attempt to hide it.

I chanced a glance up at Hades through my eyelashes to gauge his reaction, only to be entirely distracted by his face.

Oh dear.

He was very impressive looking. Taller than me by a full head, with shoulder-length, curly dark brown hair and a long dark beard. His skin was paler than mine, probably from a lack of sunlight, but it made his almost coal-black eyes stand out in even starker relief. The furrow between his brow was so deep, I wouldn't be surprised if his face was in a constant frown, but it didn't look harsh and angry like I expected.

His black chiton was fastened at one shoulder with a bronze brooch depicting a screech owl, and golden chains rattled at his hip where they were secured to his leather belt.

I'd intended to say something. I wasn't sure what exactly, just something to let Hades' court know that I wasn't an easy target, but his stupid face distracted me entirely.

I added it to my list of crimes he'd committed against me.

"Come, Kore," he said in an infuriatingly soothing voice. That was going on the list too. "Let me show you your rooms."

Not my rooms. I'm not staying. Demeter will be here before nightfall to collect me, and she'll bring the entire realm down in a rage when she arrives.

CHAPTER 6

As tempting as it was to march off in a huff—to be anywhere except where the god who'd just ripped me away from my home was—I followed Hades through the corridors of this unfamiliar palace with my head held high. There were too many eyes around, watching and judging and finding me lacking, which wasn't too different from my life in the upperworld, but it stung nonetheless.

I could save my anger and tears for somewhere private.

"Why are you doing this?" I hissed under my breath, stubbornly keeping my arms tucked at my side when Hades looked like he was going to offer me his.

Did he not realize that he'd kidnapped me? That I was here against my will? He seemed genuinely surprised that I wasn't throwing myself into his arms.

"Walking you to your rooms?" he asked, glancing at me as though it was obvious. "Because you don't know the way."

I was beginning to suspect that every negative thing Mother had told me about men might be true.

"They're not my rooms, I'm not staying." My voice was low enough that he had to lean in to hear me, and as much as I didn't want to be overheard, I regretted his closer proximity almost immediately.

Why did he have to be so... imposing?

Hades frowned. "If you don't like the rooms, you can change them however you wish. I expected you would want to redecorate them."

What? He thought I wouldn't stay because of the *decor*?

Before I could point out the absurdity of that statement, an enormous beast barreled around the corner, paws slipping on the smooth marble floor in its excitement, and I barely muffled a shriek as I stumbled backward.

"Kerberos, calm," Hades said absently. The creature immediately skidded to a stop, sitting on its haunches, tongues—plural—lolling out of its heads—also plural.

Three tongues.

Three heads.

One enormous dog-like body, covered in thick black fur.

"This is Kerberos," Hades stated, gesturing at the... dog? A black-scaled serpent rose from behind the animal, tongue flicking out to taste the air, and I realized with dawning horror that it was the beast's *tail*.

I liked to think I wasn't the fainting sort, but this monster was really testing that theory.

"He is *supposed* to be at the Port of Charon, guarding the gate," Hades continued, his tone slightly exasperated. "I suppose he wanted to meet you."

Kerberos wriggled impatiently on the spot, paws tapping softly on the ground as though he was fighting to keep still. All three heads appeared to be happy, giving me dog-like smiles complete with tongues out, though I noticed the head on the furthest right seemed the *most* happy, drooling all over the spotless floor and panting excitedly. He looked almost... silly.

The snake tail looked decidedly less excited, though I supposed I'd never seen a happy snake for comparison.

"Hello," I said lamely, waving at the beast, who was only a few inches shorter than me. Kerberos seemed to take that as an invitation, bounding forward and nuzzling my shoulders and arms, all three tongues licking my skin.

"Kerberos," Hades sighed, before shooting me a troubled look. "He's usually much more fearsome than this. I wouldn't have appointed him as Guardian of the Gate otherwise."

I nodded, slightly confused, as I hesitantly reached out to pat Kerberos' back, hoping that would be sufficient to satisfy the beast and then he'd leave me alone. It sounded like Hades was worried that I wouldn't find Kerberos scary *enough*, which made no sense because I found him plenty terrifying, despite the puppy-like licking.

With a head butt that showed me just how much strength he was hiding, I landed on my backside with a thud, a moment before Kerberos threw himself backward on my lap, all four paws in the air, his request for a belly rub obvious.

Should I…? I mean, it couldn't hurt.

If Kerberos was the Guardian of the Gate, he would probably be a good creature to have on my side.

Tentatively, I began rubbing his belly, amazed at how *adorable* he was, for a three-headed dog with a serpent tail.

"How will you feel if a soul escapes the underworld because you weren't doing your job properly?" Hades asked Kerberos solemnly, arms crossed over his chest. "You're embarrassing yourself. This undignified behavior doesn't befit the Guardian of the Gate."

That was quite the solemn lecture to deliver to a dog—or a dog-like beast—over a few belly scratches, I thought, slightly perplexed. *Was fun not allowed here?* Probably not.

Kerberos climbed to his feet with a quiet whine, the silliest-looking head giving my palm a final slobbery lick before he bounded off down the hallway, the way we'd entered.

Hades sighed, muttering something about responsibilities as he stepped toward me, extending a hand like he was going to help me up. Affronted by the gesture, I climbed to my feet on my own, daring him to take a step closer.

With a slightly confused expression, he gestured forward, continuing down the corridor. *He was the strangest kidnapper ever,* I decided, following in a daze. In all Mother's horror stories about Olympian gods stealing away their conquests and ravishing them, it had always sounded a lot less cordial than this interaction had been.

Hades pushed open a heavy door while I waited behind him, before standing back to let me enter. *I think not.* I glared at him, crossing my arms— still wet with dog drool—over my chest and staying in place. Whatever prison he was leading me to, he could go in first. Hades eventually conceded, walking through the enormous doorway and shooting me another somewhat puzzled look in the process.

I'd assumed the King of the Underworld was terrifying. An ominous, nightmarish deity with the kind of chilling smile that promised pain and retribution.

Hades... was not that. He was certainly intimidating, but not in the ways I'd expected. He'd kidnapped *me,* and yet he had the nerve to look at me like *I* was the bewildering one in this situation.

Was he lulling me into a false sense of security? Was his confusion an act?

Perhaps it was my curiosity about his strangeness that persuaded me to follow him into the sitting room. It was infuriatingly lovely, with high ceilings and marble columns arranged in a rectangle in the center of the space, framing a sitting area with a luxurious klinai to lie on, covered in crimson silk, with brightly colored woven cushions at the headrest. There were wooden stools scattered around for visitors to sit on, the legs carved into the shape of lion's feet. The relief on the walls was dark red and gold, depicting what I assumed were different areas of the underworld, and the black and white mosaic floor at my feet spiraled toward the middle of the room where an enormous asphodel flower had been painstakingly made from tile.

Unlike my mother's palace, there was complete privacy—thick wooden doors and gleaming marble walls that would keep the sound out. There were no windows, but that made it easier to forget that I was in the underworld. All told, I found it a lot less unpleasant than I should.

In fact, it was beautiful. A beautiful room, fit for a queen of any realm.

A nymph stepped forward from next to one of the columns on the furthest side of the room, making me start. For a nymph, she was surprisingly harsh in appearance—her skin was as pale as moonlight, especially in contrast to her inky black hair that hung in a silky wave down to her knees. Her black eyes were sunken, the planes of her face sticking out in sharp relief. The chiton she wore was as dark as her hair, draped artfully over a slim frame.

I'd met my fair share of nymphs in my time, but none of them had been as solemn-looking as this one was.

"This is Orphne. I have asked her to be your attendant," Hades said off-handedly, moving back toward the door when a man appeared, silently requesting his attention.

Asked her to be my attendant. Not *commanded* her to be.

Hades ran an unusual court here.

"Unfortunately, I must leave you while I sort out a dispute." Hades sighed, looking irritated. "Ask Orphne for anything you need, I'll return when I can."

I opened my mouth to object as he followed the man who'd come to talk to him back into the hallway, pulling the door shut behind him and leaving me alone with the stone-faced nymph.

Why was I offended? It wasn't like I *wanted* to spend time with him. It just seemed sort of rude to kidnap someone and then immediately abandon them. It was a lot more difficult to demand he take me home when he wasn't here.

"Kore," Orphne murmured, bowing uncomfortably low. At my mother's court, only she was treated with that kind of reverence. "I hope you find these rooms to your liking. There's a bedchamber and private bathing pool through this way, and that door connects to Hades' chambers."

"Does it now?" I asked dryly, glaring at it. "This is the queen's quarters."

"It is," Orphne agreed, inclining her head. "For the future Queen of the Underworld."

"That's not me," I replied primly. "I'm going home, I don't belong here. Something I'll remind Hades of when he returns," I added under my breath, wandering around to take in the details of the sitting area.

I glanced at Orphne out of the corner of my eye, catching the surprise on her face before she masked it. Did she really expect me to stay here? What had Hades said to give her that impression? Or did she just think so highly of the underworld that it never occurred to them I'd want to leave?

Orphne must have forgotten how delightful sunshine felt on the skin if she thought life down here was preferable.

"What did he say about me coming here?" I asked, running my fingers over a beautiful wooden cabinet engraved with the bland, colorless flowers of the underworld.

"Just that you would arrive at some point and would I attend to your needs and assist you in arranging the wedding ceremony."

I whirled around to look at her, pinning her with perhaps a harder glare than she deserved. "There will be no wedding planning."

Orphne's face remained carefully blank as she inclined her head. "I am at your disposal."

Wedding planning. Ridiculous.

"Where has he gone?" I asked, turning to stare at the door Hades had departed through. "Surely there's nothing pressing that requires his attention down here. Everyone is dead." I glanced at Orphne. "Nearly everyone."

The corners of her mouth tipped up for a moment before her stoic expression was back in place. "If you've only seen death from the upperworld, it is easy to think that the dead don't require much ruling down here."

"And that's not the case?" I asked, sitting on the klinai for lack of a better idea and motioning to Orphne to sit too.

"Souls have nothing but time. The Judges of the Dead determine where each one goes when they arrive, and most end up in Asphodel Meadows. There are six factions there, and souls usually align themselves to one or the other right away, out of fear, I suppose. There is violence among them, but mostly, the king leaves them to it. They maintain the balance of power between them—if one gets too ambitious, the others cut them down. They've been more restless than usual, so Hades is forced to intervene."

What *was* this place? Everything from the way the souls acted to Hades' hands-off approach to managing them was the complete opposite of the world I'd come from.

"I assumed souls just sort of... floated around, I guess," I admitted, shifting uncomfortably in my seat.

If Orphne wanted to laugh at me, she politely disguised it.

"That would make life much easier for Hades, but no. They have entire lives here, and keep us rich in gossip with their goings on. Lovers' spats are particularly common. People moving on to new lovers after their partner dies, or forming new relationships with other souls, that kind of thing."

That was... quite intriguing, actually.

No. No, I refused to be intrigued.

"Well, as busy as he is, Hades will need to find time for an audience with me," I clipped. "I refuse to stay here. He can't keep me here. Frankly, my mother will start a war over this if he doesn't return me, so me staying is in no one's best interests."

My throat burned, and I stood hastily, muttering some excuse under my breath as I shut myself in the bedchamber before Orphne could see my tears, refusing to admire the beautiful furniture or soft linens in here. I refused to like anything about this place. I wasn't going to stay.

My mother would come for me.

I curled up in the luxurious bed I'd been given and cried until, with nothing else to do, I fell asleep. *Alone.* Either Orphne hadn't been instructed to sleep at my side to supervise me, or she was politely giving me some space, but I had the feeling that it was the former.

I doubted Hades was interested in safeguarding my virtue. The opposite, if anything.

Since I had no windows to see the sky and there wasn't a sun here anyway, there was no way of knowing how much time had passed. How long had I been left here alone? How long had it been since I'd been taken from the garden?

Surely, Mother knew by now—we'd been due to leave for Artemis' temple at any moment. She was probably on Olympus already, raging and demanding my return, assuming I'd been snatched by an upperworld god. No one ever gave much thought to Hades.

He deserves to be ignored, I thought bitterly.

I sat up in the absurdly soft bed, pulling the silk sheets up around me and tucking my knees to my chest. Another idiotic tear escaped me and I rubbed it away roughly with the heel of my hand, repeating the gesture on the other cheek before conceding defeat and letting a few more fall.

I'd always been helpless by my mother's design. The only thing I was good at was repressing my magic, making myself as small and invisible as possible so as not to inconvenience anyone. That helplessness was almost crushing now—I had no idea how to get out of here, if I even *could* without an escort, and no clue how to tell my mother where I was so she could come and collect me.

And even that idea was a little embarrassing.

Hades had brought me here because he'd believed me suitable *queen* material, and I was sitting here wondering when my mother would fetch me and take me home.

It was humiliating. Frustrating and humiliating.

Not for the first time, I wished I had a little of Despoina's bravery. She wouldn't have cried. She would have... stolen a sword and sliced off Hades' head. It probably wouldn't have helped, but she'd have at least *done* something.

Maybe I could pretend to be brave too, just this once. It didn't seem like Hades was going to hurt me, I could push the boundaries a little, couldn't I? If it meant getting out of here?

"Kore?" Orphne called hesitantly as I sniffed. "Can I get you anything? A bath, perhaps?"

Oh dear, her kindness was only making me cry harder. She was a stranger, and she was treating me with more understanding than many of the nymphs I'd known my whole life.

"A bath would be nice, thank you," I replied, my voice wobbling despite my best intentions. I took a few deep breaths to steady myself before climbing out of the bed and smoothing down my chiton and opening the door to the bedchamber for Orphne to enter. She didn't look at me with the thinly veiled disappointment that the nymphs in my mother's court always did, which was nice. Instead, she set down a length of fabric on a chest at the end of the bed and a jug of wine that I wouldn't touch on the table.

I didn't know much about this realm, but I knew that consuming food or drink of the underworld was the fastest way to be tied to it forever.

"A courting gift from Hades," she said, gesturing at the fabric before bowing and moving into the bathing chamber. With a resigned sigh, I unfolded the dark green linen, edged with intricate gold embroidery. It was a chiton, much like the color I already wore—Demeter's color—though *far* more regal. Where the chitons Mother preferred me in were made of wool with extra draping at the top, this one was thin and, once pinned into place, designed to better showcase the feminine form. The nymphs at home often wore them, creating fashionable sleeves by securing the fabric over their forearms, and tying them tightly beneath the bust.

My cheeks heated, and I was confident my face was glowing gold with the hot ichor in my veins. Envisioning myself in an elegant, fitted chiton was making me feel strange—more womanly and desirable than Kore the Maiden was supposed to feel. Shaking my head at the absurdity of my reaction, I quickly refolded the fabric and set it down on the chest.

I'd bathe, then put the chiton I was already wearing back on. I didn't want Hades to get any ideas about me accepting gifts from him.

The bathing chamber was an enormous pool of water that seemed to be filled from a hot spring as I couldn't see a well or fire in here to heat it. The entire room was tiled with a beautiful glass mosaic, trapping the steam in, and Orphne waited with an amphora of olive oil to cleanse my skin before I climbed in the water.

"Is the chiton to your liking?" Orphne asked lightly as I undid the belt at my waist and brooches at my shoulders, stepping out of the garment and setting it on a bench at the side of the room.

I gave her a withering look at her fishing for my approval, surprised at how confident I felt around her. At home, I was careful to always act in a way that my mother wouldn't find objectionable when I was in the nymphs' presence, knowing they'd all report any infractions as soon as they occurred.

"I'd like to put my one back on after the bath," I told her, ignoring the small flash of disappointment in her eyes as she rubbed the olive oil onto my skin and efficiently scraped it free with the strigil to scrape away any dirt and sweat before I entered the water. Once complete, she moved back, and I climbed the steps to the bath, lowering myself into the warm pool.

"Can I get you anything else?" Orphne asked.

"I don't suppose you can find out when Hades is going to return to speak to me?"

"Of course. He came earlier, but I told him you were sleeping and he didn't want to wake you." Orphne inclined her head, backing out of the room and leaving me in the peaceful quiet of the bathing chamber. The water was scented with some kind of herb, not the lavender that I usually used at home, but perhaps something unique to the underworld and soothing nonetheless.

For the briefest moment, I entertained what it would be like to be the Queen of the Underworld. I wasn't so attached to my principles that I wasn't tempted by the idea—the luxury and freedom it would afford me would be unparalleled.

But I'd have to live here.

And I didn't think I could give up sunshine for all the riches in this realm or any other. Sunshine *or* my family. I'd been mad at my mother before Hades had snatched me away, and I was still upset at her decision to send me away, but I loved her.

I didn't want her to hate me, and she would if I married Hades. He was everything she despised about powerful gods.

"Kore."

I startled at the sound of Hades' low voice, and all but drowned myself in my haste to hide my body under the completely clear water as he strolled into the bathing chamber.

"What are you doing?!" I shrieked, banding a hand over my breasts. "Turn around!"

To my immense surprise, he actually did, though he looked infuriatingly confused about the request.

"You can't just wander in here while I'm bathing," I chastised, my mouth running away from me again as it seemed to do in Hades' presence. "I'm nude."

"That is generally how people bathe," he agreed, not sounding nearly apologetic enough for my liking. "Are there not mixed bathing chambers in the upperworld? I assure you, I've seen the nude female form before."

My jaw dropped in unmitigated outrage before I slammed it close, sternly reminding myself that I had no business feeling... whatever it was I was feeling at his admission of seeing other women naked. It wasn't jealousy.

That would be ludicrous. It was just irritation. He was irritating me.

"There are no mixed chambers at my mother's palace. No *males* live at Henna except my younger brothers, who are children, and have their own bathing area anyway."

Hades hummed thoughtfully. "Shall I leave? We can speak after you've finished bathing."

"Well, you're here now," I muttered, sinking an inch lower in the water. He was a king, and probably incredibly busy. I wasn't sure when I'd get the opportunity to talk to him again.

"All right. What would you like me to do the next time this circumstance arises?" he asked. I paused in my fussing, the water growing still around me. The question sounded genuine—like he was actually seeking guidance on how to proceed.

It was odd to be asked for my input on anything, especially considering how powerful Hades was. I'd spent my entire life *not* speaking my mind, and a small part of me was excited at this opportunity.

A small, idiotic part of me.

"You could knock and wait to be invited in?" I suggested hesitantly, waiting for him to turn around and laugh in my face for daring to dictate his behavior.

"That sounds reasonable," he agreed, nodding his head curtly, drawing attention to his thick, shiny hair. I'd barely even taken a moment to appreciate that yesterday, too busy mooning over his face. "What did you want to discuss?"

And now I was mooning over his hair. *By the Fates, Kore. Pull yourself together.*

"I would like to discuss me going home." *There, that sounded stern.*

"You are home."

"This is *your* home. I'd like to return to *my* home. In the upperworld."

Hades made a dispassionate sound, and I braced myself again for anger, tightening my arms around my body. "But this *could* be your home. You could have a position here far more permanent, far more important, than anything you would have in your mother's court. You will be free to explore your gifts as much as you like, to not make yourself smaller to fit into whatever box has been designed for you."

"I don't do that," I lied, my face growing hot and not just from the steam in the room. I *knew* I did that, knew that I had to in order to meet my mother's expectations of me, but hearing the words from someone else's mouth was mortifying. "And even if I did, it's not your responsibility to rescue me from my own life. I want to leave."

I watched Hades' back and I could have sworn he let out what looked like a shaky exhale at my words. I supposed that made sense—if he returned me, he'd have to answer for his crimes. Better to keep me here and try to convince me to stay.

"Hades," I began, softening my voice. "Whatever ideas you've formed about my life in the upperworld from whatever source is providing information about me, you're wrong. I love sunlight and flowers and fresh air. I love my sister and brothers. I *love* my mother. I'm sure you want a goddess to take as your bride, and perhaps my lineage is appealing, but I'm not suited to be Queen of the Underworld."

For the first time since he'd snatched me away, I saw a ripple of anger from Hades. True, barely restrained rage.

"Your *lineage*?" he spat, turning his head to the side but keeping his eyes averted. At this angle, I could make out the tic in his jaw, the even deeper frown lines on his forehead. "I couldn't care less about your lineage, Kore. I don't even care that you're a goddess. I wanted *you*. I only want you."

With that confusing statement, he stormed out of the bathing chamber, taking a moment to pause and gently pull the door closed behind him.

CHAPTER 7

Orphne looked at me expectantly as the King of the Underworld politely knocked on the door to my chambers, waiting in silence as he had for the past three days when he'd visited for me to grant him entry.

Why did it aggravate me so much that he was following my instructions? Perhaps because his respectfulness made it a lot harder to hate him.

"Are you ready to return me to the upperworld?" I called, the same as I had on his last visits.

"I will not return to you to the upperworld," he called back, his answer as consistent as my question. Orphne sighed quietly.

"Then you can't come in."

Hades didn't protest. He simply waited for Orphne to go out into the corridor so he could hand over the courting gifts I kept rejecting before going on his way.

Why couldn't he be more brutish? I was grateful that he seemed averse to the idea of forcing himself on me, but this unfailing politeness was maddening. It made me doubt myself, my rage. He'd stolen me away from my home, but his respectfulness had me wondering if I was even right to be enraged about it.

It had to be a trick. I refused to accept that the monstrous King of the Underworld would treat me with more kindness than half the members of my mother's court.

"Would you like another bath?" Orphne suggested, setting down another new chiton, probably as bored with my company as I was.

"I want to leave," I muttered petulantly. I wondered idly if she found me as insufferable as I'd found myself these past few days.

"These rooms? Or the underworld?"

I looked at her in confusion, mildly hopeful.

"How loyal are you to Hades?" I asked tiredly, on the off-chance she was a traitor lying in wait for the perfect opportunity to betray her king. I'd think less of her if she did, but I'd save those judgmental thoughts for when I was back home, at least.

Orphne's lips twitched. "I am loyal to the King and Queen of the Underworld."

"I'm neither of those," I sighed. "I want to go home. My mother will be beside herself with worry."

Orphne's expression turned sympathetic. "If you consented to marry Hades, he would have the ceremony arranged and a visit to your mother organized within the day."

I gave her a disbelieving look. "Mother wouldn't let a pesky little thing like marriage stop her from bringing me home and getting revenge on Hades for daring to take me. Besides, I know Hades thinks he's saving me from some terrible fate, but I *like* my life in the upperworld."

Most of the time.

"Would *you* guide me back to the upperworld?" I pressed, seeing little point being coy about it now when I'd already made my intentions clear. "My mother would reward you richly, you know. Give you a place in her court, wealth, whatever it is you wanted."

"Ah, no." Orphne shot me an apologetic grimace. "I don't need those things, and even if I did, I wouldn't leave."

"Are you a prisoner here, too?" I asked sympathetically, garnering a shocked look in surprise.

"No, of course not. The underworld is my home. I love it here. You're not a prisoner either, Kore," she added gently.

"The fact that I'm here against my will suggests otherwise," I replied dryly.

"Well, yes, that's true. But you can leave."

"Hades said—"

"Hades said he wouldn't return you," Orphne interjected softly. "Not that you couldn't leave. He specifically instructed me not to stop you should you choose to go."

"Oh."

That made no sense. Why go through all the trouble of kidnapping me, just to let me walk away? Then again, leaving the underworld probably required some near impossible journey, and that was why Hades felt comfortable allowing it.

Maybe I could steal his chariot.

"Perhaps if you explored the underworld a little, you would see it through the eyes of those who live and like it here? Discover why it is Hades believes you're so well suited for this life?" Orphne suggested gently. I had no doubt about that, but I wasn't sure I *wanted* to. "I know it must seem strange and dark here compared to the upperworld, but for many of us, it's a place to belong when we don't fit in anywhere else."

Orphne glanced down at her feet, and my gut twisted in sympathy. I could see why she would struggle to fit in among other nymphs—she was quiet, demurely dressed, with a serious disposition. I'd never met a nymph quite like her before.

She looked up, giving me a wry almost-smile. "Forgive me, Kore. I didn't mean to speak so frankly. I certainly don't think you are in need of somewhere to fit in." I blinked at her in surprise. "You're a beautiful goddess, daughter of Demeter. You must find the underworld horribly isolating compared to your life there," Orphne laughed quietly.

"I wouldn't say that," I mumbled. I supposed from the outside, it looked like I had the ideal life in my mother's court. While I was hidden away as best my mother could manage, it was no secret that I'd been fathered by the King of the Gods. It probably seemed like a gilded existence to anyone who didn't know me.

It was strange that Hades appeared to know so much about my life and had clearly talked about me at least a little to Orphne, yet he hadn't mentioned the more tragic aspects that he'd disapproved of in the bathing chamber. If he hadn't told her out of respect for me...

I didn't know how to feel about that.

"If you wanted to look around, there are ways you could see things without walking through the palace and interacting with everyone," Orphne said slowly. "Ways you could explore unseen."

"Like what?" I perked up immediately, memories of spying on mortals and immortals alike with my siblings running through my mind.

"If you wanted to be really bold, you could, er, *borrow* Hades' helmet from his rooms. It confers invisibility on the wearer."

"Borrow without asking?" I laughed, noting the way she'd hesitated before she'd said it.

"Hades means to make you his queen, whatever is his is yours. He wouldn't protest," Orphne replied, lifting her chin slightly. I highly doubted that. "But if you'd prefer not to borrow his belongings, there are passages through the palace that few have access to. I could show them to you."

It probably would have been sensible to say no. A not-insignificant part of me worried that there *would* be things I liked about the underworld. Liked enough to tempt me away from that damned oath that would undoubtedly weigh heavily on me the moment I was back in the upperworld. Liked enough to make me forget for a while how desperate I was to see my family again.

But a tour around the underworld was the perfect way for me to plot my escape, and I'd be foolish to turn it down.

"I suppose it couldn't hurt to see what all the fuss is about," I replied slowly. "Though I already know I won't want to stay."

"Could you promise to keep an open mind?" Orphne asked with a smile.

"Sure." I shrugged. "You show me the underworld, and I'll keep an open mind about it."

Orphne led me out of my temporary rooms and into the quiet marble corridor. I looked around, expecting to see someone else, but there was no one. Hades kept this wing of the palace very private.

It was certainly different from Henna and the constant stream of nymphs who invaded my personal space. *It was nicer,* I begrudgingly admitted. Peaceful.

"Welcome to the Whispers," Orphne breathed, silently prying open what appeared to be an engraved marble panel in the wall, disguised behind some ugly statue of a nightmarish underworld creature, revealing a wooden spiral staircase.

"What is this place?" I asked, ducking my head under the low entry panel to peer up the staircase. Even with my superior eyesight, it was *dark*.

"They're passages connecting most of the palace. Very few people even know they exist."

I could see why. Secret tunnels could be a very powerful and very dangerous tool.

"Why are you showing *me* this?" I asked, genuinely puzzled. Maybe Orphne was a traitor to Hades after all.

"It's the best way for you to see the palace for yourself, without influence from anyone else who lives here. To see *Hades* for yourself."

That may be so, but it still seemed awfully trusting of Orphne to reveal such a potentially dangerous tool to me based on nothing but the fact that Hades had formed some kind of one-sided attachment to me.

"Hades isn't usually like how he is with you," Orphne went on, fidgeting with the fabric of her chiton. "Maybe if you see him as he is, you'll want to stay."

I was confident that made no sense—if he was *worse*, I wouldn't want to be around him, and if he was better, I'd be offended that he was terrible around me. Orphne seemed uncomfortable enough without me pointing that out, though.

Maybe she was starved for female company down here and that's why she was putting in so much effort to convince me to stay?

"Well, let's take a look then," I sighed, peering apprehensively into the darkness again. "Won't there be *things* in here? Creepy things?"

Ridiculous, I chided internally. *You are an immortal goddess.*

Still, the underworld was full of monsters and critters I'd never encountered in the upperworld, it couldn't hurt to check.

Orphne gave me an understanding smile and shook her head. "There is nothing in this palace that exists unless Hades allows it to. There is not a speck of dust within these walls, no insects, no mud is traipsed across these marble floors. He is a god, one of the most powerful, and the firstborn of the Olympians. He takes great pride in maintaining a home as grand as any found on Olympus."

I nodded stiffly, gesturing for Orphne to enter first. I didn't want to admit that I was indeed impressed by the gleaming marble palace. That his home was, in fact, beautiful, if not a little devoid of life and color. Not that I'd ever been to Olympus, but it seemed very grand and imposing to me.

I followed Orphne into the darkness, carefully pulling the hidden entrance shut behind me. I could faintly make out the walls and low-hanging roof overhead, but I wondered why we hadn't brought a torch with us.

"Oh," Orphne said softly, turning back to face me. "I thought you might allow yourself to illuminate the space. I shouldn't have assumed."

I blinked, feeling slightly idiotic for not thinking of it sooner.

"I'm regularly surrounded by mortals," I muttered by way of embarrassed explanation. "I have to dampen my form so as not to kill them on sight."

It had become my default state of being—so much so that it took me a moment to remember *how* to let my more majestic, divine form surface. My features remained unchanged, but my skin, hair and eyes glowed with a warm golden light, a manifestation of the power buried deep within.

What else had I forgotten after keeping my gift repressed for so long?

Orphne's face came into focus, illuminated by my light. "How beautiful. Hades glows silver."

She began climbing the narrow stairs, and I followed, wondering why he *hadn't* been glowing silver in the times I'd seen him. Everyone who lived here was dead or immortal. There was no need for him ever to disguise his divine form here.

The marble walls felt cool and solid on either side of me, and for a long time as we climbed and wound through passages, there was no sound at all except for our footsteps. Orphne pointed out hidden exits from time-to-time, and I made a note of them for my future escape attempt.

Occasionally, Orphne would turn and press her finger to her lips, but I never heard more than a faint hum from the walls. Then again, I supposed the wing of the palace that Hades had brought me to had been deserted. Eventually, Orphne led us up a ladder-like staircase and the murmur of voices grew louder and more definable.

"Up here," Orphne breathed. "Perhaps hide your shine now," she added apologetically.

I did so happily, unused to walking around, glowing like the sun. It would draw attention to me, everything I'd been encouraged against doing my entire life.

Orphne ushered me closer, and I carefully climbed up on a thin ledge, not much wider than the branch of a poplar tree, and inched across to where she stood. There was a small horizontal gap in the slabs of marble, just wide enough to see through. We were looking into the crowded throne room, though we could only see a narrow section between two columns that contained a round dais and black obsidian throne Hades sat on, listening to an advisor who whispered in his ear.

Even his throne was stark and plain, like he'd conjured up the first option that came to mind that would get the job done, with no thought as to whether anyone else would be impressed by it or not. I couldn't imagine how liberating it would be to care so little about other people's opinions.

If everything in this realm existed because of Hades' say-so, maybe the small nook we were hiding in had been set up as somewhere for his closest confidantes to watch his interactions and monitor for any sign of treachery or dissent within his court. It wasn't so different from the nymphs my mother entrusted to do the same. They just sat in the open and pretended to be vapid gossips instead.

The shadowy nature of Hades' court was oddly thrilling. Or I was just starved for adventure. Unlike the supervised explorations I'd gone on with my sister all those years ago, I felt in the lead here. While Orphne was with me, I didn't think she'd interfere or hold me back for my own good.

I hadn't had much of a chance to look at the souls when I'd arrived, and I took a moment to examine the petitioner who was next in line to speak to him, nervously twisting her hands. She was different from the living mortals I'd encountered in the upperworld, that much was certain. It was like their inner light had extinguished, they still looked human but *not* somehow. Sort of grayish, dimmed. All wore simple plain black chitons, with no adornments.

This petitioner was an elderly woman, her body hunched with age and her face creased with deep wrinkles. That was the body she'd died in, and therefore the form she'd taken to the underworld. I wondered if she resented that she wasn't going to appear youthful for the rest of eternity, but then again, perhaps not. Not all mortals reached the age this woman had. I imagined there was a sense of pride and accomplishment for her, having survived the harshness of the mortal world so long that she bore the mark of that success on her body in the form of wrinkles and white hair.

The advisor moved away, and I paid even closer attention as the woman approached, moving with surprising spryness. I supposed even if she *looked* old, the aches and pains that would have bothered her in the upperworld had disappeared with her death.

To my surprise, the woman shook the moment she was in Hades' presence, bursting into violent sobs that wracked her entire body. I glanced warily at Orphne, who was watching with a dispassionate look on her face, like she saw this kind of display often.

"I want to remember," the old woman sobbed. "Please, o great Hades. I can't remember. Please help me. I *need* to remember."

Remember what?

I craned my neck, trying to catch a glimpse of Hades' face, but I could only see a little of his profile, faintly illuminated by that silver glow Orphne had mentioned. What I *could* see, I didn't expect, but then again, none of his reactions had been what I'd expected so far. Why should this be any different?

He looked *uncomfortable*. It was a strangely humanizing expression for an immortal, immensely powerful deity. Kerberos trotted into the room, all three heads held up regally, and came to sit at Hades' side. His hand found the animal's fur almost instantly, the flex of Hades' fingers only visible to Orphne and me in our spot slightly behind the throne.

He *was* uncomfortable. Had Kerberos come to keep him company, to soothe him? The goofiest of the three heads began turning toward us, sniffing the air, but a sharp movement from Hades stopped it from moving any further.

"You need to stop drinking from the Lethe," Hades stated flatly. Of course, the Pool of Lethe, of forgetfulness.

"I *can't*. I've tried. I know the waters make me forget."

She was weeping loudly, and most of the courtiers who'd been standing around watching turned away in distaste. Were the waters of the Lethe addictive? Perhaps forgetting was the easiest way to pass eternity, and the souls took too much. The idea struck me as tragic, but that was easy for me to say, wasn't it? I couldn't truly comprehend the lengths mortals went to in order to survive, but I had seen firsthand that they often did *terrible* things. Things that I imagined would haunt them if they had forever to reflect on it.

Perhaps the Pool of Lethe was a kindness Hades had given the souls here.

"I can't restore the memories you've lost. The goddess, Lethe, controls the magic of the waters, and I can't undermine another deity."

His words were delivered factually, if not a little coldly. He was incredibly powerful. Was he really claiming there was *nothing* he could do? Surely, in this realm, he was all powerful. I'd never seen my mother turn someone away because she *couldn't* help, though occasionally she roped in other gods to assist with a request.

"Restrain me," the woman begged. "Put me in a dungeon. In chains, anything. Just until I can resist the urge. Please, please, o Hades, great King of the Underworld."

Judging by the lack of reaction from everyone around him, this request wasn't unusual. Hades sighed heavily, still stroking Kerberos and staring at the woman for a long moment before tipping his chin at one of his attendants who stepped forward with chains similar to what Hades had attached to his belt, and began wrapping them around the crying woman's wrists.

Hades glanced away, toward where we were, though I wasn't sure if he *knew* we were here or not, and I took in his surprisingly sharp cheekbones, his dark lashes resting against his skin as he looked down. The clench of his fist on the arm of his throne and the slight tremor of his beard that I'd noticed before when his jaw ticced.

This was not a happy god.

Strangely, no one looked overly terrified about that fact. When Mother was unhappy, everyone held their breath.

"He doesn't like this," Orphne murmured. "The souls get addicted to the numbness the Lethe provides, then it's hard to stop. Chaining them up is the only thing that works, but it takes a toll on Hades to hurt those he's meant to protect."

She'd grown incredibly still next to me, and the air between us was heavy with expectation. She wanted me to react, to care perhaps. To express some sort of emotion or *something* for the King of the Underworld.

I didn't want to admit even to *myself* that I felt a frisson of sympathy for him, let alone admit it to anyone else. *He'd stolen me away from my life and my home.* And yet, Hades wasn't the indomitable force I thought he was.

If anything, he seemed a little lonely. Perhaps even overwhelmed.

"There has to be a better way," I muttered, trying to see the other petitioners and if they had the same vacant look in their eyes that the woman had.

"Perhaps there is, but Hades hasn't found it. Maybe you will," Orphne offered, staring into the throne room.

Me?

Orphne truly had the wrong idea about me if she thought I could solve a problem that the King of the Underworld hadn't been able to solve. One of Kerberos' heads began drifting back to us, but Hades set a hand on the side of his face, pulling its wandering attention forward.

"I've seen enough," I whispered, barely loud enough for myself to hear, let alone Orphne. And yet, despite how quiet I'd been, I was sure I caught the briefest glimpse of Hades turning toward where we stood before I climbed off the ledge and waited for Orphne to lead me back through the darkness.

CHAPTER 8

Every time I chained up one of the souls in my care, it cost me. Not only was I cutting off the ability for me to draw power from them when they were in chains, but it left me in a *foul* mood.

The Pool of Lethe had come with the underworld when I'd inherited control of it. I hadn't put it there, and the goddess, Lethe, refused to reduce the potency of the waters or provide any kind of solution to counteract the effects, no matter how many times I asked her.

I caught myself tapping my fingers impatiently on the arm of the throne and forced my hand to still. It would not do well to fidget. Not with so many eyes already on me, questioning my authority, my decisions, my very sanity. The court was always like this whenever I had to deal with someone suffering from the effects of the Lethe—they found my solution distasteful, even though none of them had offered any of their own.

"O great Hades."

I did my best not to let the disdain show on my face as Linus, of Thrace in his mortal life, appeared at the front of the line. He was an impressive musician—a son of one of the Muses, I couldn't remember which—and liked to show up at my court to sing his long dirges about how he missed his life in the upperworld. It was all very tedious, but the courtiers and other souls seemed to like his singing, so I supposed I was meant to just put up with it.

"I have composed my latest song in your honor. It is an ode to love, to commemorate your future bride."

I nodded, gesturing for him to proceed before returning my hand to Kerberos' fur.

Linus began a slow, grim lament to the futility of love that had everyone in the court smiling idiotically, but I couldn't bring myself to care. Not when new magic had been stirring in the palace walls, unbeknownst to most of those who lived here, who weren't as attuned to the slight shifts and invisible tremors rippling through the air.

It wasn't an overwhelming power, but it was faint and distinctive. Kore had stopped dampening her glow, if only for a little while.

Unfortunately, I doubted it was because she felt relaxed enough to walk around without hiding her impressive form. It was more likely that she was inside the Whispers and had needed the light to see by. Still, I'd take what progress I could get.

Hopefully she'd grow so comfortable wearing her true form that the idea of returning to a life of concealing herself would be untenable. I personally found it incredibly uncomfortable to suppress my divine form, but it seemed polite to do so in her company when Kore wasn't wearing hers.

Linus continued, working himself up to his big finish as Kore's energy retreated back through the Whispers to her rooms. It was unfortunate timing that she'd been here to witness me sending a soul to the dungeons, though I suspected Orphne had wanted something like that to happen. Even before she knew about my obsession with Kore, Orphne had been very vocal about my need for a wife. She seemed to think I was lonely and overworked.

One of those may have been true.

Kerberos growled in irritation as Linus began his series of bows to everyone in the throne room, and finally the incurable showoff had the sense to look unnerved, though he didn't leave. Instead, he broke into some long-winded explanation of his inspirations that I couldn't have been less interested in hearing.

Should I go back to Kore's rooms and try to visit her again now she'd demonstrated some interest in leaving her chambers? This was all very new to me. I'd never contemplated a *relationship* before, and I wanted to do it right—in a way that made her comfortable and happy—but Kore hadn't seen me, hadn't allowed me into her rooms, since our interaction in her bathing chamber. She'd been very distressed when I walked in on her, and I couldn't help but wonder if that was why she kept refusing me entry. That, or my leaving in a temper.

I hadn't meant to grow angry. It was just that she'd spoken of herself like she was nothing more than her lineage. Like the only plausible reason I could be interested in her was that she was the daughter of two Olympians, and therefore suitable bride material.

It enraged me that she'd think that way.

Why did she think that way? How did I change it? I needed to fix it.

Every deity I'd ever encountered had an overabundance of confidence. They thought themselves too good for everyone and everything. Every deity except Kore, who seemed to think she was entirely unexceptional, only made interesting by her parents.

Kore's parents were the least interesting thing about her.

They might be the only thing I *didn't* like about her.

Linus was still talking at me, and Kerberos finally gnashed his teeth, fed up. I gestured discreetly at Keuthonymos, my quiet and stalwart attendant, who expertly interceded to move Linus along. It had taken decades for us to get to this point—I used to just sit and wait until whoever was speaking was done, no matter how long it took or how much Kerberos growled and complained. It was Keuthonymos who'd suggested a polite way of moving them along so I could talk to more people.

"Time for a break!" a feminine voice announced. I gritted my teeth, gripping the arms of the throne so tightly that the stone was at risk of crumbling under my fingers.

"You overstep, Minthe," I warned her as she sashayed into view, planting herself between me and the waiting petitioner. Kerberos rose from his seated position, everything about his posture confrontational. He'd never liked Minthe. My heart had stopped in my chest when he'd headbutted Kore, thinking he'd taken a dislike to her as well. I could have never predicted he'd lie in her lap and pout until she scratched his belly.

"You work too hard, I just want to make sure you take breaks," Minthe cooed, flipping her emerald green hair over her shoulder, and flicking Kerberos a wary glance. "Of course, I assumed that now you'd brought a bride back to the underworld, she'd be doing all of this for you. Where is the famous Kore?"

I didn't always understand women—almost never, in fact—but I was fairly confident that Minthe's intentions were malicious. I'd shared her bed a few times before I'd known about Kore, a decision I regretted immensely, and Minthe had been vocal about desiring a more permanent place at my side on a throne of her own.

"That's none of your concern."

"Kore's new here, she might need a guide—"

"Kore has me," I cut in coolly, offended at the very concept of other people spending time with her when I hadn't yet had the privilege.

"You cannot be serious, Hades," Minthe repeated in disbelief. All three of Kerberos' heads growled in unison, even the usually more placid one. "You're the King of the Underworld, you can't spend your days showing her around the place. You barely have enough time for all your responsibilities as it is."

That was true, but I rejected the words on principle because they'd come from Minthe's mouth.

"Kore is the future Queen of the Underworld. She gets the best of everything, including the king himself as her guide. I'm done with this conversation. If you want to speak to me, you can line up with the other petitioners."

Minthe looked as though she was going to object, but Kerberos launched forward, snapping his teeth close enough at her pale chiton to leave a slight tear in the fabric. Minthe stumbled back, eyes wide, and the group of nymphs she usually consorted with tugged her back among them, bowing apologetically to me while Kerberos continued to make his displeasure known.

I hoped that would be the end of it. It didn't matter to me if every person in my court disapproved of Kore, I wasn't going to give her up.

I stormed through the palace toward my wing—*our* wing, now that Kore was here—in a foul mood. Not at all how I intended to present myself to the love of my life to offer her another courtship gift after multiple rejected attempts, but the entire day seemed to have conspired against me.

In sending Onesimos to Tartarus, I'd created a gap in the power structure in the Meadows. Various souls were fighting for dominance, including those from other factions who wanted to try their luck at a more prestigious position. If they needed to fight, they were more than welcome to do battle, but certain lines couldn't be crossed without consequence, and the contenders drew closer and closer to those lines each day. One soul had already fallen into Phlegethon's flames while attempting to wrestle their opponent into the fiery river, and I was not in the business of losing souls.

Fortunately, there was an abundance of new souls coming across the Styx, more than usual each day.

Unfortunately, Kerberos always seemed to sense when I was frustrated, regularly abandoning his post at the gate to check on me. That would be just what I needed after Thanatos' catastrophic mistake with Sisyphus—one of the many new souls who were lining up for judgment wandering out of the underworld because my appointed guardian kept slacking off.

"Hades," Keuthonymos called, jogging to catch up to me, shoving his pale hair out of his eyes. "Might I have a moment of your time—"

"Can it wait?"

Keuthonymos hesitated, glancing past me at the corridor that led to my rooms.

"Is it about Kore?" I asked impatiently. Every soul, nymph and deity in this realm seemed to have formed an opinion of her, and they hadn't even met her yet.

"The discontent around her presence is growing quite unmanageable." I narrowed my eyes at Keuthonymos, whose sole purpose was to *manage* things. If he wasn't managing them, then what was the point of him? "Not that I can't cope," he added hastily.

"Everything about this conversation suggests otherwise. What is it you'd have me do, Keuthonymos? Why is it you've chased me down the corridor?"

"Marry her," Keuthonymos said, trembling as he held eye contact. "By force if you have to."

"Excuse me?"

The passage dropped in temperature, thin cobwebs of ice creeping along the walls and floor. Keuthonymos glanced at them nervously.

"Once she's your wife, she's untouchable. It doesn't matter what the Olympians say, it doesn't matter what your courtiers say. Marry her and she's unconditionally yours."

It wasn't as though the idea hadn't crossed my mind, but I couldn't do that to Kore. I didn't just want her to *be* here, I wanted her to be *happy* here.

"If other people take issue with my relationship with Kore, that's *their* problem to deal with, not mine, not Kore's."

"With all due respect, Hades," Keuthonymos pressed, visibly straightening his posture and holding his ground. "It will become your problem—*Kore's* problem—if it goes unaddressed. There are many who feel she isn't a suitable wife for the King of the Underworld. She has presented no powers to speak of, has no experience in ruling anything, is too afraid to even leave her chambers—"

The ice around us solidified before snapping with a large crack, showering the floor in sparkling shards.

"I will take Kore as my wife when she is ready, and not a moment before," I growled, my voice as flinty and cold as the ice chips that littered the floor. "Anyone who disagrees with my approach can take it up with me personally. By all means, send them my way."

"Hades—"

"I love her. I won't see her suffer any more than she's already suffering."

A quiet flare of power glinted and disappeared in the wall next to me. A flare as bright and golden warm as the sun, bright and alive with life.

Kore had been in the Whispers. She'd heard every word I said.

CHAPTER 9

If Hades furiously defending my honor and announcing that he *loved* me had told me anything, it was that it was time to go. His courtiers didn't want me here—despite Hades' misguided impression that my presence here would be a happy surprise—and Hades himself was clearly far too attached. Terrifyingly so.

I love her.

I shook my head, trying to dislodge the memory of his words that had been haunting me for days, putting an abrupt end to my cautious explorations in the Whispers. *Love.* Impossible. How could he possibly love me? He didn't even know me. I'd sent him away every time he'd tried to visit, we hadn't spent enough time together for love to be even a remote possibility.

There was a strange fluttering in my stomach whenever I recalled those words and the vehemence in which he'd said them. A fluttering I attributed to flattery. It *was* flattering, in spite of everything. I'd always been envious when the nymphs at Henna bragged about the poetry that lovesick men had written in their honor, craving that sort of attention for myself. I never thought that once I had it, I wouldn't trust it. That I'd want to get as far away from it as possible.

I had to plan my escape. Despite the entirely warranted misgivings of his court, Hades wouldn't return me to the upperworld, and as close to two full weeks had passed, I had to concede that Mother wouldn't think to look for me here.

If I wanted to leave, I'd have to rescue myself.

I'd spent days in the Whispers, memorizing Hades' routine, and occasionally listening against the door that connected my rooms to his. I hadn't been as subtle as I'd hoped to be, and I knew Orphne was already getting her hopes up, thinking my sudden interest was something to do with a growing fondness for the King of the Underworld.

I just wanted to know his schedule.

It was a full one. Hades spent every moment of his time either in the throne room with petitioners, or being called away to the Meadows to sort out some dispute or another. The only deviations he had were to knock on my door, and he *never* visited his own chambers, not even to sleep.

That idea sat somewhat uncomfortably with me, but I forced myself to ignore that irksome, niggly feeling that may have been pity.

"Shall I leave you to rest?" Orphne asked as she did every day after straightening out my rooms.

"Yes please," I replied, forcing myself *not* to look at the heavy carved wooden door that separated my sitting room from Hades' lest I give myself away. My voice already sounded higher pitched than normal, though Orphne fortunately didn't seem to notice.

When I was confident Orphne was long gone, I quickly moved about the room, ready to wrap myself in the absurdly luxurious dark red himation Hades had left with Orphne for me. I'd done so well at ignoring the beautiful courting gifts. *So* well. The problem was that I was vain and Hades had exceptionally good taste, and that was a dangerous combination for my principles.

Everything he'd given me was so lovely—silky fabrics that clung to my body, dark jewel colors that Mother wouldn't have selected for me, golden bangles so polished I could see my reflection in them. *I was leaving anyway*, I reasoned. What was the harm in using the gifts while I was here? It wasn't like I'd get to enjoy things like this when I was back home at Henna.

Before I could pull the cloak on, there was a knock at the door that made me freeze. Had Orphne returned? That would be unlike her. Hades had already tried to visit me earlier, it couldn't be him. It deviated from his routine. And yet...

"Kore?" Hades called, knocking again. I gripped the himation tightly in my hands, trying to decide what to do. Should I just speak to him? Maybe talking to him now would work better, throw him further off my trail when I left. There was a dull thud while I deliberated, like his head had landed against the door.

"I know you don't want to see me. You heard what I said to Keuthonymos in the corridor, and it's made you want to see me even less. I didn't even realize that was possible," he muttered, sounding remarkably annoyed about the fact.

I wrapped myself in the cloak, tiptoeing closer to the door to listen. Not that I was curious or anything. I just *wondered* what he was going to say.

Perhaps I was a little curious.

"I don't know why I'm here," Hades mumbled under his breath, his voice so quiet that I pressed my ear against the door. "Maybe I thought you would require assurance that just because I'm in love with you doesn't mean I expect your love in return. Not yet, anyway. Perhaps not ever, though it would be nice."

I tugged the cloak tighter around myself, swallowing so thickly through the sudden tightness in my throat that he probably heard it through the heavy wooden door. There was such a strange swirl of emotions going through my head that I couldn't even begin to make sense of them.

"I've never loved anyone except you," he continued, even quieter now. "It's a terrible feeling, really. Like ripping your own chest open and watching it bleed. I wouldn't recommend it to anyone."

Another dull *thud* that made me wonder if he really was knocking his head against the door, and then he was gone as abruptly as he'd come.

Like ripping your own chest open and watching it bleed.

I loved my family, but I'd never been *in* love before. Never experienced that kind of all-consuming want that made you do stupid things for someone, like my mother sneaking away with Iasion at that wedding.

Or Hades kidnapping me from the upperworld.

The cloak suddenly didn't feel adequate for the chill that had set over me. I'd never asked to be the object of Hades' affections. I hadn't *tried* to cause him pain. I barely knew anything about him! I had to get back to my real life, for both of our sakes. This... whatever it was, had gone on long enough.

Confident that Hades had retreated down the corridor, I carefully opened the door that connected our bedchambers, peeking through it like I'd wanted to for days.

Silence.

Our rooms were almost a mirror image of each other, only the depictions on the frescoes were slightly different, and I was surprised all over again at the grandeur of the accommodations Hades had given me. Even if I'd been *planning* on marrying him, I probably would have expected less grand rooms until I was officially his wife.

I shut the connecting door behind me, darting into the bedchamber on the other side of the room and taking in my surroundings. Unlike the one in my bedchamber, Hades' bed had no soft cushions or luxurious blankets. There was a single dark blue blanket, so impressively flat and smooth that I would bet every piece of jewelry I'd ever owned that it had never been slept on.

It was so *sad*. It wasn't that immortals needed sleep—we could function perfectly fine without it—but it was a luxury. Resting our minds, inviting the Oneiroi visit with the dreams they wove, or just surrendering to blissful oblivion for a few hours was the kind of luxury that couldn't be bought. Hades' life must be stark indeed if he didn't even allow himself this very ordinary pleasure.

Not that I felt sorry for him.

I didn't feel anything for him.

I refused to.

In the corner was the item I'd come here for—the Helmet of Invisibility—and I forced myself to focus on that instead of my stupid pity for my kidnapper.

The bronze, rather unassuming helmet sat on a marble plinth at the edge of the room, almost daring me to take it. Why was it so unprotected? Was everyone so fearful of Hades that they just didn't come in these rooms at all? Or was there some kind of unseen magic guarding it that would immediately notify him if someone touched it?

Without having any experience using my own gifts, I was at a disadvantage in understanding how the other gods' worked too. I was at a disadvantage in many ways, and I intended on raising all of them with Mother when I got home.

There's only one way to know if the helmet is protected, I resolved. I strode confidently toward the plinth—more confidently than I felt—and picked it up with both hands, holding it just an inch above the marble for a moment to see if anything happened.

Nothing.

Would I know? I felt like I'd know. I always sensed when divine magic was used around me, and the reason I wasn't allowed to use my own was because it left a trace.

A more patient, less impulsive person would have set the helmet down. Walked away. Left it a day at least to see if there was any reaction.

But I wasn't a more patient person. Or I wasn't *here*. Something about the underworld made me reckless.

I lifted the surprisingly light helmet, setting it over my head and adjusting it until it was comfortable. *Was it working?* I didn't *feel* invisible. I held my hand up to my face and could still see it perfectly.

There was a hand mirror on a table in the corner and I crossed the room, sucking in a quiet breath when my reflection didn't appear. It *did* work. I could see my own limbs in the flesh, but I was invisible to the outside world.

I was almost giddy with the possibilities.

Except I'd have to be sensible with this newfound power. If I failed to get out of the palace before Hades realized the helmet was missing, he'd undoubtedly store it somewhere more secure. He was adamant that he wouldn't provide any assistance in my escape attempts, and borrowing his things probably counted as assistance. Not that I had any idea of how I'd return the helmet when I was done with it, but that seemed like a problem for me to deal with when I was safely back in the upperworld.

Mother will handle it, I thought uneasily, slipping through the adjoining door that connected our rooms. Strangely, after an entire lifetime of Mother handling most everything for me, I wasn't looking forward to returning to it. I liked the freedom I had here, liked that Hades for whatever reason seemed to genuinely respect my words when I spoke.

No, no, I didn't like that. I didn't like anything about him.

He'd *kidnapped* me. I was losing my mind.

Without Orphne here, I had no one to test my newfound invisibility on, but I was too curious to wait for her to return, so I headed through the sitting room and out into the empty corridor. This wing of the palace was always so quiet. I supposed it made sense that if Hades didn't spend any time here, his courtiers didn't bother to either, but it still struck me as strange compared to my mother's court with the open walls and courtiers who showed up whenever they pleased.

I turned a corner toward where I thought the throne room was, passing two giggling nymphs who paid me no mind. Emboldened, I moved closer to the souls milling about around entryway, seeing how close I could get. It was so… *odd.* When people looked at me at my mother's court, it was normally with pity.

Not having anyone look at me with thinly veiled sympathy was *glorious.*

"When are we starting?" someone muttered. "He's usually here by now."

"There were issues in the Meadows again," the woman next to him replied. "There's been a power struggle since Hades dropped Onesimos into Tartarus, and the souls seem to think he'll be busy enough with his new bride to not pay attention. If you lived over that side of the Meadows, you'd know how violent it's gotten."

"I belong to Eupraxia's faction, we're too small to get involved in all that," the man sighed, though I missed the rest of their conversation as I continued making my way around the edges of the crowd. I should have immediately made for the exit, but I wanted to see the throne room in all its glory just once. The tiny sliver I could make out from the Whispers had only made me curious to see more.

Why was Hades dropping his own people into Tartarus? Didn't he derive his power from the souls in the underworld? It seemed illogical to then throw those souls away, and if there was one thing I was fairly certain Hades *wasn't*, it was illogical.

He was stubborn, though. I could believe that he'd be too stubborn to explore other paths if he'd already set his course.

There was a big enough gap between groups that I could slip into the throne room, immediately making my way to the very front near the dais where none of the petitioners dared to stand, sticking close to a column.

A green-haired nymph with a smile that promised misery stood closest to the dais, possessing the kind of unwavering confidence that said she was used to being there. *An ex-lover, at the very least,* I thought, only slightly bitterly.

"I wonder if this vaunted future *queen* of ours will make an appearance today," she laughed, loudly talking to her companions. I froze in place, sliding my gaze to the circle of tittering nymphs she stood amongst. "How can Hades expect her to rule by his side when she's too much of a coward to leave her bedchamber?"

I narrowed my eyes, hands flexing incessantly at my side as I fought my gift back out of habit. If ever there was a time to let it go, it was now, though I had no idea what would happen if I did.

Surprisingly, my rage wasn't purely on my own behalf. They were *laughing* at Hades too. Brazenly disrespecting his authority just feet away from his throne. How was it possible that they felt comfortable enough to do that?

"He must see some potential in her that we don't, Minthe," one of the nymphs offered placatingly.

The first one who'd spoken—Minthe—shot her a derisive look. I hated to admit it, but she was exceptionally beautiful, with long emerald hair, pale green skin and dainty features. She'd be the picture of kindness and innocence, were it not for the vicious smirk.

"You know how Hades is. He *fixates* on things, gets an idea in his head and refuses to be moved until someone moves *him*. That's all this is. His latest idiotic fixation. The sooner he's encouraged away from this lunacy, the better off we'll all be. Demeter's darling daughter can go back to the upperworld where she belongs."

That was theoretically what I wanted as well, so I didn't know why I was so offended when *she* suggested it. If anything, she could be a potential ally in getting me out of here.

"Minthe," one of the other nymphs laughed. "Even if you do successfully drive the useless goddess away, how many times does Hades have to reject your suggestion of marriage before you believe him?"

Minthe's face flushed with fury, and my flesh ached with the effort of keeping my magic contained. Nothing would give away my presence sooner than... whatever it was that I wanted to do to Minthe.

It wasn't jealousy.

I refused to accept jealousy as an explanation for my abrupt desire to *unmake* her somehow, to watch her suffer.

Thankfully, before I could act on my sudden bloodthirsty desires, Hades made his grand entrance, which wasn't grand at all. My mother would wait until everyone was standing at attention before a procession of nymphs would lead her in. No such thing for the King of the Underworld. He strode in from a gap between two columns, looking harried, not sparing anyone a glance as he threw himself down onto his throne.

An attendant approached, clearly ready to relay important information about those waiting to see the King of the Underworld, and no one seemed perturbed by Hades' behavior. Was he always this rushed? This impatient? This *unhappy?* He certainly didn't seem like a ruler who relished the trappings of power.

The courtiers moved closer to the dais while the line of souls that cut through the middle of the room straightened slightly. Unlike at my mother's court, the courtiers seemed to have no interest in those who'd come to make their requests, not a single iota of curiosity.

Then again, I supposed the stakes were low. The souls weren't going anywhere, they wouldn't be struck down by a vengeful deity if their request was too bold, nor would they be rewarded with the kind of gifts that only temporal beings could truly appreciate.

They just *were.*

Leave, I told myself. I was meant to be finding a way out of here, and hovering in the corner watching Hades on his throne got me no closer to that goal. But I could admit to myself that I was just the slightest bit transfixed.

I had grown up hearing about those who wore power like fine jewels. They showed it off, reveled in it, and ultimately when they grew bored, discarded it. Zeus spent far more time pursuing carnal interests than ruling. Poseidon fared only a little better.

Hades was no such king.

Hades bore his authority, his responsibility, his *power* like Atlas bore the weight of the Earth.

There was a strange aching sensation in my chest, my fingers flexing in the folds of my chiton like I could go up to where he sat and take some of that burden for my own.

It was an absurd notion. That wasn't why he'd chosen me as his bride, and I wouldn't have the faintest idea how to carry such a weight even if it was. I was a goddess who didn't know how to use her power, snatched away from everything I'd ever known because I was available. A pretty vessel for growing future gods and goddesses in.

That sobering thought sent me quietly backing out of the throne room before the first petitioner could speak, winding my way through the crush of souls waiting for his attention and out onto the palace steps. I didn't belong here. Not in this palace, not in this realm.

I paused for a moment when I got outside, looking at the dark, intimidating landscape around me. Mountains so tall they seemed impossible to climb on one side. The dancing flames of the Phlegethon on the horizon. I swallowed thickly. No ordinary mortal soul could find their way out of the underworld without Hades' express consent, I knew that, but I was an immortal goddess. Surely, if anyone could, it was me.

The mountain range was to my left, and I was confident we'd been flying *towards* that, rather than over the top when Hades had dragged me down here, though my memories of the chariot ride were fuzzy and tinged with terror. To the right was a strangely barren, rocky area, except for an enormous pool that wasn't surrounded by souls, unlike the Lethe, which I assumed was the crowded pool on the other side of the palace. I'd never get past there without bumping into someone.

I rushed down the marble steps, keeping my himation tightly wrapped around my body so the fabric didn't whip anyone as I passed. My feet landed on the cool stone path, and I turned right, following the trail and cursing my lack of observational skills the entire way. If I ever got abducted again, I was going to pay much closer attention to my surroundings.

The sheer number of souls lining up to get to the Lethe was so overwhelming that grounds at the front of the palace were crowded with them. It was almost impossible to navigate through the throng without bumping into someone, though I wasn't entirely sure they'd notice even if I *did*. These souls were in even worse shape than the woman I'd seen begging Hades to lock her in the dungeon—at least she'd been *trying* to fight the effects of the Lethe. There was no spark to the souls here the way there was with most of the petitioners who fought for Hades' attention in the throne room. These just seemed to *exist*.

There had to be something Hades could do about this. Some way he could block off access to the Lethe, to stop the souls from accessing such a cruelly addictive substance.

I had to believe it was cruel, that it was out of his hands, or I might turn around and go back out of some misplaced sense of sympathy.

You don't belong here, Kore. Don't look back.

CHAPTER 10

The crowds thinned out as I walked on, the path growing rocky and uncomfortable beneath my feet, unlike the smooth worn stone near the palace.

The sky seemed darker here. No, it *was* darker here. In fact, it grew darker and darker as I went, like night was falling, but when I turned to look back, the sky above the palace was as grayish purple as ever.

With growing unease, I realized that it wasn't night that was making the sky darken, but this *place*, wherever it was. A place where even the lost, forgetful souls didn't venture.

My steps slowed as I traversed the rocky path downward, rounding a corner to find yet another palace, illuminated only by the fiery Phlegethon. Unlike Hades' gleaming marble dwelling, this one looked to be made of obsidian, the shining black reflecting the sparking flames that shot out of the river.

It was what I had *expected* the Palace of Hades to look like. Dark, imposing, cold.

I paused, taking a moment to sit on the ground with my himation tucked underneath me, softening the uncomfortable rocks beneath me somewhat.

Now what?

This gloomy palace was built right on the banks, and I was in no rush to test out my immortality in a divine fire river. I would have to go around it, between the palace and the abandoned pool, to what I thought was the west of Hades' home. I'd be doubling back, moving closer to Hades rather than further away, but I couldn't see another way around.

Curse Hades and his flying chariot. I doubted he'd even once worried about how to cross the Phlegethon.

The dark palace was built farther down the slope, but there was a narrow ridge on the hill that I could perhaps inch around, so long as I kept my back to the cliff face.

It would be fine.

The worst that could happen was falling into the terrifying castle of darkness. Nothing at all to worry about.

I didn't dare to breathe as I clambered up onto the ledge, pressing my back and my palms against the rough-hewn rock and sidestepping my way around the slope. Looking at my feet made me more off-balance, so I chose to go slowly by feel and watch the palace instead.

What was it? Who resided there?

Perhaps that was where Hades went, and that was why his rooms were always empty. Then again, it didn't really *feel* like him. And there was no shortage of dark and shadowy deities in the underworld that could feasibly call such a nightmarish-looking hall home. Rumors from the upperworld said that Kronos himself—the last King of the Gods—lived here somewhere, having been released from Tartarus. I'd rather return willingly to Hades' palace than encounter Kronos.

Each step felt so precarious, so filled with fear that I'd make a mistake and fall into the unknown at the bottom of the hill, that for a moment I wondered how mortals did it. And by it, I meant *anything*. They were so fragile that with every misstep, they could suffer death or permanent injury, and yet they persisted with each step through life anyway.

Perhaps some vague part of me had always felt like I was better, braver, more impressive than the mortals who came to my mother's court, begging for whatever scraps of grace she would show them. I'd leave the underworld with a newfound respect for those mortals. For what it was to experience true, genuine *fear* and carry on anyway.

My foot slipped, and despite my flailing attempts to grab at something, I was already falling, sliding down the slope toward the base of the dark palace with no way of stopping.

I bit my lip hard enough to bleed to hold in my scream, hoping the sudden collapse of rocks and debris looked like a landslide as I came to a painful stop in a pile of dirt. The dark palace loomed above me, eerily silent. *Run,* I told myself, wincing as I climbed to my feet. My himation and chiton were torn and filthy, and ichor welled at every cut and scrape on my palms and legs, running in rivulets down my skin.

Curse it all. A trail of golden droplets on the ground was as good of a giveaway as anything. If I could get to that abandoned pool, just over the rise of the hill, I could at least rinse off the evidence. Though even that was a risk—it definitely *wasn't* a pool of forgetfulness, I knew enough to be certain there was only one. But I didn't know what it *did* either.

I chewed on my lower lip for a moment, but there was a clanging sound from inside the dark palace that made up my mind for me. I ran around the edge of it, wincing at the pain in my feet, heading north to where I knew the pool was, and began climbing, hastily grabbing on to roots and rocks and anything else I could find. The movement split the cuts on my palms open further, and I cursed silently at the smears of gleaming gold that remained everywhere I touched.

The moment I got to the top, I collapsed on my back, giving myself a moment to recover. The injuries were hardly grave, but I'd never experienced anything like them in the upperworld—no simple rock there would have been able to pierce an immortal's flesh. The sensation of *pain* was strange.

Unpleasant.

Just another reason for me to get out of this realm.

I glanced down, realizing that in shifting around the hill, I could now see the entrance to the dark palace. Above the enormous doorways was a carved relief, and I could faintly make out three feminine figures. I squinted, wondering why their faces looked so strange. *Blindfolds.* They had been depicted with blindfolds covering the upper halves of their face. I couldn't see what it was they appeared to be holding between them, but I could make an educated guess.

Three blindfolded women could only be the Moirai—Clotho, Lachesis, and Atropos. The Fates themselves. I shoved myself to my feet, stumbling backward onto the stone path at the top of the hill. The more distance I could put between myself and the Fates, the better.

I didn't want to see them. I didn't want to converse with them. Perhaps it was cowardly, but the idea that they might tell me something I didn't want to hear—like that my future was *here*, in the underworld—was terrifying. I'd rather not know.

Instead, I raced across the wide path, leaving golden footsteps in my wake and picking up my pace when I realized I wasn't alone. Someone, or some*thing*, was definitely chasing me, but I was too afraid to glance back lest it give them the chance to catch up.

Stupid, stupid, stupid.

I should have stolen a weapon.

Something barreled into my back, pushing me to the ground at the edge of the enormous still pool. I stiffened instinctively, waiting for some underworld beast to tear into my flesh, but instead I felt rough wetness on the backs of my shoulders and neck, huffs of hot breath puffing over me as whatever it was panted.

"Kerberos?" I wheezed, face pressed uncomfortably into the smooth rocks that lined the edge of the pool. "Could you let me up?" I asked hesitantly, remembering the unusually conversational way Hades had spoken to him.

Kerberos yipped, clambering off me and dropping down on his haunches, waiting patiently as I pushed myself up into a sitting position, wincing at the fresh injuries on my hands from my fall. I wasn't sure if he could see me or he was just following my scent, but Kerberos shuffled in closer, nosing my arm before finding a wounded palm and licking the ichor clean off it.

"I don't know if that's good for you," I murmured uneasily, trying and failing to deter him. Ichor was fatal to mortals, but Kerberos was a monster of the underworld. Surely there wasn't much that could take him down.

He resumed his work, sniffing around until he found the other hand, before nosing down my body and licking the soles of my feet while I tried not to kick him away on instinct. It would certainly solve the trail problem even though the wounds hadn't closed yet.

I took a moment to examine my surroundings, and from up here, I could see a much easier path between the pool and the dark palace than the one next to the fiery river I'd followed before, so long as I stuck close to the water I'd get past to whatever lay beyond.

Maybe... Maybe I could convince Kerberos to take me to the gate he was meant to be guarding. Maybe I didn't have to stumble along blind at all, if I could somehow get the three-headed dog beast with the snake tail on my side.

Kerberos finished tending to my injuries, and I took turns at scratching behind each set of ears in gratitude for a moment. I didn't like the idea of using him to escape, and I hoped Hades wouldn't punish him for it. Kerberos attempted to plant his enormous body on my legs, and I laughed silently, arranging him until all three heads were in my lap, the rest of his body spread out on the rocks. What was the harm in taking a short break? I needed to give my feet time to heal anyway, or I'd just undo all his hard work. There was a long twig on the ground next to me, and I snatched it up, using it to poke at the surface of the dark blue pool in front of me, sending a small ripple out.

Nothing.

It was strange to see the mirror of the Pool of Lethe deserted, when the other side of the palace was so crowded with souls. What about this water was so off-putting to them?

Maybe I should throw a rock?

Deciding that would be the best way to find out if there was a creature lurking in its depths, I picked up the biggest loose rock within my vicinity and hefted it toward the middle of the pool, where it landed with a dull crash. Kerberos let out a loud snore from my lap.

"Well, I'm certainly glad I wasn't swimming," a voice said from behind me. I let out a blood-curdling shriek that would have alerted whoever it was to my location, even if they didn't seem to already know, given how close they were standing to me. Kerberos leaped up, positioning himself defensively in front of me for a moment before making a dismissive huffing sound and flopping back down half on my lap.

"Do you scream like that for Hades? Is that why he wants to marry you?"

The teasing quality in her voice made me blush. Surely she couldn't be alluding to what I *thought* she was alluding to?

"Who are you?" I demanded, twisting to face the smirking goddess staring down at me, certain I'd never seen her before. She was tall and elegant, with dark brown skin, deep purple eyes, and black curly hair, tied in a golden ribbon.

"Will you take off the helmet?" she asked, squinting at Kerberos like she was trying to figure out what exactly he was lying on.

My first instinct was to say no, but she'd mentioned Hades wanting to marry me, so I supposed she knew who I was already. I didn't think I'd ever get used to that—the mortals who showed up at Henna were surprised to discover Demeter even *had* a second daughter.

"Fine," I muttered, yanking the helmet off my head and setting it down on the rocks next to me.

"Prickly little thing. No wonder the King of the Underworld likes you." The goddess stared at me, cataloging my features. "He's rather prickly himself, but unfailingly civilized, even perhaps when he ought not to be. Sometimes we need to be a little aggressive to get results, wouldn't you agree?"

"He stole me from my home, I hardly consider that unfailing politeness. Who exactly are you?" I pressed, sinking my fingers into the fur at the back of Kerberos' neck, the act of petting him helping me to keep my head.

"Mm, Lethe mentioned something about your arrival here," she mused, ignoring my question. "It's very out of character for Hades to behave that way. You must have been in dire straits indeed for him to feel the need to come to your rescue in such an unorthodox fashion."

"I didn't need rescuing," I snapped, growing exasperated. "Who are you? How do you know Lethe?"

"She is my perfect opposite, of course. My counterbalance. Sometimes I visit her down here to see how she's been doing, how many memories she's stolen, that sort of thing."

Stolen indeed, though the goddess said it with no trace of judgment whatsoever.

"If you are her opposite," I began slowly. "Then you must be the Goddess of Memory. Mnemosyne."

"Very good. You're more than just a pretty face and an impressive scream." She looked inordinately pleased that I'd gotten it right, and I fought the idiotic urge to preen. I blamed it on a lack of compliments in my life.

"I'm not a pretty face," I muttered. "Or an impressive scream."

"Oh, my dear, you very much are. I know you might not wish to be reminded of such—but your parents are exceptionally lovely, and you've inherited their breathtaking features."

She was right, I didn't want to be reminded of that.

"Do you know if anything lives in this pool?" I asked, poking it with a stick again.

"Nothing," Mnemosyne said lightly. "This pool is unoccupied and unnamed."

"Why?" I wondered out loud, not particularly asking Mnemosyne but rather musing to myself. Everything in life had a balance, a counter. For darkness there was light, for heat there was cold.

For forgetfulness, there was memory.

"This is meant to be *your* pool," I realized, pointing an accusing finger at her and giving her my best hard glare, channeling Demeter's ferocity.

"So it is," Mnemosyne replied cheerfully. Clearly, I needed to work on my glare.

"Well then, why isn't it?"

"Hades never asked me." She shrugged. "It's his realm, after all. If he wants to chain his subjects in the dungeon to suffer through the effects of Lethe's magic, well that really seems like his prerogative."

"He never asked you," I repeated flatly. Kerberos huffed indignantly, and I was almost certain he understood every word we were saying.

"I mean, must I do everything? It's his job to work this sort of thing out. Though perhaps that's why he's gone and found himself a queen."

"I'm not his queen."

"Not yet, though he's given you all the authority of one," Mnemosyne remarked. Had he? I doubted that was true, but if she believed it to be so, then what was the harm in trying my luck?

I was leaving anyway, may as well do a good deed on my way out.

"You will occupy this pool," I commanded without a shred of confidence that she'd listen. "You will bless its waters. Your gift will counter the effects of Lethe's, and restore the memories of those who seek to have them restored."

Kerberos lifted all three heads off the ground, peering up at Mnemosyne whilst also shuffling his position as though he could fit his entire body on my legs like a kitten instead of the enormous beast he was. The snake tail hissed as he rolled on it, and Mnemosyne took a wary step backward.

"Okay."

"Okay?" I repeated hesitantly.

"You are the future Queen of the Underworld, I can hardly say no to you. But you'll need to do your bit too."

"What's my bit?" I asked suspiciously.

"Well, you'll have to bless the waters too, after I claim them. It's *your* underworld, I can't just be going around laying claim to things without approval. I'd cause a scandal."

This conversation was making my head hurt. "I doubt that's true, and even if it was, I don't know how to bless things. And it's not my underworld."

"You've been given the authority of a queen by Hades," Mnemosyne insisted. "Only he or you can bless the waters. And as for how, just walk in and let your magic fill the pool. It's very easy."

Easy for someone who used their gifts, perhaps.

Before I could point that out, Mnemosyne strode past me and hopped into the pool, which immediately glowed an impressive shade of cerulean, as though it was welcoming her home. Mnemosyne waded toward the middle, the water only coming to her waist, skimming her hands over the surface and humming off-key as she went.

"Are you doing it?" I called out, waiting for some explosive display of magic. My own gift was rising, at a slightly alarming rate if I was honest with myself. I flexed my hands repeatedly to try and keep it at bay.

"Oh yes, all done, my future queen," Mnemosyne replied cheerily. I got annoyed all over again that all this time when souls had been chained in a dungeon to save them from themselves, all she had to have done was paddle through a shallow pool for a few seconds. It was just like a god to let people suffer just for the sake of it. "Your turn now."

Kerberos climbed off me, positioning himself next to the helmet and watching as I picked my way over the rocks to the water's edge.

"Will you tell Hades that it's done? That he can now send souls here for healing?" I called to Mnemosyne, hesitating on the bank.

"Hades? Oh no, I don't think I will. Of course, if he *asks*, I'll be entirely forthcoming, but I do *so* hate visiting the palace. Hades is such a miserable host, and he has acquired the most unhappy nymphs I've ever encountered for his court."

"Well, how is he going to know to send souls here if you're not going to tell him? How will the souls know to drink from your waters? I can't do it, I'm leaving."

"Mm, quite the conundrum you have there." Mnemosyne flopped back, floating on the water, resuming her tragic humming. "Hop in, it's lovely and warm."

Fates, spare me.

While I didn't know what I was doing, my magic seemed to. It was practically beating at my skin, desperate to escape the prison I kept it in. I'd been so scared of using it my entire life that it still felt *wrong* to entertain the idea, even though I knew I was being illogical. Hades didn't want me for my magic.

For reasons I didn't understand, he wanted me regardless.

"This better work," I muttered, my divine form emerging the moment I dipped a toe in the water. I waded further in, my golden glow illuminating the pool, glittering shapes that I couldn't quite make out dancing over the surface.

Nothing about it was a conscious decision. In the back of my mind, I knew I vaguely *wanted* to bless the waters, that I wanted it to work and for the souls to have somewhere to go to heal their memory, but I wasn't in charge of whatever my magic was doing.

If I was in charge, I'd use less. My limbs were feeling strange and heavy, and my head felt odd. Like it was spinning in circles.

Mnemosyne said something, but her voice sounded as though it was thousands of miles away. And then I heard nothing at all.

HADES

CHAPTER 11

"Hades," the waters of the Stygian Marshlands that ran behind the palace whispered to me. *"Kore has lost consciousness."*

I jumped to my feet, storming past the line of petitioners waiting to speak to me without an explanation. How had this happened? She'd been fine. The rivers had been reporting to me on Kore's wanderings from the moment she'd left. I'd nearly gone to drag her back multiple times already, but I'd told her I wouldn't interfere if she tried to leave.

I hadn't realized how hard that would be, knowing she was out there, walking around, exposed to the harshness of the underworld. Only the assurances I'd received from Phlegethon had given me any reassurance, and it wasn't much—before she'd lost consciousness, I knew she'd fallen down the cliff above the Halls of Night.

She'd taken a detour, but Kore had been traveling in the right direction. Alarmingly so. If she'd gotten to the edge of the pool, she'd have seen the increasingly long line of souls that lined the bank of the Styx, waiting for judgment. Following it back to the start, back to the *gate*, would have been nothing.

I was selfishly glad she failed, and furious at myself for it. She was *injured*. Every tiny cut and scrape was an indictment on my ability to keep her safe and comfortable in this dangerous realm. I'd never be able to convince her to stay if I couldn't keep her from harm.

I nearly called for my chariot once I was on the palace steps, hoping it would get me to her faster, but a golden glow further down the path had me breaking into a run instead. *Kore.* In her blinding, brilliant divine form.

Unconscious.

Kerberos moved slowly and carefully, with Kore draped over his back, stopping when I got to him. Swallowing thickly, I lifted Kore into my arms, her head lolling back, the tips of her golden hair brushing against the ground.

I should have ignored Orphne's advice to give Kore freedom to explore and learn about the underworld for herself. This would have never happened if I'd locked her safely in her rooms, and I doubted that seeing the starkness of this realm had endeared her to it.

"Clear the way," I instructed Kerberos, striding toward the palace with my future bride in my arms.

If anyone tried to speak to me on the way back to Kore's rooms, they'd find themselves in the pit to Tartarus before the day was done.

Kerberos snarled at anyone within a few feet as we made our way up the palace steps and turned away from the crowd toward our private wing. I could feel the eyes of the court on my back as I walked, but their judgment meant nothing to me.

"What happened?" Orphne gasped, pulling open the door to Kore's rooms and stepping back.

"She used too much of her gift at once," I clipped. "Leave us, Orphne. I will care for her."

Orphne bowed, immediately excusing herself while Kerberos flopped down on his belly, watching the entry. I carried Kore through to the bathing chamber, climbing the steps to the pool with her in my arms and submerging us both in the warm waters. Water was essential to life, and Kore was a goddess of life. She may not have realized it yet, but I was certain that was why she spent so much time by the lake in the upperworld. It was settling to her gift, underutilized as it was.

I carefully brought Kore's head up, resting it against my shoulder, and wrapped both arms around her middle to keep her in place. It felt too right, too perfect, too easy to have her on my lap. This was where she was meant to be. She was meant to be *mine*, and I hers.

Why couldn't she see that? What did I need to do to make her see that?

Within seconds, Kore began to stir. Her face turned toward my chest, nosing slightly at the fabric of my chiton, shifting it out of the way and inhaling deeply against my bare skin. A small, dopey smile played around her mouth, and perhaps it wasn't as hopeless as I thought.

She liked how I smelled. Surely, I could do something with that. Use it to my advantage somehow.

Then she opened her eyes, and the tenuous flame of hope I'd been nursing immediately extinguished.

Kore shrieked, flailing backward into the pool in her attempts to get away from me. I reached under the water, grabbing her hips and lifting her to sit on the bench at the edge of the bath before backing away a few steps with my hands raised.

"Be calm, Kore. I don't want to hurt you."

She pulled her legs up onto the bench and wrapped her arms around her knees. "What are you doing here? What am *I* doing here?"

The fear in her eyes was hard to take. I wanted nothing more than to close the distance and hold her again, even though I knew that would only make things worse.

"You expended too much of your gift at once. I'm not sure what you were doing," I replied carefully. Not for the first time, I wished Kerberos could speak.

Kore's brow creased as she stared into the bath water like it held all the answers. "I can't remember either. But that can't be right. I don't use my gift."

She held a hand up to her face like she was surprised to find it was glowing golden. With impressive control, she pulled her divine form within herself again, her glow extinguishing.

"Why don't you use your gift?"

Kore's affronted expression, the one she usually wore in my presence, reappeared instantly. "I'm not having this conversation with you in the *bath*."

"But we're not nude. I thought your objection to me seeing you bathe was your nudity?"

Kore gestured at the soaked fabric of her chiton on her arms, which admittedly clung appealingly to her skin. "This is basically nude, Hades. Where is Orphne?"

"I dismissed her."

"Of course you did." Kore sighed, rubbing her temples. "I will dry and dress *by myself*, and then if we must discuss anything, we can do it then. Does that sound agreeable?"

"No."

"Will you harm me if I offend you?" Kore asked, shooting me an irritated glare.

"Of course not. I would never harm you, you have my word."

"Great. *Get out, Hades.* I'll speak to you when I'm dry and dressed," Kore ordered. The fire in her eyes made my cock stir, and I decided it probably *was* the best course of action to get out of the bath before my ill-timed desire caused Kore even more discomfort.

"I'll be in the sitting room," I called over my shoulder, feeling Kore's gaze tracking the length of my body as I climbed out of the water, the fabric of my black chiton sticking to my skin.

I sent Kerberos back to the gate and took a moment to go into my rooms for the first time in I couldn't remember how long, quickly changing before grabbing a small alabastron of healing salve from the side table. The salve smelled of sideritis, and had been acquired by Hermes at my request, in exchange for a favor. It was infused with ambrosia, and would heal Kore's wounds instantly and cleanly, even ones caused by the underworld's unforgiving landscape.

Not particularly glamorous, as far as courting gifts went, and she was already annoyed with me for getting into the bath with her. I sighed heavily as I knocked on the connecting door between our rooms.

I never seemed to get it right with Kore, despite my best intentions.

"Come in, if you must," Kore muttered. I opened the door immediately, inclining my head at her. She'd dried and changed into a fresh chiton, and tucked her hands behind her back when she saw me, hiding the scrapes on her palms.

It was a chiton that *I'd* given her, made from dark blue silk. It was the first time I'd truly seen her in one of the garments I'd gifted her, and it had my possessive instincts rush frantically to the surface. *Mine.* Kore was mine. She had to be.

"Hello again," she said, watching me with wary eyes, undoubtedly wondering how I was going to respond to her venture into the underworld with my stolen helmet.

"Hello. Will you sit?" I asked, impressing myself with how even I kept my voice as I gestured to the klinai.

Kore sighed heavily again, as though I were asking the world of her, but eventually took her seat, clasping her hands together. She straightened the moment I approached, eyeing me suspiciously as I kneeled at her feet, tipping some of the medicinal salve from the small vessel into my palm before setting it aside.

"What is that? What are you—" Kore's question cut off with a surprised gasp as I carefully picked up her wrist from her lap, my knuckles brushing her thigh as I flipped her hand over, exposing the scrapes.

Several emotions I couldn't identify flitted over Kore's face, and while I struggled to understand what it was that she was *thinking*, I knew what it was she was *planning*. An excuse. A lie.

My heart thudded unevenly, a strange tightness blooming in my chest. I didn't like it when Kore lied to me. Everyone lied to me all day long, looking at me like I was too incompetent, too honest, to understand what they were doing.

It suited me just fine to let them underestimate me, but the idea of Kore lying to me felt like a betrayal.

"Don't," I warned quietly, lightly spreading the salve over each scrape on the first hand. "Keep your secrets, Kore."

Her hand shook slightly in mine, eyes downcast.

"You aren't curious as to how I got these scrapes?" she challenged softly. Stubbornly.

"Very. I'd also like to know why you don't use your gift, and what you were doing that meant you expended so much, but only if you're willing to give me an honest answer. I find hearing lies from your lips distressing."

She made a strangled noise, and I kept working in silence, finishing the first hand and then the second before rocking back on my heels and looking up at her.

"Lift your chiton."

Kore spluttered, a delightfully ungainly sound. "Excuse me? Absolutely not."

"I only wish to tend to your injuries. If I wanted to seduce you, I'd rip the garment right off your body."

Kore's face glowed more golden than I'd ever seen it, the flush spreading down her neck and disappearing past the fabric.

"Brute," she muttered, delicately bunching the material so it rose just enough to expose her ankles. She had particularly lovely ankles. I didn't think I imagined her soft exhale as I cupped her heel and lifted one foot to rest on my thigh, taking my time in removing my hand and reaching for the salve.

As much as I wanted to drag this out, I might alarm Kore if my cock sprang to attention against her foot, based on her insistence that I not see her nude and the fact that there were no grown males at Demeter's court.

Then again, Kore had been proposed to twice, and she hadn't mentioned either of those to me. Perhaps it was *me* specifically she didn't want to be around.

"Ouch," Kore winced as my thumbs pressed a little too hard into a wound on the bottom of her foot.

"My apologies," I murmured, stroking her softly with my thumb. I chanced a glance upward, finding Kore watching me closely.

"What's wrong?"

"You collapsed," I replied immediately, any faint traces of anger gone in the face of Kore's discomfort. I was supposed to be here to *woo* her, and I was getting it all wrong.

"No, there's something else bothering you," she pressed, tilting her head to the side. I wasn't used to genuine curiosity, not about me. "Your mood just changed completely."

"Yes." Even if I wanted to lie to her—which I didn't—I'd been informed repeatedly that I had no talent for it. "There are a combination of reasons why I'm upset. For one, you're hurt. That makes me angry. I failed to keep you safe."

Kore's brow furrowed. "They're scratches and they're not your fault."

I hummed, quietly disagreeing. I should have sent Orphne to follow Kore at a distance, to make sure she was safe in her attempts to get away from me. At least Kerberos had the sense to keep an eye on her.

"What else?" Kore asked, muscles flexing slightly under my ministrations.

"I remembered that you've received offers of marriage from other gods before me. It makes me feel jealous."

To my surprise, Kore burst out laughing. "Really? As far as I know, you're the only god who has ever proposed to me. Or abducted me and insisted I would be his bride." She giggled quietly to herself again, shaking her head like the idea was preposterous. "Your honesty is always so startling."

That made me feel better, though I wasn't sure from her tone if that was her intention. "Hermes and Apollo have both made you offers of marriage. You don't recall?"

Kore made a discontented sound. "I've never even met them. Hermes saw me once, and my mother immediately ushered me away. Perhaps Apollo spotted me too, he's visited her court from time-to-time. I imagine any proposals would have gone to her, and while I'd expect her to turn them down, I'll admit I'm a little disappointed she didn't even mention them to me."

"Why?"

Kore gave me a searching look. "Is that a genuine question?"

"I wouldn't have asked it otherwise." I moved my hands to rub the salve on the backs of her calves, relishing the feel of her shapely legs under my palms. "What is the purpose of asking questions if I don't want to hear the answer? I don't understand why others do it either."

"Court games, I suppose," Kore replied absently. "Every sentence has a double meaning, meant to raise your own standing at the expense of whoever you're speaking with. Every question is a trap."

I wanted to object, to claim that *my* court wasn't like that, but in truth, I wasn't sure if I could. While I did my best to stay out of it, I knew there was competitiveness within the palace walls that took place behind my back.

"To answer *your* question, why wouldn't I be disappointed? My mother always made it seem like choosing to pledge a vow of virginity was my choice, but it feels significantly less like my own decision to make when I didn't know what other options were available to me."

She would have considered those proposals as options. Of course she would, and why not? They were *Olympian* gods. I doubted they would have treated her half as well as I knew I could—*would*—but they were powerful and prestigious nonetheless. It would have gotten her out of her mother's house without having to leave the realm she loved.

"How do you know about these proposals?" Kore asked, eyes narrowing on me as I lowered her leg to the ground and gently picked up the other one, settling it on my lap.

"Zeus told me when I traveled to Olympus to ask for his blessing to marry you."

Kore snatched her foot back, tucking it up on the chaise, and looking at me with wide eyes.

"You did *what*?"

"I traveled to Olympus to ask for Zeus' blessing to marry you," I repeated slower.

"I— No, I heard you just fine. You *asked* Zeus if you could marry me? When? What did he say?"

"I did. It seemed polite. Two weeks before I brought you here. He said he thought it would be an advantageous marriage for you."

Kore's eyes immediately narrowed because she was sharp and curious—two of my favorite things about her. "That isn't his blessing."

"He thought your mother might object."

Kore laughed a little hysterically, and I took the opportunity to gently wrest her leg back so I could finish applying the salve. Everywhere I'd spread it, there wasn't a single trace that the skin had ever been injured.

"So, Zeus knows I've been here the whole time," she muttered under her breath. "Surely, he is intelligent enough to piece together that you visited him, asking to marry me, then two weeks later I disappeared, which means the only reason Mother hasn't come is because Zeus hasn't told her what he knows. Why wouldn't he have told her?"

I wasn't sure the question was for me, but I answered anyway. "Zeus won't risk making an enemy of Demeter if he can help it, because she would be a formidable foe." I looked up at her, my thumbs still pressing into the silken skin of her leg. "But so would I."

Kore swallowed thickly. "What happens if Zeus demands my return? He didn't give you his blessing, after all. And I'm nominally his child."

If, not *when*. Kore didn't have much faith that he'd come to her rescue.

I scoffed. "Zeus can't take anyone or anything from my realm without my express permission. I'm the king here, and my word is absolute."

"Then why not just *command* me to marry you?" Kore challenged, her tone defiant, if not a little tired.

"You know why. You heard my conversation with Keuthonymos."

Kore flushed again. "You didn't mean that."

"Which part?"

"The part where you said... Never mind. Any of it. All of it. You didn't mean it."

"I'm not in the habit of saying things I don't mean. I don't want to command you to marry me, Kore. You're meant to be my equal in all things. My queen."

The defiance seeped from her posture instantly, leaving something like confusion in its wake. "You've trapped me here. I can't be your equal and your prisoner."

"I won't let anyone take you, nor will I assist your departure, but you can come and go as freely from the underworld as I can. You're not a prisoner here."

Surely she knew that? She'd been wandering around unobstructed all day.

Kore laughed hollowly. "But I may as well be if I don't know the way out. Come now, Hades, don't be deliberately obtuse. You're better than that."

I tipped my chin in acknowledgment. "I want you to stay, Kore. I want you to experience this realm for yourself, to see it the way I do. To understand why you belong here."

"I've spent my life in sunshine, surrounded by flowers, Hades. How could you possibly think that this is better for me?" The frustration bled into her voice as she gestured at her surroundings. And this was the *best* the underworld had to offer.

The scrape on this leg went all the way up to the back of her knee, and I slowed my pace, taking my time to rub the salve into her skin with gentle circles that made her shudder.

"I always knew that the environment would be a difficult adjustment for you, but I hoped regardless. I've seen you, Kore. You may have enjoyed the sun on your face and flowers at your feet, but that wasn't enough to quell the boredom you *felt*. You have the fierce protectiveness and air of authority of a queen, skills that can't be taught, but you hide them all under the guise of a powerless deity when it's clear you're not. You could be anything, Kore. I just want to give you the opportunity."

She was quiet for a moment, staring at me like she was seeing me for the first time.

"You want to give me a lot more than that," she breathed, her leg trembling slightly under my fingers.

"I do," I agreed, dragging my hands away from her body while I still had some control over my cock. "But I can't force you to love me."

Kore made a choking noise, tucking her legs safely beneath her. "Marriages between gods have very little to do with love."

"My marriage won't." I stood, setting the half-full alabastron on the side table. It was a practical courting gift at least, especially if she was going to go gallivanting through the underworld alone.

Kore cleared her throat, cheeks glowing delightfully golden again. I wished she'd stop dampening her power—both because I wanted to see it and because I wanted to stop dampening mine in her presence. It was an uncomfortable sensation, like being stuck in skin that was too tight for my form.

"Why don't you use your gift?" I asked again.

"Well, I clearly *did*," Kore muttered, standing and smoothing down her chiton while I silently mourned losing the view of her legs. "Though I can't remember why, or even where I was…"

"Kerberos was with you," I said, hoping that would reassure her some. "I'll ask if anyone else saw you."

"That would be reassuring," she replied, blowing out a sharp breath. "It's strange that there's an empty spot in my memory. Strange and unsettling. I've only ever used my gifts in dire situations, when someone's been injured and I needed to help them."

"You have the gift of life, like your mother."

Kore blushed golden. "I don't use it because she doesn't want me to draw attention to myself."

I scoffed at the ridiculous reasoning. As though not using her gift would stop Kore from attracting attention. Aside from the fact that anyone with a modicum of intelligence could detect the magic she was suppressing, Kore would be plenty capable of drawing awareness to herself even if she possessed no gifts.

She had the kind of presence that illuminated the space around her, whether she meant to or not. If I wasn't in love with her, I might envy her.

For a king, I was distinctly lacking in *presence*.

"I guess I don't need to bother with all of that here," Kore said wryly. "Mother didn't want me to attract the attention of a powerful god who might wish to make me his wife."

I flashed her a grin. "Too late for that."

Kore pressed her plush lips together, almost as though she was trying not to smile. Was that too much to hope? I wanted her to stay, to marry me and be the queen she was always meant to be, but I knew she'd never love me the way I loved her. How could she? There was everything to love about Kore, and nothing in particular to love about me.

I hoped she would at least give me her smiles though.

"You, uh, probably have a lot to do," Kore said, glancing awkwardly at the door. "Thank you for the, you know." She gestured at her legs, hidden by the silk fabric.

"Of course," I replied, vaguely insulted she'd thank me for healing the scrapes she should have never received, but not for offering her a throne. "I'll send for Orphne to keep you company."

I would never understand women.

CHAPTER 12

The Goddess of Failed Escapes. That's what they should call me.

I'd never had a title before, and I couldn't think of one more fitting. Not only had I failed to escape the underworld, I couldn't even remember what I'd been doing when I failed, and I'd *lost* the Helmet of Invisibility.

Hades had to have noticed—he'd gone into his rooms to change, he must have seen that the plinth was empty. Why hadn't he brought it up? Was he waiting for me to confess? He'd specifically told me not to lie, as though giving him the truth was an option.

I burrowed down under the blankets, yanking them over my head like I could hide my embarrassment from myself. I wasn't going to confess, no matter how nice he was about my strange fainting episode and healing my scrapes.

He was no hero. I wasn't about to start feeling any kind of gratitude toward him when he wouldn't take me back to the upperworld. I wouldn't have been injured in the first place if he hadn't stolen me away from my home.

"Kore," Orphne called hesitantly, while I hid under the covers, contemplating my lost helmet dilemma. "You have another, er, visitor."

"Tell him no," I replied idly, probably deriving too much enjoyment out of sending Hades away.

"It's not Hades, it's—*Oof*."

I sat up in bed, frowning as I pushed the blankets down. "Orphne, are you okay?"

Before she could answer, the door flew open with a bang that made me jump, and a blur of black fur came careening toward me. I landed flat on my back, Kerberos' enormous paws pinning my shoulders to the bed as his three tongues licked my face excitedly.

"I'm so sorry," Orphne panted, leaning against the doorway. "He's very strong and doesn't understand instructions."

I snorted at that. Kerberos understood just fine.

"Kerberos, stop," I told him sternly. "Get off me."

With a whine of protest, Kerberos flopped dramatically onto his side, sending a few silk-covered cushions tumbling to the floor.

"You know that was naughty to barge in like that," I chastised, giving him my most serious-looking face. "You owe Orphne an apology. And next time you want to see me, you can knock on the door with your paw and wait nicely for Orphne to tell you to come in. Don't worry, she'll let me know that it's you and not your terrible master, so you'll be allowed in."

Orphne made a slightly strangled sound from the doorway, while Kerberos gave me an impressively reproachful look with all three of his heads.

"Do we have a deal?" I asked. The heads barked once in unison, and I took that as agreement. "Good."

I glanced over at Orphne as I rewarded Kerberos with ear scratches, and she looked on the verge of passing out.

"I'd heard that he carried you back to the palace when you lost consciousness," Orphne murmured. "But actually seeing you interact..."

"He's really very friendly," I assured her. Orphne hummed warily, and Kerberos huffed what sounded like an offended doggy laugh.

"Shouldn't you be at the gate? Doing Gate Guardian things?" I asked Kerberos. He burrowed closer toward me, closing his eyes and feigning sleep. "Silly puppy. If you want company, I can always walk you back there?" I added hopefully.

He harrumphed, the middle head opening one lazy, judgmental eye.

"Or you could walk me back to where I fainted, wherever that was."

I'd definitely gotten away from the dark palace, but everything after that was a blur. And I *needed* to find that helmet. Aside from the fact that I needed it for my escape, I felt more than a little guilty that I'd lost such a powerful item. Who knew what would happen if that got into the wrong hands?

"You're certain you're feeling better?" Orphne asked nervously. "You've been so tired."

"I suppose that makes sense if I expended too much of my gift," I agreed with a shrug, frustrated that I had no recollection of *why* I used it. "I'm feeling better now though."

More than better, if I was entirely honest with myself. The constant strain of repressing my gift had eased for the first time in decades. I felt lighter and freer than I had in so long, and knowing that I was going to have to give this feeling up when I was back in the upperworld was crushing.

Kerberos laid his heads over my chest and stomach, snuggling in as though he'd picked up on my melancholy mood.

Maybe, once I was home, I could convince Mother that more good than harm came from me using my gift? Surely, after all of this, she couldn't continue to treat me like a child. Whatever happened, however it was I eventually returned to the upperworld, I wouldn't be the same Kore I'd left as.

"Hades came by earlier, but I told him you were still sleeping so he left your gift with me." Orphne held up another expanse of exquisite silk, this time in a dark red the color of rich wine. It was edged with gold embroidery in an elegant geometric pattern, and I almost hated how much I liked it.

"I suppose it would be wasteful to be given such a beautiful piece of fabric and *not* wear it," I replied slowly, already envisioning the striking dark color against my pale hair.

I rejected Orphne's offer to do my hair because I hoped to find the helmet and it fit more comfortably when I wore it loose, and shooed Kerberos into the sitting room so I could dress.

It was too strange to change in front of him when he was as intelligent as he was.

"Perhaps you could visit the throne room today?" Orphne suggested, settling for combing my hair once I was changed and adorned in a tasteful amount of gold jewels. "I know Hades would welcome your presence. He has been so busy at the Meadows that the line of petitioners is growing unwieldy."

"Wouldn't that just distract him?"

"I doubt he'd mind," Orphne pointed out, mouth twitching into an almost smile. "As you may have gathered from when we visited the Whispers, Hades doesn't particularly relish his role speaking to the petitioners. Someone has to do it, and there's no one else, but it doesn't come easily to him."

I believed that. From every conversation I'd had with Hades, it had grown increasingly clear that he was literal to a fault. He took words at face value, didn't understand why others didn't do the same, and seemed to find it hard to couch those literal words in ways that made other people comfortable. Probably because he didn't see the point, but that wasn't always helpful when dealing with scared or emotional souls.

It made me feel oddly *protective* of him, which was absurd, since he was one of the most powerful gods in existence and didn't need protection from anyone, least of all me.

"The courtiers aren't always very sympathetic to him," Orphne continued. "They make their opinions known."

"Why doesn't he stop them? No one would dare talk about the way my mother ran things in her court."

Orphne shot me a wry smile, setting the comb aside. "Your mother has other courts to compare to. She'll have visited other Olympians' homes, seen the way they do things, judged them and known she'd be judged in return. Hades has none of that. Zeus, Poseidon and Hades drew lots to see who would have dominion over each realm the moment they were free of Kronos' prison. Hades got the underworld, and departed for it immediately. He doesn't know how other courts do things."

Perhaps not, but there was no reason he couldn't have learned, if he'd wanted to. While Hades may not visit the upperworld or Olympus in person, there was a consistent supply of souls who *could* provide him with information—plenty of mortals spent time among the gods, if they were favored by them. No, Hades didn't care about how other courts did things.

"What do the courtiers say about me?" I blurted out. Orphne's hands stilled for a moment before resuming combing. I'd overheard a little, but I was sure there was more.

"There *was* some talk of your suitability for the role, from vapid gossips who don't know any better. Who are jealous because they'd like to be queen themselves. There's less talk now though. The underworld is a little more chaotic than usual—not even a mysterious future queen is enough to distract from it."

"What do you mean by chaotic?" I asked, frowning. It hadn't *seemed* overly chaotic when I'd been wandering around, injuring myself and failing to escape. Then again, I couldn't remember all of it.

"It's not noticeable here at the palace. Charon deposits new souls at the port, and they slowly make their way along the riverbank to the hall where the Judges of the Dead reside to face judgment on where they will end up. There's always a line of souls waiting to be seen, but now there are *so* many souls, there's almost no room for more on the bank. The Meadows was already in uproar with one of the factions currently leaderless. It's not a good time for there to be a sudden influx of new dead."

"Does that happen often? A lot of new souls arriving at once?"

"Occasionally." Orphne shrugged. "War always means lots of death."

My gut twisted uneasily, both at the thought of a war among mortals happening above us, but also, selfishly, at what that would mean for me. The gods were infamous for picking sides in human battles, happily involving themselves in mortal conflicts. Wars meant the gods would be busy, and if they were busy, they wouldn't be looking for me.

I knew Mother loved me. Everything she'd ever done had been because she had my best interests at heart—even if we disagreed on what those best interests were—but war...

Mother was still a goddess. And goddesses were tempted by the promise of violence and notoriety.

Not to mention Zeus. Unless he was completely obtuse—and I hadn't ruled that out—then he was aware of my location. I'd assumed that he wouldn't be able to withhold that knowledge from my mother for long, but if there was a war going on, he would have plenty of excuses to avoid her.

I had long ago given up any notion of Zeus caring for me as a daughter—he'd sired me, as well as half the population of the earth in his wanderings—but perhaps in the past few days, a sliver of vulnerability had gotten the better of me. Perhaps I wished that for once in my life he'd care enough about me to go against the will of his wife, Hera, the fearsome Queen of Olympus who saw every child of her husband's infidelity as a personal offense against her.

He wasn't going to. I knew that with absolute certainty now.

"Well, since I'm dressed, I may as well see if Kerberos wants to go for a walk," I announced, hoping I didn't sound suspicious at all. I needed to find the helmet before someone else did, and I couldn't do it without Kerberos' help. I needed to get home.

Kerberos trotted cheerfully into the Whispers at my side, and I let myself light up like a candle while I navigated the narrow passages.

"Can you get me out of the palace without going through the entry hall?" I murmured, resting a hand on Kerberos' back. One head butted affectionately into my shoulder, and I hoped that was a 'yes'.

Occasionally, I caught pieces of conversation at the gaps between the marble, and after Orphne's explanation, what I overheard made a lot more sense. Lots of mentions of the 'judges' and the 'lines' and complaints that Hades wasn't doing enough.

How readily they complained, with no expectation of repercussions. If the trees had told my mother that her courtiers were saying things like this—even things *less* inflammatory than this—she would have carried out an execution. Not that I thought her system was better, but it bothered me how little respect anyone seemed to have for the King of the Underworld who never so much as slept because he was too busy running everything with almost no help.

Kerberos occasionally made a rumbling sound of disapproval as we passed them, probably hearing even more than I did with his canine ears.

He led me through narrow halls I hadn't been through before, eventually stopping at a low panel with a thin sliver of light around it, and nosing impatiently at the wall. I had to kneel to push it open, and Kerberos squished all his heads through at once, his body scrambling after, while I crawled behind him, desperately hoping that no one was watching from the other side because this was very un-goddess-like behavior.

I silently pushed the panel shut behind me, finding myself in a deserted corridor—no, a gallery. There were sculptures everywhere, mostly depicting various monsters that were said to reside in the underworld.

I wondered if they'd been gifts. I would have hidden them in an abandoned corridor too.

"Kerberos?" I whispered, peering around the artwork. Where had he gone? For such an enormous beast, he could certainly move quietly when he wanted to. I inched around another sculpture, looking for him, when a strangled shriek made me pause.

Great, just great. Kerberos had led me into some kind of torture chamber.

On silent feet, I edged forward, using the sculptures as shields, following the sound of a feminine voice making agonized sounds.

Crouching beneath a statue of the Furies, I leaned around the side to peek out, catching a glimpse of a bronze skinned nymph, facing me, with an enormous bearded god behind her, his fingers pinching her nipples in a way that may have been painful or possibly pleasurable, it was difficult to tell.

For a moment, my heart felt like it stopped in my chest, because the only large bearded god I'd met here in the underworld had claimed to love me, and I decided I didn't like the idea of his hands on someone else's nipples, regardless of the fact that I'd repeatedly told him I wouldn't marry him.

But the god lifted his head, and I realized that it wasn't Hades. Whoever this was, his beard and long hair were wilder than how Hades kept his, and Hades would never wear a chiton like this one, in such bright, fantastical colors, embellished with jewels.

"Thanatos," the nymph moaned, arching her back. Despite the sounds, the look on her face seemed to imply she had no problem with whatever it was he was doing to her breasts.

Thanatos. God of Death.

He was... not what I expected, to say the least. He was so *vibrant.* Maybe he'd spent so much time in the upperworld, collecting souls, he'd taken a liking to the vivid colors of the mortal realm.

"It's been so long," the nymph moaned. "You work too hard."

"I have been recently," he muttered. "Be good and take the edge off for me. I'll fuck you raw afterward."

I sucked in a breath at his crude words while the nymph dropped to her knees with a thud in front of Thanatos, smiling adoringly up at him. He wasted no time freeing his manhood from the folds of his garment and feeding it into her waiting mouth.

By the Fates.

It wasn't unlike the fantasies I'd had before, based on that one hazy memory from the forest I'd snuck out to with Despoina, but I hadn't gotten a view like this last time, and I knew I'd be recalling these details in the future when I gave myself pleasure.

Not imagining Thanatos, of course. *Certainly* not imagining Hades. Just a nameless, faceless god who sort of resembled Hades by pure chance.

Thanatos tangled his hands in the nymph's hair, keeping her in place while his hips thrust rhythmically, his teeth embedded in his lower lip and head tipped back in ecstasy. This was carnal. This was lust.

I should leave.

It seemed very intimate.

Well, they shouldn't have done it in public then, I decided. Maybe they liked being watched.

The nymph reached under her chiton, rolling her hips against her hand while he stilled, groaning loudly as he expelled his *seed* in her *mouth*.

I hadn't seen that part last time, we'd left too early. I hadn't really thought too much about the male release and how... *messy* it was.

Appalling. If Mother truly wanted me to take an oath of virginity, she should have encouraged me to witness whatever this nightmare was.

Then again, the nymph was disconcertingly comfortable with it, so maybe it wasn't as bad as I was making it out to be in my head.

"Not in my corridors. Why is that such a difficult concept to comprehend?" Hades clipped, marching past them without breaking his stride. Thanatos laughed, making no attempt to stop what he was doing. I barely contained my gasp of surprise, shrinking further down behind the statue, the cold marble of the floor pressing into my skin. Hades stalked right by my hiding place, his eyes trained forward, until he vanished among the sculptures.

Too close.

The only thing worse than being caught by Thanatos and the nymph was being caught by Hades himself.

Despite Hades' words, Thanatos and the nymph—Daeira, judging by the word he kept moaning over and over again—seemed to have no intention of stopping. He hauled her to her feet, spun her around and bent her over with a hand in the center of her back. She moaned—in pleasure?—as she braced herself against the base of a statue of poor Kerberos, and Thanatos thrust into her in one rough movement.

She made a rather alarming howling sound, but moved her hips back eagerly to meet his movements, and I watched, fascinated at the position they were in. *This*, I recognized. From the orgy, from animals in nature, from my own sordid fantasies. At the relentless pace Thanatos was moving, the complaints nymphs often had about their aching sex the morning after seemed warranted.

My cheeks glowed with heat, and I pressed my hands to them, worried that my face would shine bright enough with embarrassment—or whatever other emotion it was that I was experiencing and didn't want to admit—to give me away. The idea of *sex* had always been an abstract dream for me, an unidentifiable man roughly taking his pleasure and giving me mine in return.

But now, I was struggling to call up that same fantasy without Hades' face taking the place of that featureless man. Without hearing the low voice he'd used when he'd told me to lift my chiton to tend to my injuries. There was a fluttering sensation near my stomach, every part of my body feeling more alert than it should.

I didn't want to stay in the underworld, but I could admit that I could do worse as far as husbands went than Hades. At least I was attracted to him. The idea of bending over the way Daeira was and presenting myself to the King of the Underworld, feeling his strong hands gripping my hips, his body covering my back...

I discreetly fanned my burning face.

This was a dangerous line of thought. I couldn't afford to mix the curiosity I'd always harbored about sex with my increasingly complicated feelings about the God of the Dead. Not if I wanted to be able to return to my life in the upperworld. To return to normal.

And I did want that.

Didn't I?

Surely, Mother wouldn't send me to Artemis' temple after this. She'd want to keep me closer, if anything. Leashed to her throne perhaps, back in the heavy woolen chitons I'd come to resent slightly, my face a perfect mask of indifference as I watched her go about her day, saying nothing.

Was that what I wanted? Could I really go back and act as though nothing had changed? As though I hadn't changed?

Daeira made another horrendous squealing noise, eyes rolling back in her head as she stilled, and Thanatos threw the fabric of her chiton up over her hips, pulling his member free and jerking it repeatedly, spraying her backside in more seed.

That is quite enough, I thought to myself, tiptoeing backward on silent feet, darting between sculptures again. My heart was beating so loudly in my chest, I wondered if it was going to give me away. I needed to find some ice cold water to shove my face into.

Where was Kerberos? The traitorous dog beast, leaving me here.

Fortunately, the gallery seemed to have doors at either end, and I escaped out of the one Hades had probably entered the room through, bringing me into yet another marble corridor with no distinguishing features. *Wonderful.* I couldn't even remember how exactly I'd gotten out of the Whispers, so there was no chance of me escaping back that way.

"Kerberos!" I whisper yelled, following the faint sound of voices that probably originated from the throne room and front steps I'd been trying to avoid. "Kerberos! I'm very annoyed with you."

For reasons I couldn't explain to myself, I veered away from the increasingly loud voices at the last minute, taking a sharp turn into a narrow, poorly lit corridor that seemed to slope downward where the air was cold and stale. There was a tug in my chest, dragging me down, and by the time I realized it wasn't my own will pulling me forward, I couldn't turn around. Something was compelling me, encouraging me to... something.

The marble walls gradually morphed into worn stone, and there was an incessant drip somewhere further ahead that struck me as unusual, if only because it was the kind of thing Hades would remedy—every other part of the palace was flawless.

A tapestry that covered most of the wall captured my attention, and I paused to look at it, the yank in my chest abating for a moment. Maybe this was where it was taking me to? Why would such a beautiful piece be hidden away in this neglected part of the palace?

It was so intricate, and the shining gold and silver thread woven in so exquisitely, there was no doubt in my mind who had crafted it. Only Athena—Goddess of Weaving, among other things—could create such beauty in tapestry. I carefully lifted a torch from a sconce on the wall, holding it high above me to illuminate the details.

There were seven figures in all. Zeus and Hades dominated the image, and it was clear that this tapestry had been made specifically for Hades with Zeus' stamp of approval. Kronos, the former King of the Gods, lay on the ground at Zeus' feet, sickly and pale, clutching at his belly.

I stepped closer to the tapestry to get a better look at the fawning, ridiculous expression on Hades' face, stifling a giggle. The Hades of the tapestry looked at Zeus with such devout admiration that I wondered if Athena had ever *met* Hades. Surely, no one who had met him would think him capable of such a reverent expression.

I supposed it made sense. The only one of The Twelve who spent any time in this realm was Hermes, and he was a liar and a thief who could hardly be relied on for an accurate account of Hades' nature.

Perhaps if Hades spent more time in the upperworld, his fellow immortals would know him better. As far as I knew, the only times he'd left his realm were to ask Zeus' permission to marry me, and then again to steal me.

I was struck by a petty urge to hold the flames closer to the obsequious Hades' face, and I couldn't decide whether my hatred of him or my hatred of the depiction that did him no justice motivated me.

You don't hate him, my mind supplied. I had, once. Somewhere along the line, that hatred had morphed into a combination of curiosity, pity, and begrudging attraction.

Very begrudging.

None of it mattered, I couldn't stay here. Orphne had asked me to see this world for myself, and I had. I saw much that it had to offer, and the lonely, untouchable god who held it together. But I also saw a dark and barren wasteland. Endless acres of harsh plains under a swirling purplish sky. Jagged mountain ranges and rivers of soul-destroying fire.

No life-giving sun or clear rushing streams touched this land. The clouds here churned, but never parted to reveal glorious blue hiding beyond.

The waters here weren't filled with abundant life, but with flames or addictive memory-stealing magic.

How could the Daughter of the Harvest be happy here? Whatever Hades had claimed about loving me, he either hadn't considered such a thing or he didn't care. Both, in all likelihood. *Immortals were not known for their happy marriages*, I thought wryly as I passed the depiction of Hera on the tapestry and set the torch back in the sconce. Before I could turn around to go back the way I came, that insistent tug in my chest returned, reminding me how I'd ended up down here and encouraging me to go further into the dark corridor.

At this rate, I was never going to get that helmet back.

The yanking sensation became more pronounced, and I rounded a corner to find an enormous black archway—*completely* black, like there was some kind of void within it. There was no door, just... nothingness.

I hadn't seen anything like this in my other explorations, and while the wise thing to do would be to leave it alone, I was too intrigued and perhaps feeling a little reckless.

What if it was a way out?

I took a steadying breath before crossing the threshold. The instant drop in temperature was the first thing I noticed. It was the kind of chill that came with snow, except there was none that I could see because I couldn't see *anything*. Even the brightly lit hallway behind me only illuminated a couple of feet into the archway, enough to make out the stone floor and nothing else, as though the darkness swallowed up all the light it could reach.

What *was* this place?

There was a *whoosh* and a rush of ice in the air that made me realize I wasn't alone, and I sucked in a startled breath, looking around in alarm.

"If you take just a few more steps, you will fall so far that the realm of Hades will seem as far above you as Olympus seems now." The voice was dark, masculine, and utterly terrifying.

"I've never been to Olympus," I replied faintly, for lack of a better response, taking a large step backward.

Tartarus. This archway led to Tartarus, the deepest layer of the underworld and home to the worst kind of souls, plus gods so ancient they made the Olympians look like newborn babes. I must be speaking to one now.

The thought made me feel slightly ill. Should I bow?

"Erebus, my love, you are frightening her," an awe-inspiring feminine voice called out from somewhere else in the darkness, though I had no idea where. This time I bowed reflexively. Erebus, God of Darkness, and his consort, Nyx, Goddess of Night.

"You need not bow to us," Nyx said mildly, her voice sounding slightly closer now. "Not when you are soon to have a position much grander than ours."

I straightened, opening my mouth like a gaping fish before closing it again. "I'm not certain I will ever be in a position grander than yours, Goddess," I replied eventually, choosing my words carefully.

Nyx hummed. "I am. As are my daughters."

She had many daughters, but I knew it was the Moirai she was referring to. The Fates, who saw everything, and held every mortal's life thread in their hands.

"I invited you here because I was so eager to meet you for myself," Nyx continued. "Unfortunately, I'm unable to venture into the underworld without Hades' approval, but this is something of a neutral ground. A meeting place for Hades and Tartarus to discuss prisoners who perhaps need a more severe punishment."

"Oh. How nice," I replied meekly, wondering how I was going to get out of here. That insistent pull had been Nyx's *invitation*, and I had no doubt that she had more compelling ways of bending both gods and mortals to her will, if she wished to use them.

"They call you Bringer of Destruction." Erebus' rough voice rumbled in the darkness, making me jump.

"Me? I'm not... I would never bring destruction," I replied in surprise. What possible destruction could *I* bring? I was insignificant in nearly every way that mattered. Perhaps I was the bringer of my *own* destruction, but certainly not anyone else's.

Another thoughtful hum from Nyx. "Is destruction such a terrible thing? Sometimes clearing away the old is needed to make room for something new."

"Maybe," I agreed tentatively, not wanting to argue with her. "If the old needs to be rid of, then yes. I suppose."

There was a long enough silence from the abyss to make me panic that I'd said the wrong thing.

"You know," Nyx said eventually. "In my generation, a goddess knew her own worth. We were not bargaining chips to be married off."

I pressed my lips together before pointing out that there *were* only two goddesses of her generation and they were both terrifyingly powerful. Nyx's sister, Gaia, was the Goddess of Earth and an eruption of violent rage waiting to happen.

"No one is marrying me *off*, Goddess. Hades has taken me against my mother's will. Against *my* will," I corrected hastily. Both. Either. Whatever.

"Zeus refused to either give his blessing or his refusal, unwilling to risk either Hades' anger or Demeter's." I didn't think I imagined the derision in Nyx's voice. How did she even know all of this? Did her daughters fill her in? "But Hades took you anyway. If you weren't a bargaining chip among the gods *before* Hades took you, you certainly are now. For the first time in his existence, Hades has something to lose. Something that the Olympians can hold over his head."

I swallowed thickly, slightly ashamed that the idea hadn't occurred to me earlier. He was still wrong for taking me, of course, but for the first time, the fact that Hades claimed to *love* me felt like it had a ring of truth to it. Why else would he do this? Why else would he compromise himself this way?

"It seems to me that you have more power and opportunity than you've ever had in your life," Nyx continued. "Are you using it well?"

The fact that I'd been creeping around the palace, failing to escape and losing bits of my memory, then watching the underworld immortals being intimate in a corridor would indicate that... no, no, I hadn't been using it well.

"I don't want to stay here. I hoped this archway was a way out," I replied, a touch defensively. I had no idea if Nyx would immediately report me to Hades, but to my great relief, she only laughed.

"Then you are very lost, little goddess. Though I suppose if you fell into Tartarus, you would certainly be free of Hades' clutches."

Free of the underworld, only to end up somewhere *far* worse.

"Turn around, Bringer of Destruction," Nyx encouraged, using that terrible epithet again. "You could be so much more than what you are, or you could return home. Or perhaps both, the choice is yours. Either way, you are far too full of life for Tartarus. Turn around."

I didn't need any further encouragement. I gave Nyx and Erebus a hasty bow before quickly backing toward the thin light, stumbling awkwardly back into the relative warmth of the underworld.

Who knew I'd ever feel relief at being in Hades' palace again?

"What were you thinking, Kore?" Hades' voice boomed from behind me. I whirled around, sucking in a startled gasp. "What possessed you to walk into Tartarus?"

CHAPTER 13

Hades strode away without a backward glance, and for lack of a better idea and direction, I followed. Besides, Nyx's words had been illuminating.

Illuminating and frustrating.

He'd taken an even greater personal risk than I realized, and for *what*? Me? That hardly seemed like a worthwhile sacrifice.

Possibly now wasn't the best time to raise those frustrations, since he was angrier than I'd ever seen him, but I was plenty angry myself and I wanted some proper answers. Angry at *him*, for taking such a huge risk for *me*.

"Stop," I snapped, nearly tripping over my feet in my efforts to keep up with his long strides. To my surprise, Hades stopped instantly, turning to look at me. The torch he was standing next to half illuminated his face in the dark of the stone corridor, his features set into a harsh mask of barely restrained rage.

"You're angry," I stated.

"I am *furious*."

I pursed my lips, his tone immediately raising my hackles. "If you don't want people to wander through the gate to Tartarus, perhaps you should consider putting up a sign. Or better yet, a door. I don't see why you're mad at me—"

"I'm not angry at you, I'm angry at *myself*," Hades interjected, shoving both hands back through his hair. "This corridor isn't accessible to anyone but us—you have full access to every area of the palace, as you should. I should have taken more precautions. Should have at least warned you of the dangers. What if you'd fallen? It's so dark—"

The wind seemed to vanish from my sails. "I'm fully grown, Hades. It isn't your responsibility to ensure my safety."

While I wasn't sure I'd have been able to fight the pull of Nyx's invitation even if I'd tried, the ominous black archway of nothingness should have probably been a big enough indicator to stay away.

"I'm responsible for the safety of everyone in my realm," he replied instantly, hands flexing incessantly at his side. It reminded me of the times I'd watched him talking to petitioners, and the way he'd gripped the arms of the throne so tightly, I thought the entire marble slab would crumble to dust until Kerberos came to soothe him.

"I'm not a resident of the underworld. You don't need to worry yourself with my safety." I'd been trying to *leave*. I was going to leave. I didn't want his concern. It made me feel strange and guilty, like I'd been doing something wrong by wanting to return home.

"I worry about everything to do with you."

"Take me back to the upperworld and I'll stop causing you so much stress."

Hades laughed humorlessly. "The only thing that would cause me more stress would be not seeing you each day."

"I don't understand any of this," I said slowly, shaking my head. "You barely know me. You *don't* know me. I just... why *me*? For all the risks you've taken in acquiring me—" Hades shot me a distasteful look at my choice of words. "—I can't understand why you picked me of all the goddesses you could have stolen. Was it because I hadn't sworn the oath yet? Was I just the closest one at hand when you burst out of the ground?"

I'd asked him why me before, and I still hadn't received a satisfactory answer, and his claim to *love* me had made it all the more confusing. The look of offense on Hades' face was slightly comforting—I didn't *want* to be just the first goddess he was able to get his hands on, and I had no idea what that said about me. About us.

"Of all the questions you could have asked, this is what you want to know?"

Frustrating, insufferable god.

"You don't think it's pertinent?"

His frown deepened, the furrow between his brows growing more pronounced. He was quiet for a moment, and I realized he was actually *thinking* about it. I'd asked the questions somewhat facetiously, but he was giving it genuine consideration.

"Come with me," he said suddenly, turning around and resuming his rapid pace down the corridor. *Spoken like a god who was used to having his orders followed.* I contemplated refusing just to be difficult, but I got the sense that Hades would happily acquiesce to my wishes, and then I'd be the one who looked petulant and stubborn.

Traits no one in my upperworld life would have accused me of having, but that somehow, Hades brought out in me.

With an exaggerated sigh so he'd know how much his bossiness annoyed me, I trailed after him, climbing upward until the worn stone walls became smooth marble once more. It wasn't until the murmur of voices grew louder that I realized we were approaching the entry hall, filled with underworld residents who'd last seen me when Hades had carried my unconscious form back through the palace.

Not that I cared what they thought, I reminded myself. *Their opinions don't matter to me.*

And yet, I hesitated for a moment, anyway. Hades glanced back, raising an eyebrow slightly. Surely, there was another way out of here that didn't rely on going past his entire court. Had this been intentional on his part? To force me out of seclusion?

No, somehow I didn't think so. It wasn't his style to be underhanded. When Hades wanted something, he was brazen and unapologetic about it.

"What is it?" he asked, genuinely perplexed.

"Nothing, let's go." The fact that he'd asked had eased the tension that had been building in my chest. I'd heard enough to know that his court already didn't like me, so what difference did it make if I showed my face or not? Hades didn't let their opinions bother him, and in this one instance, I decided to follow his lead.

I straightened my spine, falling into step next to him as we walked through the crowded entryway, silence settling around us despite the sheer number of souls and courtiers milling about. I glanced discreetly at Hades, finding him wearing such a fearsome expression on his face that it was no wonder that no one was daring to speak.

He caught my eye before I could glance away, and I pressed my lips together to avoid laughing at the furious look on his face. His beard twitched ever so slightly, those dark eyes softening for just a fraction of a moment, before he returned his gaze to the crowd, mask of anger firmly back in place.

My cheeks heated, and I desperately hoped I wasn't glowing in front of the entire court. There'd just been something so... *intimate* about that expression. Something that was just for me.

It made my chest feel strangely tight.

Hades led me down the steps, pausing at the bottom before letting out a distinctive whistle and looking skyward. I tipped my head back, sucking in a quiet gasp of surprise as his chariot appeared in the sky, pulled by the four enormous steeds who'd dragged me down into the underworld in the first place.

"They just come when you whistle for them?" I asked in awe, absently committing that unique sound to memory. Just in case.

"Of course." Hades shot me a curious glance. "There's no room for them at the palace, they're free to roam until I have use of them."

The beasts landed with a quiet thud, pawing impatiently at the ground as Hades gestured for me to climb onto the chariot.

"I don't suppose you're taking me home," I murmured when I was close enough that no one would overhear. Close enough that I could feel the heat of his body before he even offered me his hand to help me step onto the platform.

That cypress and narcissus scent that was purely Hades was so distracting, I nearly missed his answer, delivered with a quiet chuckle. A *chuckle*.

"No."

There was no time for a witty reply. Not when he stepped up behind me, thick arms boxing me in so he could take the reins, solid chest pressing almost obscenely against my back.

Definitely obscenely against my back.

An image of Thanatos pressing against Daeira's back flashed through my mind, and this time I knew my cheeks were glowing.

With quick, efficient movements of the reins, Hades directed the chariot into the sky, and I gripped the edge tightly as the ground fell away beneath us.

"Are you frightened?" Hades asked cautiously.

"No," I lied. Perhaps *other* gods were used to flying, but I absolutely wasn't. My mother's domain was very much on land.

"Don't lie to me, Kore," Hades reminded me, a hint of agitation in his voice.

"Don't ask me questions I don't want to answer then," I snapped.

Hades went quiet for a moment, and I wondered if he was contemplating throwing me off the back of his chariot.

"How am I to know when I'm asking a question you don't want to answer? Is there a way of knowing *before* you lie?" he mused. "It's easier when I can see your face. Your nose twitches right before you tell an untruth."

Of course, he'd been paying attention. Of course he'd picked up a tell I didn't even know I had.

"You can't know," I sighed, all of my irritation now directed squarely at myself. I'd never been so snappish with anyone else in my entire life. "You can't know unless I tell you. So if I don't want to answer a question, I'll just tell you that."

Hades hummed, a pleased sound. "That sounds like an acceptable solution. We're landing now."

My stomach churned uneasily as I chanced a look down. *Fates, we were high up.* The treetops seemed thousands of miles away from here, and before I'd panicked and forced myself to study my hands again, I hadn't been able to see anything *except* trees, so I had no idea where we were supposed to be landing or why.

We started our descent, and I gripped the chariot harder, feeling suddenly lightheaded. With infuriating calm, Hades transferred the reins to one hand and banded an arm around my waist, holding me close.

"You're taking liberties." It was meant to come out as a growl, but my voice trembled.

"Yes. You're welcome."

A surprised laugh burst free as the horses' feet landed on the ground, running a few steps until we came to a proper halt in a small clearing among the barren trees. As much as I hated to admit it, his embrace had made me feel slightly more secure.

"I'm not going to thank you, and you can let go now," I said primly. I could have sworn I felt his own silent laughter at my back before he released me, stepping off the chariot and holding out a hand for me. I ignored it, jumping to the ground and enjoying the feeling of soft earth beneath my feet again.

The ridge of mountains that I'd only seen from a distance were close now, looming over this quiet patch of trees we were standing in.

"This is the Forest of Kore."

I made a sound somewhere between a surprised laugh and a strangled cough. "No, it isn't."

Hades shot me a sidelong look. "Yes, it is. It's my land. I can name it whatever I like."

"Well, it's my name and you can't use it," I retorted, crossing my arms over my chest. "Besides, it doesn't even suit this place."

I wasn't even sure it suited *me*.

I dropped my arms, wandering away from the chariot and the grazing horses, running my fingers over the blackened bark of the poplar trees. It looked dead, and I should have hated it, but surprisingly, I didn't. The starkness, the contrast of the black poplars and the drooping willows with no leaves, the foreboding presence of the forest itself... It was all oddly beautiful in its own way. My mother bent her natural surroundings to her will, each tree, each plant was a reflection of her.

This place was wild and untamed. It was a reflection of nothing but itself, and there was something rather magnificent about that.

"I think this place suits you well," Hades murmured, eyes tracking my movements. I clasped my hands in front of me, self-conscious that I'd been wandering around fondling trees while he stared at me.

"Kore isn't the right name for this forest," I replied stubbornly. "It's too upperworld for this place. Why did you bring me here? Presumably it wasn't because you need help renaming clusters of trees?"

Hades watched me for a beat before answering. "You seemed to be under the mistaken impression that I brought you to my realm because it was convenient. Because you were the closest eligible goddess, or some other such nonsense."

He began walking, and I fell into step behind him, wondering what it was he was going to show me in this forest to dispel that notion. Faintly wondering if I even wanted to see it.

I love her. I won't see her suffer any more than she's already suffering.

Those words were scarier if he'd actually meant them.

Hades stopped, pointing up at a patch of sky. For a long moment, I wondered what it was that I was supposed to be looking at. But then I realized that it wasn't just the usual strange sky of the underworld I was seeing, but what seemed to be a *ripple*. A ripple of water.

"Lake Pergusa," Hades clipped.

I felt like I'd swallowed my own tongue. Lake Pergusa. The lake I visited nearly every day of my life.

"I have watched you for years. The first time was accidental. I happened to be passing through here, and I looked up to find you staring down into the water, smiling at something your sister was saying. You were the most beautiful creature I'd ever seen."

I stared up at that window into my old life, unable to meet Hades' eyes. My heart thudded so loudly, I was sure he could hear it.

"Over the years, those smiles grew further and further between. You seemed sad, lonely despite being constantly surrounded by company."

I understood exactly what he meant, because Hades seemed that way to me. Surrounded by courtiers and souls, but somehow apart from them too.

The reflection of the lake rippled and shifted, like a strong gust of wind had blown over it, and I swallowed past the lump in my throat, remembering the bliss of a cool breeze over sun-warmed skin.

I'd always felt like that lake was somehow alive, staring back at me when I sat by the water, pouring my grief and frustration into it without saying a word. Hades gently cupped my jaw, turning my face to him.

"I've seen you, at your brightest and your darkest. You're observant, intelligent, thoughtful, and controlled—all excellent traits for a queen. Besides that, you are radiant, lively, and beautiful. Filled with life and light that was evident even in the upperworld, and is almost blinding in the underworld. That was why I found your question—*why you?*—so frustratingly ridiculous. It seems obvious why *you*. Who else could it possibly be? Who else could even compare?"

He delivered the most achingly romantic words I'd ever heard so factually, like it was the most obvious thing in the world, and he was borderline exasperated that he even had to explain it to me.

"That's the nicest thing anyone has ever said to me," I replied quietly, fighting to maintain eye contact when I was so overwhelmed with emotion. I exhaled a long breath before I did something truly ridiculous, like burst into tears.

"Then why aren't you smiling?" Hades asked, almost accusatory.

"The kindest thing anyone has ever said to me came from my kidnapper. It's somewhat bittersweet."

Hades tilted his head to the side, still cupping my jaw. "It *could* have come from your betrothed, if you'd just agree to marry me."

I laughed—though judging by the look on his face, he hadn't been joking—and moved to take a step back, though my body refused to cooperate with my mind.

My mind said, 'this is too intimate of a position to be in with the god who stole you away from your life and claims he's going to marry you.'

My body said, 'he called you beautiful and intelligent, and he smells like cypress and narcissus, and looks like every vague fantasy you've ever had. What exactly are you fighting?'

Not him. This life, an eternity in the underworld, I was definitely fighting those things, but I wasn't fighting Hades. Not anymore.

"This is where you kiss me," I whispered, my voice shaking slightly.

Hades exhaled quietly. "Oh good, I hoped so."

There was no more hesitance as he pulled me into him, his hand firm on my jaw while his other arm banded low around my waist, pinning me in place against his hard body. Hades encouraged my head back, and I stared up at him, forgetting to guard the emotions on my face as I looked into his dark eyes, trying to make sense of everything I found there.

Those eyes dropped to my lips, and I parted them instinctively, my breathing growing labored in anticipation. *He was drawing this moment out,* I realized. Almost like he was savoring it. Or memorizing it.

No one had ever looked at me like they couldn't imagine anything more exquisite than being in my presence. The hopefulness in his gaze sent a sharp pang through my chest.

The scratchiness of his beard against my cheek was chased by the softness of his lips. He repeated the gesture on the other side, brushing the tenderest of kisses against my skin, then another on my forehead that made unwelcome tears well in my eyes.

"Why are you doing this?" I asked weakly.

"Because I love you."

Only the sudden feeling of his lips against mine stopped me from sobbing. His movements were gentle, giving me a chance to pull away whenever I wanted it to end, but I *didn't*. I didn't ever want it to end, and that was the most frightening thought I'd ever had.

Hades' tongue swept my lower lip, and I opened for him on instinct, my entire body melting against his as he explored my mouth. Each teasing stroke of his tongue seemed to echo throughout my body, every inch of me growing warm, needy.

An embarrassing noise of pleasure escaped me, and it only spurred Hades on. My feet left the ground as he hauled me upward, and I draped my thighs over his hips instinctively, burying my fingers in his beard and clutching him to me, kissing him like I'd die if I didn't.

"Kore," he rasped against my mouth, one hand cupping the bare skin of my backside as my chiton trailed behind me, his manhood thick and hard between us. "I've wanted this for years, my self-control is growing thin."

I pressed my forehead against his, closing my eyes and maintaining my grip on his jaw while his hands flexed against me, needing a moment to compose myself. Despite the intimacy of our position, I felt perhaps safer and more comfortable than I'd ever felt in my life.

Like I'd truly found a home of my own, and it was in Hades' arms.

"We can't do this," I whispered. "I can't stay. If you truly loved me, you'd understand that I could never be happy here."

His grip grew just shy of painful. "I would give you everything, Kore. Everything that is within my power to give."

"I know. But the things I need *aren't* within your power to give. You can't give me sunshine and flowers and the salty ocean breeze. You can't give me my family."

Despite how tightly he was holding me, the moment I shifted my thighs, Hades released me. I slid down his body slowly, and it took everything in me not to climb back up him and shove the thin layers of fabric between us out of the way.

I shouldn't have been surprised that my words hadn't put Hades off. If anything, he looked *more* determined.

"I'm not going to give up, Kore. Until the world stops turning, I will belong, heart and soul, to you."

"I don't know how to respond when you say things like that," I muttered, my heart fluttering idiotically in my chest. Needing to put some distance between us, I wandered away to examine the trees again with far more intensity than required. Was it obvious by looking at me that we'd been kissing? I'd never been kissed before, and my lips felt swollen and tingly. I was sure everyone would be able to tell.

"I stand by my words, but fine. I'll give you a reprieve from my declarations for today," Hades said. "In the meantime, will you promise not to visit Tartarus alone again, Kore? If you'd fallen off the edge... Your fate wouldn't have been up to me. I am the king of my realm, Tartarus is the king of his."

I spun around to look at him, surprised by the genuine concern in his voice.

"Nyx and Erebus wouldn't have let me go any further," I replied, strangely confident in that fact. Even if it was just because Nyx seemed to derive some kind of entertainment from watching my life falling apart around me. "She was the one who, er, encouraged me to the archway. She wanted to meet me."

"Obviously. You're the future Queen of the Underworld."

I gave him a withering look.

"You said no more declarations." I hesitated for a moment, wanting to confide in someone about what Nyx had said, but not sure whether I wanted to confide in *him*. Then again, maybe if I told him what Nyx had said about me, he'd be more inclined to get me away from his realm. "Nyx said the Fates call me the 'Bringer of Destruction.'"

Hades frowned, and my stupid fingers twitched like they wanted to smooth away the furrows on his forehead. Idiot fingers. Idiot body.

"Do you know why they'd say that?" I pressed, watching his reaction carefully. "Don't lie to me, Hades," I added, mirroring back his line.

"I don't lie," he clipped. "I suppose it's to do with the greater number of souls who have entered the underworld since you arrived."

"You mean the greater number of *deaths* in the upperworld since I *left*," I said wryly, giving him a pointed look.

"That is another way of looking at it," he agreed, tilting his head to the side. "I prefer my way."

Then I truly *was* the Bringer of Destruction. Maybe it wasn't a war. Maybe people were dying somehow because of me.

I stared up at the small window to Lake Pergusa, wondering if this little glimpse of the upperworld had always been visible or if it was somehow connected to my life. It seemed obnoxious to think that, but I couldn't deny there was some kind of *energy* between Hades and me that felt like it was bigger than us. Like we were on a path that had been laid out for us long before we even existed.

"I promised you that I won't visit Tartarus alone, you have my word," I said quietly. "But I want a promise from you."

Hades watched me warily, undoubtedly expecting another request about going home. He was too selfish to promise to take me back to the upperworld. I wasn't even going to try.

"Promise me that when I am back in the upperworld—" Hades made a sound of discontent. "—that you won't watch me anymore."

Hades' face was the picture of alarm. He looked like I'd asked him to hand over the keys to his kingdom, rather than my simple and very reasonable request that he not stare at me every time I visited the lake.

"Why?" he demanded, closing the distance between us. "Why do you want me to promise you that?"

I didn't mean to touch him. My hand seemed to find his face of its own accord, my fingers lightly stroking his rough beard, the silken skin of his cheek, then through his surprisingly soft hair.

"Because it makes me sad, Hades, thinking of you here all alone."

"Then don't leave." He captured my hand before I could pull it away from his hair, turning it to place a soft kiss on my inner wrist. I knew I'd just presented a vulnerability on a platter for him, and that he absolutely wasn't above reminding me of just how lonely he'd be if I left, but I found I didn't mind too much in that moment.

Maybe I'd gifted him a weakness, but it was one I was okay parting with.

"I have to." I pulled my hand away, shooting him a rueful smile. Fates, I still needed to find the helmet before he noticed it was missing. And hunt down Kerberos, because I had words for that dog. "We can go back to the palace now. Your warnings about Tartarus have been noted."

Hades looked at me for a long moment, an internal war raging behind his eyes that I couldn't even begin to comprehend. "As you wish, Kore."

HADES

CHAPTER 14

The Judges of the Dead were so busy, they barely acknowledged me as I walked past the seemingly endless line of waiting souls to the enormous desk where the three of them sat at thrones only marginally less grand than mine.

"Finally," Minos grumbled from his position in the center of them as I rounded the table to stand behind his chair. Aiakos and Rhadamanthys tended to make the judgments, with Minos observing and contributing when a decision couldn't be reached between them. "I wondered if you'd ever bother to visit."

"You're not the only one who's been busy," I replied calmly. "Though I concede that I should have come earlier. Another war in the upperworld?"

I had been paying even less attention to the goings on of the upperworld than usual. Without Kore up there, there was no point. Nothing to capture my interest.

Minos snorted. "You," he called, pointing at the next soul in line—a young man on the cusp of manhood. He'd evidently been given proper burial rites, which meant any injuries he'd suffered or the ravages of illness had been wiped clean before he'd entered the underworld, and I wondered idly what had killed one so young. It wasn't unheard of to send boys into war when there weren't enough men left to fight.

"Tell the King of the Underworld how you died," Minos commanded. Aiakos shot his fellow judge an irritable look from his spot to the left of him, undoubtedly annoyed at their process being disrupted. I would find that aggravating too.

"Famine." The boy's voice trembled as he spoke, his eyes cast down.

I frowned. *Famine?* The upperworld had food in abundance. Only those who'd gravely offended Demeter died of famine. A sense of unease unfurled in my gut as I moved back down to the line of souls, some old, but many young. Mothers holding babes, children clutching one another, young men who should have been filled with life practically shaking with rage.

"What killed you?" I asked an older woman, second in line.

"Famine, o great Hades," she replied gently, bowing her head. "Nearly all of us in this line, I should think. The ground is dead. There was fruit and wheat one day, the next it was all gone. Nothing will grow. The animals have starved, there is no meat."

I gave her a curt nod, retreating back to the judges' table. *Famine.* Demeter was starving the earth in her rage. Or perhaps her grief.

Minos twisted, sparing me a pointed look. "I take it you don't need me to explain *why* famine would suddenly be ravaging the mortal population?"

"I don't."

"Does it bother you?" Minos pressed, narrowing his eyes at me. He'd once been mortal himself, perhaps it made him sympathetic to their plight.

"Why would it?" I shrugged. "My power comes from souls. The more here, the better off I am. Demeter will presumably adjust her behavior when she realizes that her rage is doing me a favor."

"You aren't endearing yourself to the mortals," Minos pointed out, as though that would influence my decision in the slightest. The mortals in the upperworld already feared and despised me in equal measure. If they wanted an underworld god to idolize, they would soon have Kore. Just as soon as she agreed to be my wife.

It had to happen. We'd made progress. We'd kissed, and it had been at *her* request. That had to mean something.

While I certainly didn't think every kiss I'd ever had was going to lead to marriage, Kore wasn't like the others. Physical intimacy was new to her, surely it *meant* something.

Then again… what if it didn't?

Not bothering with goodbyes, I headed back to the open plains to call for my chariot, leaving the Judges to their important work. At this rate, they'd ask to retire even sooner than the last ones had. New judges were appointed by Zeus—usually former human kings that he'd sired because he was determined to spread his seed as prolifically through the upperworld as possible. When the Judges felt they no longer had a good grasp on humanity, on what made one's actions good and worthy of either reward or punishment, they stood aside.

Perhaps Minos, Aiakos and Rhadamanthys would be the first Judges to retire from sheer exhaustion.

I exhaled heavily as the chariot began its descent toward the palace steps, bracing myself for the litany of questions that were about to be hurled my way. Finally, Kore could stand to be in my presence and looked at me with something other than burning hatred, yet I'd spent the days since sorting out disputes amongst angry souls, struggling with the sudden influx of dead that were invading their space. It was a necessary part of my role, but I never got comfortable interacting with people all the time.

The souls and courtiers left me alone when I'd walked through the palace with Kore. Perhaps they found her more intimidating than they found me.

"Hades!" Thanatos boomed, barging through a group of nymphs, stopping to smack one on the rear as he passed. She giggled madly, staring after him, and I tried to determine if that was the one he'd mounted like an animal in my sculpture gallery or not.

It was hard to tell with Thanatos. He always had some nymph or another over, on, or underneath him.

"Thanatos. Did you need something?"

He snorted. "No. I'm on my way out again—you know how it is, people dying everywhere, souls to collect—but I thought you might like a reprieve from all the..." He trailed off, gesturing vaguely at the crowd. "All the *this*."

I grimaced, falling into step beside him as we walked into the palace. We didn't spend all that much time together, but his presence appeared to be enough of a deterrent to keep anyone else from approaching, probably assuming we were discussing some important business.

"How's your queen?" Thanatos asked bluntly. Aside from the embarrassing Sisyphus incident, Thanatos had always been my favorite of the immortals who lived in the underworld. He never said things he didn't mean, which made him easy to understand.

"Still very much *not* my queen."

"I don't mean to offend you, Hades, but are you any good with women? I could always give you tips."

I cut him a sidelong look. "I have no interest in replicating the exhibition you and Daeira put on in the gallery. You really need to stop doing that in my corridors."

"Tell her that," Thanatos replied, holding up his hands in surrender. "She likes being watched—the more the merrier. You should be glad I managed to drag her to a quieter part of the palace," he laughed.

I didn't bother much with regrets, but not enforcing my no-fornication-in-the-corridor rule more harshly was one of them.

"The moment I arrived at the front steps, she was lifting her chiton. That would have given those gossiping nymphs something to talk about," Thanatos continued, a smug grin on his face while I shook my head in disapproval.

Who knew what sort of ideas Kore had gleaned about sex from watching *that* encounter? While Daeira had undoubtedly been satisfied, it was a confronting introduction to intimacy for a goddess named 'the Maiden.' If only she'd encountered almost any other member of my court in a dalliance—Thanatos was a famously rough lover, it made him popular among the nymphs, and while Daeira had clearly been enjoying herself, Thanatos had her bent over like a breeding mare.

I hated that Kore might assume anything about lovemaking based on *that* performance. Especially since I'd gotten carried away kissing her shortly after, grabbing her naked backside beneath her chiton like I had every right to.

"Well, if you want my opinion on your wife problem—"

"I don't."

"—what you need to do is let some of this go for a while. Show her that she can count on you for support and guidance in this realm that's so foreign to her. I know it pains you to drag yourself away from your duties for even a moment, but your lady love might need some extra reassurance, don't you think?"

I paused, giving Thanatos a long look. That advice had been... not terrible. I knew from Hermes' scathing remarks on it that the gods in the upperworld and Olympus didn't work as hard as I did. Maybe the extensive hours I spent in the throne room or the Meadows were distressing to Kore.

He grinned at me. "Not just a pretty face and a cock the nymphs can't stay away from, am I?"

"If you're hoping for a compliment, you'll have to keep waiting. After the Sisyphus incident, it'll be a hundred years before you get any praise from me," I replied dryly.

Thanatos rubbed the back of his neck sheepishly. "Try out my advice. If it works, then maybe you'd be so good as to knock a decade or two off the grudge you're holding."

"No." But I wandered off toward Kore's rooms anyway, considering Thanatos' words. I'd come every day, of course. I briefly stopped at Keuthonymos' rooms to pick up the helmet I'd sent him to collect for me, tucking it under my arm as I returned to our wing of the palace.

I knocked, taking a step back and waiting for Kore's usual rejection. Perhaps if I told her we'd retrieved the helmet, she'd at least grant me the pleasure of her time. Maybe even another kiss, if I was supremely lucky.

"Are you ready to return me to my home?" Kore called. If I didn't know any better, I'd say there was an almost playful lilt to her voice.

"You are home."

The door swung open, and Orphne stepped out of the way to reveal my future wife kneeling on the ground, giving the supposedly ferocious Guardian of the Gate a belly rub while all three of his dog heads drooled happily on the marble floor. Even Kerberos' snake tail, usually the least trusting part of him, looked unusually content.

Orphne had flattened herself back against the wall, eyeing Kerberos nervously. He had quite a fierce reputation among the residents of the underworld, despite his recent efforts at undoing it.

"I'm going to replace you, Kerberos," I said flatly. "I will go to the upperworld and fetch a regular dog and make him immortal, and he will stay diligently at his post and you will be disgraced."

Kerberos whined in protest, making no attempt to actually get up and return to the gate.

"He's so mean, isn't he?" Kore cooed, looking adoringly down at him. How did I get her to look at *me* like that? Surely I was more pleasing to the eye than a three-headed dog with a serpent for a tail. "Stealing us away from where we are happiest and forcing us to go where he wants us."

I frowned. Did I do that? I supposed my actions could be construed that way, even though I *knew* Kore could be happier here than in the upperworld, if she would give it a chance.

"Kerberos," I snapped in irritation. "Go back to the gate."

He rolled onto his front and pushed up on his paws, giving me the most sullen look I'd ever seen on any of his faces. As he passed, he made sure to nuzzle my arm, and I supposed that meant I was mostly forgiven.

Kore stood up, rearranging the folds of her garment. It was the first chiton I'd given her—a dark green like she always wore in the upperworld, but made from a silk that clung tightly to the generous curves of her body and edged in a gold the same color as her eyes and hair. As lovely as she looked, it was the memory of how her skin felt beneath the chiton that had my cock stirring. Kore froze as she spotted the helmet under my arm, a golden glow rushing to her cheeks.

"Orphne, could we have a moment?" Kore asked, her voice higher than usual.

"Of course." I heard the door click shut behind me, leaving Kore and I alone, just a few feet between us. I wanted to kiss her again, but she'd seemed so pained afterward when she'd said we couldn't do this. That she couldn't stay.

I didn't want to cause her pain. I'd never wanted that, and yet it was all I seemed to do.

I set the helmet down on the side table, knowing she'd probably use it to try and escape again. As much as I hated the idea, I'd seen for myself how comfortable she was exploring the palace when she was wearing it, and I held out hope that she'd see enough of the underworld to fall in love with it and stay.

Kore flexed her fingers before bunching her hands into fists at her sides. It was a movement I'd seen her do multiple times before, and I found it curious. Most deities were more prone to stillness than fidgeting.

It probably had something to do with the magic she refused to use.

"You know you don't need to hide your divine form here," I reminded her, standing in place as Kore threw herself down into the klinai. The rather ungainly gesture nearly made me laugh—I'd never seen a deity move with anything less than purposefully fluid grace. "No one here would perish if they saw you as you truly were."

"Then why do you hide yours?" Kore countered, glaring at me. There was no trace of the demure, placid smiles I'd seen by the lake whenever she talked to members of her mother's court, but I'd never liked those smiles anyway.

"Because you do. I don't want to make you uncomfortable."

"That's very thoughtful of you," she replied quietly. "I wish you wouldn't make it so hard to dislike you."

I didn't respond, trying to understand if she wanted me to apologize for that or not. I didn't *want* to apologize for that.

Eventually, a golden glow emanated from her skin, her features becoming sharper and slightly less mortal-like. Not wanting her to be more uncomfortable than she already was, I exhaled and let my own form appear, a faint silver glow casting from my body.

She gave me a small smile that may have been gratitude. Not quite the beaming looks of excitement I one day hoped to see directed at me, but it was progress.

"You found the helmet," Kore stated, looking warily at it. "I asked Kerberos to take me to it, but he led me... somewhere else. I meant to tell him off earlier, but he rolled over and demanded belly scratches and I forgot to be annoyed with him."

"I really should consider a more terrifying guardian," I muttered.

Kore laughed. "Orphne is afraid of him. I think he's just taken a liking to me. Where did you find the helmet?"

"Next to the western pool, not far from the palace. The rivers communicate with me and with each other, but not the pools. Keuthonymos had to go out and search for it on foot."

Kore's blush grew bright. "I suppose you want me to apologize for stealing it."

"You can't steal from me. Everything that I possess is yours to enjoy as you see fit. Keep the helmet, you use it more than I do."

"Oh no, I couldn't," Kore protested, though her eyes lingered on it.

Waiting—hoping—for an invitation, I moved closer to the klinai but didn't sit. "I'd rather you have the helmet if it means you're more comfortable exploring the underworld. I saw you in the throne room."

"You *saw* me?!" she all but shrieked. "You can *see* me when I'm wearing the helmet?"

I gave her a long look, trying to place where her confusion was coming from. "Well, yes. I'm a very powerful god."

"Of course you are," she muttered. "Of course you saw me sneaking like an idiot, thinking I was so discreet."

"I noticed you exploring the palace and observing the goings on. How does that make you an idiot?"

"Because I thought I was invisible. I was *acting* like I was invisible. You should have said something."

"If you'd wanted me to see you there and comment on your presence, you would have taken off the helmet," I pointed out. "Likewise, when you were watching Thanatos and Daeira in the gallery. If you'd wanted me to comment on your presence, you wouldn't have hidden yourself behind a statue."

Kore's eyes went comically round as she stared up at me in horror.

"Oh no," Kore groaned, burying her face in her hands.

"That particular sculpture is rather awkwardly shaped," I continued. "Lots of gaps between limbs to spot bright golden hair."

"Did *they* see me?"

"I don't believe so. They probably would have put on more of a show for you if they did."

"You really have a knack for saying the most uncomfortable things."

I nodded solemnly. "I've been told that before."

"I didn't *mean* to walk in on them. Kerberos led me in there for some reason, then they'd already started and I didn't know how to get out without drawing attention to myself. And Kerberos just vanished! He just left me there..."

She was babbling. I tilted my head, trying to understand this new side of Kore that I was seeing. This flustered, talkative side. I *liked* it, just like I enjoyed when Kore snapped at me before immediately looking guilty about it. It was a raw, honest side of her that I wasn't sure many others got to see.

"You don't need to make excuses," I said slowly, not wanting her to feel uncomfortable. "They weren't meant to be doing that in the corridor, I should have enforced my own rules better. As for Kerberos, there's a hidden exit from the gallery that will take you outside the palace walls—he'd probably been intending to lead you there."

"Oh. Right."

"I imagine it was a rather confronting introduction to intimacy. Thanatos is not known for being gentle with his partners." Fates, this was one of the more uncomfortable conversations I'd had in my long existence.

"For your information, it was *not* the first time I witnessed something like that." Kore shot me a defiant look. "I've seen mortals copulate before."

"Fuck."

"Excuse me?"

"Copulating is too polite of a term to describe what Thanatos and Daeira were doing. They were fucking."

Kore made a strangled sound. "*Fucking* in the corridor."

My cock stiffened painfully at hearing that word on Kore's lips. I hadn't intended for the conversation to take this turn, but I was too selfish to change the topic to something more civilized.

I wanted to hear more filthy words out of Kore's mouth.

"Yes. They regularly *fuck* in the corridors. Daeira likes an audience, so I'm told. So does Thanatos, I assume, given how many times I've seen him in the act. Presumably, he believes his sexual prowess to be so great that it deserves to be witnessed."

"You sound like you disagree," Kore said, her tone flat though her eyes sparked with that same hunger I'd seen when we kissed.

"My partner's approval is more than enough for me," I replied simply. There hadn't been many, but they'd never left unsatisfied.

The room warmed in temperature, the palace responding to my heated emotions. Kore delicately tugged the fabric of her chiton away from her skin.

"If you're telling me that in the hopes I'll give you my maidenhood, you're sorely mistaken."

"I expect you'll want to save that for our wedding night," I agreed. Kore threw her hands up in exasperation, cheeks glowing once again.

"How many times do I have to tell you we're not getting married?"

"As many times as you like, Kore. As I told you, I won't give up hope, not while the world turns."

Kore let out a quiet growl of frustration. "Stop being so nice! No one has ever talked to me like this before, and then someone finally does and it's *you*."

Maybe I should stop making such bold declarations to her. "I don't wish to distress you."

Kore raised an eyebrow, silently gesturing at the room around us.

"That's different."

"How?"

"Because you needed to be away from the upperworld, from your mother's court and rules to appreciate the distress you were feeling *there*."

"I don't know what you—"

"You are a powerful goddess in your own right, Kore," I interjected. "And yet you spend your days sitting at your mother's feet like an expensive decoration."

That information had been gleaned from a disgruntled soul, punished at Demeter's court for harming one of her precious trees. He hadn't even known Demeter *had* a second daughter until he was at the court, because Kore was never talked about at Demeter's insistence.

Kore deserved better. I was determined to make her see it.

"How dare you." Kore jumped to her feet, closing the distance between us. She glared up at me, golden eyes burning with indignation. "My mother does not see me as a *decoration*."

"Then she just treats you like one."

"You *insufferable*," she growled, taking another step closer toward me, "infuriating, miserable bastard—"

I caught her wrist as she moved to poke me in the chest, using my grip to yank her against my body and banding an arm around her waist.

We leaned into each other at the same time, lips crashing together with no finesse, each fighting for dominance, fighting to say through kisses what we refused to hear in words.

I want to hate you, Kore's lips told me.

I'll make you love me, mine replied.

Kore gasped in surprise as my tongue swept over her lower lip, and I didn't hesitate to press deeper, exploring her mouth, imprinting myself on her. I'd been Kore's first kiss, and I wanted to be the only first kiss she ever had. I didn't care if that made me a greedy, insufferable bastard or whatever it was she'd called me.

With surprising confidence, Kore hitched a leg over my hip, her hands exploring my arms and chest almost frantically as her hips rolled against me.

"Admit that you want more from your life than what you had in the upperworld, and I'll make you come," I rasped, gripping her chin and tilting her head back to kiss her neck.

"No."

My stubborn goddess. It took everything in me to loosen my grip and begin moving away, but Kore's fingers tightened on my arms, holding me in place.

"Wait! You can't stop now."

"Mm. Why not?" I dipped my head again, brushing softer kisses over her skin, inhaling her lavender and sunshine scent.

"Because I want to *finish*," Kore snapped.

"Then admit that you weren't as happy in the upperworld as you keep trying to make out," I suggested, wrapping a hand behind her neck and letting the other trail over the ample curves of her body to settle on her hip.

"Maybe I'll just go and find Thanatos and an empty corridor instead—"

The thin tether of my self-control snapped at the very idea of her with another. I spun her to face the klinai, using one hand in the center of her back to push her forward. Kore caught herself with her hands braced on the seat, sucking in a surprised breath.

"If anyone is bending you over furniture, it's me."

I slid my hand into the side split of her chiton, gliding my palm up her thigh, but making no move to go any further. This had been too much, I'd let jealousy cloud my mind. Kore wasn't experienced enough for this kind of rough treatment—

"Well? Are you going to *fuck* me or not?"

My cock swelled so rapidly, it *hurt*.

"No." My hand slid over the curve of her backside before moving in between her legs and I tugged the inside of her thigh, encouraging her to widen her stance. "But I'm not going to leave you seeking satisfaction from another either."

My fingers rubbed teasingly over her slit, testing her reaction.

"Have you thought about this before, Kore the Maiden?"

She made a small growl of displeasure, rocking her hips back against my fingers. "I'm a maiden, not an idiot. And if you don't get on with it, I'm perfectly capable of satisfying myself."

Interesting. It appeared that I'd been completely wrong about Kore in that regard.

I gripped her hip, forcing her to stay still while I took my time tracing her cunt with my middle finger, stroking her silky flesh, teasing her wet opening, before gliding my digit toward her clit without quite touching it.

"What do you think about when you're satisfying yourself, Kore?"

"Plenty of things, and they never require this much conversation," she hissed. She tried to shove her own hand between her legs, and I quickly pulled her arms behind her back, holding her weight up before returning my finger to her perfect cunt.

"Too much?"

"Not enough," Kore moaned breathily, arching her back. Did my sweet, strong, independent Kore like being at my mercy? My cock wept at the thought.

"You are a revelation," I murmured, sinking one finger into her cunt, closing my eyes for a moment at the feeling of her tight, wet heat. Despite my tight hold on her wrists, Kore writhed against me, pushing her backside against me as she attempted to get more friction.

"Your fingers are so much bigger than mine," she sighed, and I nearly came then and there, imagining her riding her slim delicate fingers. "More, please, more."

I added a second finger slowly, feeling her walls stretch around me at the thicker intrusion. If it pained her, Kore gave no indication.

"Brace yourself on the seat," I ordered, guiding her body down. I angled myself to her side, keeping two fingers buried in her cunt while reaching around her front to stimulate her clit with my other hand, my cock rubbing shamelessly on her bare thigh with only the fabric of my chiton separating us.

"Hades," Kore sobbed. "I'm so close."

Reassured that I wasn't being too rough with her, I picked up my pace, soaking the fabric of my chiton with my release as Kore found hers, her cunt squeezing my fingers.

I took my time releasing her, slowly stroking her inner walls until her body went limp before pulling my fingers free and bringing them to my mouth. My eyes nearly rolled back in my head at the taste of her. Kore tasted sweeter and more divine than any ambrosia ever could.

Kore straightened, golden eyes flashing as she watched me suck her release off my fingers, her hand brushing against the damp patch of skin on her thigh.

Perhaps I wasn't good at reading emotions, but I was confident in that moment that Kore was feeling as vulnerable as I was. Her chest heaved, nipples visible through the silk chiton.

The silk chiton that *I'd* given her. It made something territorial in me rise up fiercely.

I wanted Kore more than I'd ever wanted anything. When I'd first been assigned the underworld, I'd spent a century mourning the life I could have had. Hating the solitude this realm forced on me. Wondering what the relationships between the other gods were like, and if they remembered me at all.

All I'd wanted in those early years was to find a place on Olympus. It was the only thing I'd ever wanted for myself until Kore, and my craving for her overshadowed it by so much that it was laughable.

"That was just... physical," Kore rasped, hesitating for a moment before she continued. "It didn't mean anything."

"Don't lie to me, Kore," I reminded her, inclining my head respectfully as I backed toward the door. Enough. I'd pushed her far enough for today. Pushed us *both* far enough for today.

"It *can't* mean anything, Hades. I can't let it."

I wanted to hear the lie in her voice, but I wasn't sure I could.

CHAPTER 15

Idiot, I thought to myself, pacing in my room for the millionth time. *Idiot, idiot, idiot.*

That kiss—that first impossibly perfect *kiss*—had been bad enough. Sweet, romantic, but with a powerful undercurrent of sexual desire, it was everything I'd imagined a first kiss would be.

But *this*. I glared at the klinai as though the furniture was personally responsible for turning me into such a harlot. Or rather, for making me act on those harlot-like tendencies I'd always had, because Hades was all of my darkest fantasies come to life. Firm, commanding, yet entirely focused on my pleasure.

Furious at the renewed ache between my thighs, I stormed into the bathing chamber, roughly pulling off my chiton as I went and dropping it onto the ground before submerging myself in the hot waters. Annoyed beyond measure, my fingers immediately delved between my legs and I worked my sensitive nerves raw to wring another resentful orgasm out of my body before collapsing against the side of the bath.

There was no mindless bliss this time, just an ever-increasing well of self-loathing threatening to spill over at any moment.

Hades loved me, or at least he thought he did. I shouldn't have been encouraging his feelings for me. I shouldn't have been entertaining my own traitorous feelings for him.

I shouldn't, I had a life to return to. I *shouldn't*, but I still wanted to.

I'd wanted him to *fuck* me because his rough, possessive desire was everything I'd ever wanted. Every sordid fantasy I'd ever had since I'd watched that orgy in the forest had prepared me for this, and yet hadn't prepared me at all because the reality was so much better.

While I'd never liked being Kore the Maiden or wanted to swear the oath and commit to a life of perpetual virginity, I'd also never had the desire nor the opportunity to do something about it.

To get rid of that pesky virginity that followed me around, informing others' opinions of me and what options were available for my future.

I could be free of it all forever. No matter what happened, if Hades took my maidenhood, the oath would become a distant memory. An ignored request that I'd never have to think of again.

I didn't want to be the Maiden, and the moment Hades' lips had met mine, I'd realized that I had the opportunity *not* to be.

But I'd asked him to fuck me and he'd said no.

Humiliating. Utterly humiliating. How was I supposed to look him in the eye after we'd done what we'd done?

Some of that humiliation gave way to an almost suffocating wave of guilt. I'd let the tongue he'd insulted my mother with into my mouth without a second's hesitation. I wanted to make this irrevocable choice with him—only him, because he stirred up feelings in me that I didn't think I was capable of feeling—yet he'd kidnapped me and ridiculed my life at Mother's court. What did that say about me? What would my mother think of me?

I'd always known she'd be ashamed of the sort of thoughts I had on the rare occasions I was alone in my bed, but being with Hades would be irrefutable proof of the kind of goddess I was. The kinds of things I wanted that I was never meant to want.

I couldn't even avoid him, because he'd be back tomorrow like he always was. Hades was persistent, and he was lonely.

Lonely, and unpracticed at the art of talking to, well, anyone really. Anyone who wasn't his subordinate. Which I probably was, but I was refusing to act like it because I wasn't about to show respect to anyone who'd kidnapped me. Besides, I got the distinct impression that he liked it. Not that I was *going* to become queen, but if I did, what kind of queen would censor herself around her king? He deserved every tongue lashing I gave him.

I stiffened as the outside door opened and closed with a quiet snap, hoping he wasn't back already. I needed more time to collect all the stray emotions that I wasn't meant to be having and shove them deep inside myself, where they could never surface again.

"Kore?" Orphne called. "Hades suggested you might want company."

"Of course he did," I muttered. Because he was always thoughtful, even if it was in a sometimes abrupt manner, and probably realized that I needed a friend—which Orphne was rapidly becoming. "I'm in the bathing chamber," I called out for her benefit.

If Orphne disapproved of me getting into the water without going through the cleansing and scraping ritual first, she hid it quickly, standing in the doorway and holding up yet another piece of fabric. It was the most gloriously rich shade of Tyrian purple I'd ever seen, and I'd never owned such a large piece of it before. It must have taken thousands—*tens of thousands*—of the sea snails to produce, and hours upon hours of labor.

It was so... regal.

"Another courting gift?" I sighed, flattered and a little overwhelmed by his generosity.

"He didn't say this was a courting gift." Orphne looked thoughtful for a moment. "Actually, he sort of shoved it into my hands on his way out to the Meadows, looking rather distressed."

"Oh." I sank down a little further into the water, rubbing at the sudden ache in my chest. Was this an apology gift? If anyone had to be sorry about what had happened earlier on the klinai, it was me. I'd asked him for more, and immediately afterward, I'd lied to his face and tried to push him away.

"It would pair beautifully with the gold asphodel brooch he gave you a few days ago," Orphne suggested, admiring the fabric. I hummed in agreement. I'd already gotten inordinately attached to the golden brooch depicting the asphodel flower that grew in the meadows of the underworld. While I'd been *borrowing* the lovely things he'd gifted me, I was planning on leaving them all behind when I returned home because they were gifts for the Queen of the Underworld, which I would never be.

But I might make an exception for the brooch.

It could be something for me to remember the time I'd spent here by. To remember that *kiss* by. That kiss and everything else.

Everything that was to come, because I didn't want to leave this place without shedding my identity as the Maiden, and there was no one else I trusted to help me do that except Hades. No one I *wanted* to share that with except him. It *had* to be him.

"I'll wear it," I decided, still staring at the fabric as I stood and emerged from the water. If there was one thing I knew for certain, it was that I wasn't going to get Hades to agree to ravish me by hiding in my rooms and feeling sorry for myself.

Orphne quickly helped me dry off and dress, draping a pale himation edged with gold under one arm and using the brooch to secure it on the opposite shoulder. I held up a mirror as she made quick work of securing my hair up off my neck with a gold ribbon, and I could admit while the idea of *me* becoming Queen of the Underworld was still preposterous, dressed like this, I could almost pretend for a moment that it wasn't.

It was the kind of expensive, luxurious outfit that a goddess like Aphrodite would wear. One that screamed vanity and glamor, and my mother would *hate* it. I didn't. I loved it, and I was going to silently weep when I was home and had to dress inconspicuously again.

"Beautiful," Orphne said approvingly, looking me up and down. "It would be a fine outfit to get married in," she added, a hint of mischief in her voice.

I snorted, immediately undercutting any regal, ladylike airs I'd been putting on. "Then I'll be sure to leave the outfit for Hades' future bride when I go."

Orphne smiled sadly. "I know I can't make you stay, but I wish I could. I've known Hades for most of my life, he'd be a good husband."

"Are you married?" I asked Orphne, suddenly realizing I didn't know and wanting to move away from that statement that had felt a little too close to true.

Orphne smiled. "I am, though it's an unconventional marriage, perhaps. We could go meet him, if you like? It seems a waste to sit here and do nothing when you're all done up."

"Sure," I agreed readily, too curious about what 'unconventional' meant to say no. It was the underworld—'unconventional' could really mean anything.

"Would you like to, er, travel discreetly?" Orphne asked politely, clearly talking about the helmet that had been sitting abandoned on the side table where Hades had left it.

"Not today. Today, I'll go as I am."

Orphne's smile was radiant.

Orphne led me through a combination of the Whispers and some quiet parts of the palace, down, down, down to where the air grew damp and cold enough that I undid the elegant draping of the himation and wrapped it around my shoulders and chest instead. The tunnels down here were windowless, illuminated only by faint, flickering sconces, and while I was fairly confident that we weren't heading toward the entrance to Tartarus, it definitely reminded me of that.

No, it couldn't be. Hades had said only the two of us had access to that corridor. On closer inspection, it wasn't the same worn stone walls and floor, but a glossy obsidian instead. Much like that dark palace I'd nearly tumbled into right before my memory gave out.

"Orphne," I asked, my voice barely above a whisper so as not to disturb this still, eerie place. "Do the Fates reside in the underworld?"

"Hm? Oh yes, in the Halls of Night. They're never in residence, though. Always traveling around, invisible to all but each other, allocating a thread of life to each mortal as they're born, cutting them as they go."

I thought of the number of mortals there were. Henna was a quiet place, but once I'd visited Corinth with my mother and her court, and there were *so* many more humans than gods.

"That sounds like a busy job."

"It is," Orphne agreed, seemingly gliding down the corridor, slightly ahead of me. "I mean no disrespect, but while the Olympians get all the glory, the hardest working gods all reside here, in the underworld."

I could believe that—I admired it, even. There were many things I didn't like about my mother's court, but I appreciated that she didn't shy away from her responsibilities like the other Olympians. The idea of having a position that required genuine effort was far more appealing than the idea of lounging in a cloud-like palace, drinking ambrosia, and doing nothing but meddle for all eternity.

We exited the tunnel at a rocky cave mouth, and I made a note to remember it, but after a few steps toward the bank of a dark marsh, I found that I couldn't. No matter how hard I concentrated, the moment between being in the tunnel and being out here was a fuzzy blur.

Orphne glanced back at me, smiling wryly. "You're wondering how we got out here."

"Yes." There didn't seem to be any point lying about it, it wasn't as though I'd made any secret of my desire to leave.

"It's enchanted. There are a few exits from the palace—ones that you only know about if you look—and all are disguised from the outside to prevent anyone sneaking in."

Like Hades suggested, Kerberos had probably been trying to show me one when I'd lost him in the gallery.

"Is it far?" I asked Orphne. Beyond the marshy river was an enormous plain that could only be the Elysian Fields, where the very best of mankind were sent for their eternal rest. It was pretty, for the underworld, but it needed flowers. My magic rose impatiently beneath my skin, and I flexed my hands repeatedly until the sensation went away. Last time I'd used it, I'd fainted and I couldn't even recall what I'd been doing.

Maybe my gift wasn't compatible with the realm of the dead? Like my mother, my gift was *life*.

"It is. We need to travel south of the palace, but it's easiest to come out on the northern side at the Stygian Marshlands and go by boat," Orphne replied, already walking toward the water where I supposed a boat was docked.

Or...

With a little more confidence than I probably deserved to feel—much of which I attributed to the very queen-like outfit I was wearing—I mimicked the piercing, unique whistle Hades had let out on the steps of the palace. Orphne whirled around to look at me with wide eyes.

"Did you just summon Hades' chariot?"

Four enormous beasts appeared on the horizon, a golden chariot gliding through the air behind them.

"I don't suppose you know how to drive it?" I asked hopefully.

Orphne let out a startled laugh. "Hades' steeds aren't going to respond to me. I wouldn't have thought they'd listen to you either, but Kerberos seems to understand you just fine."

I was pretty sure Kerberos understood everyone just fine. He just *preferred* not to listen.

The horses landed with a thud, whinnying loudly, and I called on every ounce of bravery I possessed as I walked toward them, holding out my hand to stroke the coat of the one closest to me. They really were majestic creatures, with inky black coats and coal-colored eyes, their bodies at least twice the size of a regular horse.

"Hello. I'm Kore." Fates, I felt stupid. "I'm hoping you can take us to... Where are we going?"

"The home of The Restless Dead," Orphne volunteered. I shot her a wary look, very much second guessing my decision to follow her. The steeds gave no indication that they understood, but they were still standing in place, pawing impatiently at the ground, and I took that as a sign they were waiting for us to mount.

"Hold on *very* tightly," I instructed Orphne, who needed no encouragement to grip the golden lip of the chariot with all of her strength while I picked up the reins, mostly for something to hold on to.

The moment we were in place, the horses took off at a run without any instruction from me, galloping along the river's edge before leaping into the air. I squeezed my eyes closed, missing the warmth and solidarity of Hades' body at my back instantly.

Okay. Okay. I definitely wasn't going to be flying out of the underworld, that was for sure.

"Open your eyes," Orphne encouraged. "Below is the hall where the Judges of the Dead sit."

"Just describe it to me. If I look down, I'll faint," I called back, keeping my eyes firmly shut. "You know it's dire because I really should be looking for a way out of this place while I have such a good view."

She shook with quiet laughter next to me. "We're moving further inland anyway. There's the Phlegethon in the distance."

I didn't need to open my eyes to know when we crossed it—the river's flames warmed us even this high up.

"Most of the land south of the Phlegethon is Asphodel Meadows," Orphne continued. "We're passing over it now. It's the flattest section of the underworld, with souls as far as the eye can see. You can make out the six factions from up here, there are thin gaps of land between their territories. How fascinating, I've never seen it from above before."

"I'll take your word for it."

This was the worst idea I'd ever had. This is what I got for showing off my temporary queen privilege. How were we even going to get down again? Would the steeds land without my direction?

We flew for so long in silence that I managed to crack open one eye to glance at Orphne, who was leaning alarmingly far over the edge of the chariot and taking in the view below. I was still too afraid to look down, but I wondered how large this realm really was considering how long we'd been in the air.

"We're landing soon," Orphne warned, right before the chariot dipped and I slammed my eyes shut again. "The land around my husband's home is rocky and unforgiving, we have to go the rest of the way on foot."

"That's fine," I squeaked. "I'd be happy to never fly again, in fact."

Orphne snorted. "Then don't whistle for the chariot next time."

"Believe me, lesson learned," I muttered, my stomach pressing against the edge of the chariot as it tilted downward. The reins dug into my palms, but I didn't relinquish my grip. Hooves hit the ground first, the sound of loose rock crunching underneath them followed by the uncomfortable bounce of the wheels as we landed.

"Never again," I muttered, stomach churning. "Absolutely never again."

Orphne alighted easily, standing behind the chariot and waiting for me to pry my fingers off the reins. "You may want to thank the horses regardless," she suggested lightly.

Nodding stiffly, I opened my eyes and stumbled to the ground, legs still shaking as I made my way over the rocky surface to pat each of the horses in turn and thank them for bringing us here. With whinnies that echoed off the tall, jagged rocks, they took off at a run and launched themselves back into the air, disappearing to wherever it was they went when Hades had no need of them.

"Your husband lives here?" I asked Orphne, looking warily around the gray, cold landscape that housed nothing but rocks. It was not the most hospitable place—there wasn't a plant in sight.

"Near here," Orphne corrected. "There are many souls in this area, they'll probably come out to beg for your assistance when they see you."

"My assistance? What would they want my assistance for?"

I searched my memory, trying to think if I'd heard of The Restless Dead before. My underworld knowledge was sorely lacking, and eventually Orphne took pity on me.

"The Restless Dead are those who couldn't pay Charon's fee for ferrying them. Instead of bringing them to the port where they travel to the Judges of the Dead, he deposits them on the shores of the River Akeron, where they stay for one hundred years, unable to pass any further into the underworld."

I swallowed thickly. A hundred years was a long time for mortals, even dead ones.

"What do they do while they're here?"

"Cause trouble, mostly," Orphne replied dryly. "There is no Pool of Lethe here. They're given no reprieve from their memories. The kinds of souls who come here without burial rites, without a loved one to give them a coin for Charon... Well, they rarely have happy memories to sustain them."

"Surely, this can't be the best way," I muttered, looking around the barren landscape. The souls were here, I could sense them, hiding among the boulders and in crevasses. Watching.

"Probably not, but Hades takes the allocation of duties very seriously. What Charon chooses to do is his responsibility, Hades would never compel Charon to change his ways."

To my chagrin, I understood that. The upperworld was filled with far more gods than existed down here, and the balance between them was a delicate thing that couldn't be messed with.

But the pain and suffering of these souls called to me. If Charon wouldn't stop leaving them here, then maybe *here* could be a nicer place for them. Somewhere with trees, at the very least. The big expanse of nothingness practically screamed for a palace or temple or *something* of its own, someone to corral these lost and lonely souls until their time came.

Stop it. Don't get attached. Don't get ideas. You are leaving.

Perhaps I'd find a way to casually drop the suggestion into conversation with Hades, since I had no doubt that Orphne would report that we'd visited this part of his realm.

"Goddess," a soul whispered, prostrating themselves at my feet. It was a young woman, barely more than a child. Her frame was frail, skin stretched over bone, and deep pockmarks marred her flesh. "Goddess, please. Help us. Give us your blessing."

Orphne stepped between us, but I touched her arm, encouraging her to move. I would be the worst kind of coward to fear someone so disadvantaged, so clearly struggling.

"What's your name?" I asked, sinking to my knees so I wasn't looming over her. She sat up abruptly, looking at me with wide eyes.

"Demetria."

Orphne made a slightly alarmed sound from behind me, probably assuming that hearing the version of my mother's name that mortals often used would make me run or send me into a rage.

Goddesses were known for their rages, after all.

I swallowed thickly, emotion clogging my throat, reminding me of just how much I missed home.

"What a beautiful name. How did you come to be here, Demetria?"

She twisted her hands in her lap. "My whole family fell ill with plague. I placed an obol under each of their tongues when they passed, but when my time came, there was no one to do it for me."

My heart ached for her. For all she'd suffered in life, and the suffering she was now experiencing in death.

"There's nothing you can do," Orphne murmured. "No soul can pass into the underworld proper until they have faced the Judges of Death."

So I was meant to just do nothing? I'd spent my entire life doing nothing, and I was sick of my own uselessness.

"I know I need to wait until my time comes," Demetria said quickly, bowing her head apologetically. "I wasn't trying to skip my turn."

Then what was it that she wanted from me? She'd asked for my blessing, but I wasn't sure that I had a blessing to give. That was the sort of thing that deities who knew how to use their magic would do.

While I very much wasn't one of those deities, my gift was rising to the surface like my magic thought I was one of those deities, even if my mind didn't.

I glanced back at Orphne, who was watching silently. Why shouldn't I let some of that magic free? Surely just a little wouldn't hurt.

"Don't leave me here if I faint," I instructed Orphne.

Deciding to just trust my instincts and hope for the best—the girl was already dead, it wasn't like I was going to accidentally kill her again—I set my hand over Demetria's forearm, looking into her eyes as my palm warmed between us.

"I'm sorry for your suffering, Demetria. You've spent too much time hurting for one so young, and I hope the Judges are kind with their placement of you in this realm, and that you find eventual happiness. That is my blessing and my wish for you."

I pulled my hand away, surprised to find that in its wake, there was a golden mark in the shape of a pomegranate flower.

Demetria held up her arm, twisting it in the dim light, making the marking glint.

Had I really done that?

I hoped it was a good thing.

"Thank you," Demetria sobbed, prostrating herself on the ground. "Thank you, thank you, thank you."

"Come, Kore," Orphne murmured. "We'll be swarmed by souls when they see what you've done."

I stood, a little dazed, and let Orphne drag me away from the girl still chanting her gratitude on the ground. As much as I wanted to help, the idea of being inundated with souls all clamoring for my attention was a little overwhelming.

"What exactly did I do?" I asked nervously, almost jogging to keep up with Orphne's relentless pace.

"Nothing bad," she assured me. "The mark shows that she's favored by the goddess, Kore. You've probably seen your mother do something similar, but you wouldn't have *seen* the mark because it attaches to the soul, not the body. They bring their favor to the underworld with them."

For all the good I imagined it did. I couldn't imagine anyone down here getting special treatment because they were favored by an Olympian.

Orphne led me through narrow rock passes and over hilly terrain in silence, stopping occasionally to look around. This definitely wasn't the usual route she took.

"This is far to go to visit your husband," I pointed out. We crested a hill, and a dark greenish-blue river came into sight, taking me by surprise.

"Well, I usually go via the water, but either way I'm immortal. I'm not short on time," Orphne laughed, smiling down at the rushing water below. "It was a nice change to travel through the skies. My husband can't leave this place, so I come to him."

"You wouldn't rather live here?" I asked, looking around for a palace, or at least a home along the river where her husband might live and coming up empty.

"I prefer the comforts of the palace," she replied with a small smile. "Besides, with such an abundance of time, having some space between us makes the moments we share together all the more special. Come, let's go."

I had no idea where we were going, but I was more intrigued than ever. We made our way down the slope, and perhaps it was a figment of my imagination, but the river water seemed to move faster.

No, I definitely wasn't imagining it.

As soon as we got to the riverbank—still no dwellings in sight—the water began coalescing somehow, taking *form*.

"What in the..." I breathed, watching with wide eyes as a man—no, a god—made of liquid ascended from the river with a beaming grin on his face.

Well, I presumed it was a grin. It was hard to make out details with the water that made up his body constantly moving.

"My love, you've brought a guest." The deep tenor of his voice took me by surprise. I supposed I thought it would come out kind of like a gurgle. "One that needs no introduction, of course. Kore, it is a pleasure to meet you. I am Akeron."

"Akeron," I repeated, looking first at him, then at the river. "And this is the River Akeron."

"It is. Or rather it is me, and I am it." He shrugged a watery shoulder, a fascinating gesture that I couldn't take my eyes off. "It's hard to say."

Orphne stepped off the bank, wading into the water, and Akeron shivered as though he was deriving some kind of pleasure from the sensation. By the Fates, I wouldn't ever be able to swim in a river again.

Still, I didn't begrudge them their happiness. I couldn't stop myself from smiling as she reached him, stepping into his waiting embrace. Her chiton was drenched everywhere he touched her, but when she leaned against his form, it certainly *seemed* solid.

I had a lot of inappropriate questions that I wasn't sure I wanted answers to.

"I hope I haven't been keeping Orphne away from you too much?" I asked, sitting on the riverbank and tucking my feet beneath my himation.

"Of course you haven't," Orphne replied, looking aghast.

"Well, I could always stand to see more of her," Akeron laughed. "But I know you've been keeping the palace on their toes. Hades may have asked us for help," he added with a sly smile.

Maybe it was sly.

Those damned watery features.

"He asked the water gods to watch over you when you left the palace," Orphne explained.

I opened my mouth before closing it again. That explained how he'd come to my rescue when Kerberos had brought my unconscious form back from that pool.

"The water gods could see me?" I asked, questioning just how effective that stupid Helmet of Invisibility actually was. Orphne's lips twitched.

"No," Akeron replied, shaking his head. Water droplets flicked off him with each movement and I pressed my mouth into a line to stop myself laughing. "There's water in every being—mortal or immortal. We have a sense for it, I suppose. All the bodies of water in the underworld are connected, even Phlegethon, that fiery showoff," Akeron continued. "We communicate with Hades that way, when he wants us to."

"All the waters have a form? Even Phlegethon?" I asked, imagining a fiery being popping out of the flames.

"The rivers do. Pools like Lethe are blessed by goddesses, we can only communicate with them through the waters when the goddess is in residence. Phlegethon and Styx both have forms—they're lovers," Akeron replied factually.

"Right. Of course," I agreed faintly, nodding my head. All the rivers were gods with bodies and lovers. I'd never felt so sheltered in all my immortal life.

Orphne captured Akeron's attention for a moment, whispering what looked like lover's words in his ear, and I turned away to give them some semblance of privacy. Akeron's river was so wide, I couldn't see the opposite bank. It just seemed to disappear into darkness, unlike the narrow, winding Phlegethon or the pools I'd seen.

But perhaps... Perhaps it was so wide because Akeron was a barrier to the mortal world, like Styx. Surely, Charon wouldn't drop souls here otherwise. I stared into the darkness across the river, straining my eyes as though if I just looked hard enough, I'd be able to see Henna beyond.

Could it be that simple? Had Orphne brought me to a possible exit, just over the other side of the river?

I inched closer to the water, contemplating just diving in and making a break for it, hoping for the best, but with Akeron still in his human-like form, canoodling his wife, just touching the water seemed almost lewd. No, I was going to either source a boat or force myself to brave the chariot again—if they'd even agree to take me across the river to the mortal realm. If they were as perceptive as Kerberos, then they probably wouldn't.

Fates, I missed my family so much. I missed Despoina's teasing, and running through the fields with the twins. I missed Mother stroking my hair, and the way her love seemed to wrap around me like a warm blanket, keeping out the occasional chill brought on by her fear. The fear she'd been right to have, since Hades had done exactly what she'd always worried about.

I missed sunshine and fields of brightly colored flowers. I missed my *life*. As unsatisfactory as it had been at times, it had still been *mine*. As generous as Hades' offers to me were, he had no right to assume that his plans for my life were more important than my own.

I had so few choices. I couldn't afford to give this one up.

CHAPTER 16

I lounged on the riverbank for hours, drifting in and out of sleep, while Orphne and Akeron played in the water—him switching between his human-like form and pure river, carrying Orphne along while she laughed lightly to herself. It was so strange to see her properly smiling that I didn't want to rush her, even if a part of me wanted to get back to the palace.

To see Hades again.

Every time I looked down and saw the beautiful purple fabric he'd given me, I wondered how he was feeling. If he felt guilty about what we'd done, and whether or not I owed him an apology for saying that it hadn't meant anything when it clearly had.

An apology that I'd follow up with a very polite request to ruin me, and not get too attached in the process.

I groaned, flopping back on the river bank and throwing an arm over my eyes. Hades had kidnapped me, and somehow I was feeling like the villainous one in our not-a-relationship.

"Kore," Akeron called, the water swirling into form again. "How can we keep you entertained? You seem so bored, sitting there on your lonesome."

I smiled as I sat back up, waving off his concern. "I'm fine. It's nice to be outside again, even though there's no sunlight here. It feels... familiar."

"Familiarity is nice," Akeron agreed, a slow smile forming. "The familiar gentle flow of the river is nice, but making waves is fun too."

"Akeron," Orphne warned, exasperated. "Ignore him. All river gods like to cause trouble because they're confined to one place. Gossip is all that keeps them entertained."

That made me laugh, a small wave of homesickness hitting me. The nymphs, as well as Despoina and I, had been much the same.

"What kind of waves did you have in mind?" I asked curiously.

"If you've been walking around unseen, you'll have heard what the members of Hades' court have been saying as clear as the waters have heard."

My smile dropped abruptly, remembering those gossiping nymphs in the throne room.

"Hades has given you the run of his realm, otherwise it wouldn't have been possible for you to walk through his private entrance to Tartarus." My word, the rivers really did gossip. How did he know about that? "Why not enjoy the perks of being a queen? Play at it for a little while. Give those jealous nymphs something to really complain about. You might find queenship suits you." Akeron winked.

That's what I was worried about. There was more than enough in this realm for me to get attached to without enjoying the power of being a queen. Even just being here, lounging by the river, had made me entertain dangerous thoughts about coming here again, spending more time with Orphne and Akeron.

"What kind of queenly things could I do?" I mused, standing up and brushing off my chiton as Akeron floated Orphne back toward the bank. "Aside from stealing chariots and helmets, and any other of Hades' possessions. What would the Queen of the Underworld actually *do* all day?"

Orphne grinned. She was so solemn looking most of the time that earning those smiles and laughs from her felt particularly rewarding. "There's never been one before. I suppose she'd do whatever she liked? Whatever the king does?"

The king did almost everything, I thought immediately. He never seemed to catch a break.

"The line of petitioners is getting unwieldy, isn't it? I'm not sure if I'd be any help—"

"You would," Orphne interjected, eyes bright with excitement. "You would be so much help. Mostly the souls just want someone to listen to them—someone important with power—and to occasionally comfort them, which isn't Hades' strong point. You did it so well with Demetria. Besides, Keuthonymos will be there to help with any specific requests."

I *was* all dressed up. And it *would* get Hades' attention, for ravishing purposes.

"You seem very excited about this," I pointed out.

"I'm hoping you find yourself addicted to the power and want to stay," Orphne agreed easily. "Come on, Akeron can take us back."

"Can he? We didn't bring the boat."

"That's not a problem," Akeron replied, definitely grinning this time. Orphne reached for my hand, encouraging me into the water, and I supposed if she was comfortable with it, then I had no reason not to be. I just had to think of the water as a river and not *her husband.*

Fates.

I slipped my hand into hers and took a step into the cool water, noticing immediately that it didn't seem to soak my clothes. I looked down at them in confusion, before looking at Orphne's soaked chiton.

She rolled her eyes. "He could keep me dry too, if he wanted to. This is some kind of territorial gesture."

Akeron chuckled, not sounding the least bit apologetic as he disappeared into the water and a sudden current picked up beneath us, moving us along.

I gripped Orphne's hand a little tighter, unsettled by sensation and the speed, the riverbank a blur of motion as we passed. There was a strange jolt, and the water temperature warmed slightly, and I didn't think I imagined the stone port that briefly appeared out of the corner of my eye.

"The Styx," Orphne called, confirming my suspicion. We'd changed rivers, and that could only have been the Port of Charon that we'd gone past. I noted an enormous pale rocky formation that I'd seen in the distance when I'd come across the Halls of Night, and then there was another jolt and we were in steaming marshland, still being scooted across the water somehow, but now whilst grass-like plants whipped at our skin.

"Nearly there," Orphne assured me, grimacing as she turned her face away from the plants. "This is the Stygian Marshlands."

The plants disappeared, and I saw the looming marble palace on the riverbank where Orphne and I had first emerged from the tunnel. Within seconds, we were dumped in a rather ungainly fashion on the rocky bank, both in dry chitons.

"Thank you," Orphne said with a soft smile at the waterway, smoothing down the garment. "I appreciate it."

"Yes, thank you," I added uncertainly, not wanting to offend whatever god was hiding within the waters.

"It's a slower and infinitely more comfortable journey by boat," Orphne assured me under her breath. She seemed happier than I'd seen her since I'd come here as we made our way back to the palace—walking around the side of it to enter via the front steps—and I vowed to encourage her to visit Akeron more. I didn't want her to feel that she had to spend every moment with me, especially since I wasn't going to stay.

The line of souls at the palace was longer than I'd ever seen it, and Orphne's relaxed posture tensed almost immediately as she took it in. "There aren't enough hours in all eternity for Hades to deal with this."

Where were all the minor gods? They had one for *everything* in the upperworld—plenty of extra hands to provide assistance in keeping things running smoothly. The other deities that lived here—like Thanatos and Charon and the river gods—all seemed to have highly specific roles, while Hades did everything else. It was unmanageable.

The nymphs who'd been gossiping about me were on the palace steps, looking down at me with clear disdain. It was hardly the first time I'd been judged and found lacking, but why should I stand for it? I could be whoever I wanted here, I wasn't beholden to anyone's rules. If there was ever a chance for me to refuse to bow my head and not draw attention to myself, it was now.

"How do I do this?" I asked Orphne, straightening my shoulders.

A smile spread slowly across Orphne's face as she glanced between me and the nymphs. "Let's go to the throne room—it's imperative that you meet the souls in the order they're lined up, or there'll be anarchy."

"Look who decided to leave her rooms," Minthe whispered loudly, laughing to the other nymphs. I marched past her with my head held high, pretending not to hear her words, knowing that no response would annoy her more than being ignored.

Two could play at court games.

It felt like I walked for miles to get to the front of the line. The souls murmured to each other quietly as I passed, undoubtedly wondering who I was and what exactly I thought I was doing. I was wondering that myself.

Keuthonymos, Hades' attendant who I'd seen here before, rushed forward to greet me as I stopped at the bottom of the dais. Hades' black marble throne loomed ominously above me, but there was no way I was going to sit on it. Apparently, I'd found a line I wasn't willing to cross when it came to borrowing Hades' possessions.

"Kore," Keuthonymos said, bowing low as though I was just as much a monarch as Hades.

"Kore has come to assist with the petitioners," Orphne said smoothly, sparing me the awkwardness of explaining myself. "As Hades hoped she would, when he conferred all the authority of a queen on her."

Keuthonymos pursed his lips, giving Orphne a wry look at the pointed reminder in her words.

"Of course, you are most welcome Kore." He glanced back nervously at Hades' throne. Probably wishing more than ever that Hades had commanded me into marriage, if only to make this logistically easier on him.

"I'll stand," I assured him. After a moment's hesitation, I released the hold on my divine form that I'd slipped around me out of habit, letting myself glow golden. There were a few surprised gasps, and the low hum of murmurs in the throne room grew louder.

"Good idea," Keuthonymos whispered approvingly. "I'll send them up."

The first petitioner was an elderly man with the same blankness in his expression that I recognized from the petitioner I'd seen with Hades. The one who begged to be locked in the dungeon. My stomach churned uneasily, and the alarmed look Orphne gave me didn't provide much reassurance.

"A goddess," he murmured, bowing low before me. "A beautiful goddess. Beautiful goddess, where am I? Why am I here? There is something at the edges of my mind, struggling to take hold…"

I swallowed, feeling every eye in the room on me. Hades probably had a list of unwritten rules in his head for how to handle those situations, something he'd already planned out in advance. I wasn't Hades though, and even if I knew what the rules were, I doubted I'd do things the way he did.

"You're in the underworld," I told the soul gently, resting my hand on his arm. "You've been drinking from the Pool of Lethe, and it's made you forget."

"Have I? I don't remember. I don't remember…"

This soul seemed worse than the one I'd watched Hades deal with. At least she'd known *why* she couldn't remember anything. Surely, there had to be some way. Some balance to Lethe's gift that would restore the memories they'd lost. My life in the upperworld hadn't been comparable to a mortal's, but the idea of losing any notion of it, of only having the underworld in my head, was terrifying. I didn't want that for these souls either.

Who was Lethe's opposite? Her balance? There had to be someone—

Mnemosyne.

The moment the name popped into my head, my missing memory returned, drifting happily into my mind like a lost pet wandering home after causing its owner acute misery.

That wretched goddess, she'd altered *my* memory.

"Go to the white poplar tree between the two pools," I announced in a clear voice, loud enough for the entire throne room to hear. "But you must fight the pull to go to the eastern pool where the other souls congregate. Go to the western pool and drink from its waters, then you will remember."

Maybe the first time he'd drank from the Lethe had been very intentional, and perhaps it was better that whatever he'd forgotten remained forgotten. Once he had his memories back, he could make that decision for himself.

"Any of you who are here because you've lost your memories, go now to the pool west of the white poplar tree and drink from its waters. Your memories will be returned to you."

"The western pool, the western pool, the western pool," the man in front of me chanted under his breath as though to remind himself, bowing low and scurrying out of the throne room. At least a quarter of the petitioners followed, peeling away from the now slightly more manageable line.

Orphne looked at me with wide, delighted eyes, and even Keuthonymos looked a little hopeful, as opposed to entirely exhausted for a moment.

"If you see Mnemosyne," I muttered, leaning toward him. "Tell her I want a word."

"Of course," Keuthonymos agreed, blinking at me.

I glanced back at Orphne, who gave me a quick approving nod, her eyes darting to where the members of Hades' court stood around watching with narrowed eyes.

Let them watch, I thought to myself. *This wasn't so hard.*

More than that, it was quite fulfilling. Not enough for me to accept Hades' ludicrous marriage proposal, but enough to give me an irritating level of pause.

"How can I help you?" I asked the young girl, who moved to the front of the line as she bowed low. How long did it take to stop feeling like my heart was being carved out of my chest whenever the soul of a child appeared in front of me?

"Oh great and wonderful goddess," the girl squeaked, her limbs trembling. "Please, please help me. My whole family was dying, but now that I'm here I can't find them."

Well, that wouldn't do.

"Keuthonymos, do the Judges keep records of the deceased?"

"They do. I can have someone escort her there to check."

"Yes, let's do that," I agreed. "As soon as possible."

One of Keuthonymos' scribes materialized from the crowd, guiding the weeping girl away, and I made a note to follow up on her later to make sure that if her family was here, they were found.

I spoke to at least fifty souls, all of whom needed some kind of reassurance. Orphne quietly explained that most of them were new, and overwhelmed with both their surroundings and the pressure to join one of the factions in the Meadows. It wasn't *hard* work, but it was emotionally draining, and my mind kept conjuring Hades' inscrutable face, trying to place him in this role, day in and day out for all of eternity, and wondering how he'd managed it for so long all on his own.

My musings came to an abrupt stop as an intimidating god, bedecked in resplendent armor, stormed into the throne room, dragging a struggling soul by the ear behind him.

The god was dressed in full for battle, carrying a spear and shield, and I realized with a jolt that it must be Ares. What was the God of War doing here? Very few gods visited the underworld, and as far as I knew, Ares wasn't one of the usuals.

"Where is Hades?" Ares barked, sparing me a dismissive look before doing a double take, his gaze tracking lasciviously down my body. He was exactly the kind of Olympian my mother had wanted me to avoid, and I fought the natural urge to hide my divine form, to make myself smaller and more invisible.

"Busy. I can deal with him," I said with more confidence than I felt, tipping my chin at the mortal he'd gracelessly deposited on the floor.

Ares shrugged, already turning away. "Fine by me. The less time I have to spend in this pit of nightmares, the better."

I bit down on my retort as Ares marched away, looking down his nose at the souls he passed. *Arrogant prick.* What did he know? Flitting from battle to battle, causing carnage as he pleased. He didn't know what it was to *rule*, what it meant to lead, to have a position with real responsibility.

The vehemence of my rage, of my defensiveness for Hades and this realm, surprised me. I quickly schooled my features into something more akin to an aloof goddess, staring down at the seemingly distraught man at my feet.

No, I wasn't an aloof goddess, I decided in that moment. Not everyone who came to the underworld was ready to be here, and if I could give them some comfort, some reassurance at such a frightening time, then I would.

Especially this man.

He looked *awful.* Beyond awful. One of his eyeballs seemed to be hanging from the socket by a thread, most of his teeth were missing, and his bones jutted out at unnatural angles. Even Demetria, emaciated and pockmarked as she was, hadn't looked like this.

"What's your name?" I asked gently, aware that the court was gathering around us in a circle, shamelessly staring at the mutilated soul in front of me.

Keuthonymos appeared between us, looking at me with alarm. "Goddess, this is Sisyphus, son of Aeolus. The cunning trickster who trapped Thanatos with his own soul chains. For days, no mortal could die because of this miscreant."

I shuddered slightly, remembering that talking decapitated head back in the forest of Henna. This mortal had been responsible for that? He seemed so... ordinary.

Where was Hades? I was completely out of my depth here.

"Please, oh great and benevolent goddess, I'm not meant to be here." Sisyphus rolled onto his front, bowing and sniffling loudly at my feet.

"It's your time," I replied softly, uncomfortable with his display. "Stand. It's time to leave your mortal life behind, and live in rest here in the underworld."

"But I'm not meant to *be* here," Sisyphus wailed. "My wife did not give me burial rites. She threw my body out onto the street, no obol under my tongue for Charon, not that it mattered since Ares deposited me here directly. I didn't look like this when I died—my body has been mutilated on my wife's orders! It's still lying in the street now, I feel the echoes of the wild animals ravaging my flesh."

Oh.

By the rules that governed the underworld, Sisyphus *shouldn't* be here. He should be with The Restless Dead until his hundred-year wait was up. No other part of the underworld should be accessible to him until then, isn't that what Orphne had said?

"Let me go back, please, oh wise and gracious goddess," he pleaded, still bowing at my feet. It was a little much, frankly, and he didn't even know who I was or whether I was worth such protestations. "Three days. I swear, three days is all I need. I'll return to my body and avenge the insult against me, against

Death itself. When I return to the underworld, it will be with the appropriate payment for Charon."

I supposed I *could* send him back if his body was lying on the side of the road, unburned by the usual funeral pyre. For his body to be left out at all where it could be eaten by wildlife was a blatant gesture of disrespect to Hades. To the very act of dying and entering the underworld.

His wife *should* be punished for that. Mortals *should* have a healthy respect for death, for the journey beyond mortality. For this entire realm.

I felt the eyes of Hades' entire court on me, waiting for my decision. Wanting me to get it wrong. What kind of goddess would I be to let a slight go unaddressed on my watch?

"One day," I said slowly, kneeling down and letting the gift of life flow from my hand to his. Out of the corner of my eye, I saw Keuthonymos shift nervously. "You have *one* day to get your revenge, then you will return willingly to the underworld and face the Judges of the Dead."

"Of course, of course. One day is plenty," he promised, climbing to his feet with impressive speed. "You are good and wise and gracious, goddess."

His praise made me uneasy, and I wanted him out of here.

"Get your vengeance and return, Sisyphus, son of Aeolus."

CHAPTER 17

"Hades!" Minthe called as I ascended the steps at the front of the palace. I closed my eyes for a moment, exhaling loudly. Could no one see that I wasn't in the mood for conversation?

I'd just thrown another faction leader into Tartarus for further disrupting the balance with the riot they'd instigated, and it was weighing heavily on me to lose another soul, even if it was due to their own actions.

"Yes?" I clipped, twisting away before she could rest her hand on my forearm. It was busy out here today, with plenty of eyes eager to witness gossip as it was being created.

"Where have you been?" she asked, softening her voice and blinking slowly at me. I disliked when she did this. She'd always followed up our physical dalliances with this particular tone and an expression that I assumed was meant to make her seem meeker than she was. It was repellent.

"Busy. Did you need something?"

"It's just that the goddess you brought from the upperworld is in the throne room, giving out orders." Minthe laughed, a high, false sound. "I know you said we were to respect her as a queen, but surely you didn't mean she should play at ruler in your realm."

"The goddess I brought from the upperworld," I repeated flatly.

"Yes. She's still in there now—I came to fetch you because even Keuthonymos is assisting her. She's telling the souls who were struggling with their memory to drink from the pool west of the poplar tree, making *pronouncements*—"

"Kore is to be my queen, she can make whatever pronouncements she likes."

Keuthonymos had found the helmet next to that pool. Kore had used her gift, *something* had happened there. That she hadn't been able to remember it meant one of the memory goddesses had been there too.

And since Lethe had her own pool, it could only be Mnemosyne.

I nearly groaned at my own stupidity. Of course, that pool should be Mnemosyne's. In fact, every time I'd encountered Mnemosyne she'd all but told me it, in her frustrating, roundabout way of talking. Why couldn't people just say what they meant?

Minthe's smile turned brittle. "She sent Sisyphus back to the upperworld."

That gave me pause, and Minthe pounced on the perceived weakness.

"Ares deposited the miscreant, Sisyphus, son of Aeolus, in the throne room. Delivered the soul here himself," Minthe recounted with relish. Ares had been *here*? He'd *seen* Kore? This did not bode well for her and me. "And he gave Kore some sob story about how his wife had thrown his body out onto the street to be attacked by wild animals, didn't give him burial rites and so on..."

Didn't give him burial rites? To disrespect a corpse was to disrespect me personally. To disrespect the very concept of death, and the necessity of the underworld. It was an insult, and it couldn't go unaddressed.

"... she said he could have a full *day* to get his revenge and then he'd have to return, but we all know he won't. He's already evaded death once, why wouldn't he try again? It's obvious to all of us that someone who is better acquainted with the underworld would be more suited to be queen. Don't be angry, Hades. I'm only telling you what we've all been thinking," Minthe added hastily.

I stared at her, trying to decide why Minthe felt comfortable speaking to me this way. "We fucked a few times. That doesn't give you an advisory role in my court."

Her ridiculous meek facade dropped, a familiar look of irritation back on her face. "I see you haven't gained any charm with this new bride you're supposedly courting," she snapped. "I'm trying to help you before you do something idiotic. As pretty as Kore is, as impressive as her mother is, she's barely even left her rooms the entire time she's been here—"

"You have a home in the underworld at my discretion, Minthe. Never forget how quickly that can change."

Mood thoroughly ruined, I stormed past her into the palace, ignoring all the bowing and scraping that was happening either side of me as I approached the throne room.

Did this mean Kore was entertaining the idea of staying? She'd said that what happened between us couldn't mean anything, but then she was here. *Standing* at the front of the line of petitioners, glowing a brilliant gold that illuminated the white pillars of the throne room.

Standing. My Kore, my future queen, was *standing.*

I silently stomped past them all, throwing myself into my throne and meeting her bewildered gaze as she twisted back to stare up at me on the dais.

"Come here," I grunted, struggling to rein in my temper.

Kore's golden eyes flashed dangerously, but she acquiesced, slowly making her way up the steps, the deep purple chiton I'd hoped to see her in dragging behind her.

"You summoned me?" she asked dryly, stopping in front of me and crossing her arms over her chest.

"My apologies," I murmured. "I see now that was rude. I dislike seeing you standing down there like a petitioner, or just another member of my court. You should be up here with me."

"There's only one throne."

"I'll share it with you."

Her face softened. "I know you would."

For a long moment—too long, considering how many other people were in the room, we just looked at one another. I understood Kore's expressions better than I understood anyone's, but I couldn't read the look on her face at that moment. If I had to guess, it was *guilt*, but that didn't seem right.

With an absent wave, I created an identical throne of black marble next to mine, barely an inch of space between the arms of them. The shocked reaction of everyone in the room didn't escape me, but it didn't matter to me either.

"It doesn't really suit you," I said with a grimace, staring at the harsh lines of the black stone. Kore was softness and life, not cold sharp edges, but I didn't know how to create those kinds of things.

"It's only temporary," Kore replied with a weak smile, taking her place next to me. Where she *belonged*.

"You created a Pool of Memory."

Kore's cheeks glowed. "It's really not as impressive as it sounds, now that I have my memory back. Mnemosyne was more than willing to do it, she was just being difficult about it."

"She's always difficult," I muttered. "And Sisyphus came."

Kore's eyes widened, a vague look of panic taking over her as though she was concerned I was going to challenge the edict she'd issued.

"I'm not angry you gave him a day to seek revenge," I clarified. "A slight against death is a slight against this entire realm, and we cannot let it go unpunished. Besides, Thanatos can always go fetch him again, I'm sure he's learned his lesson about demonstrating how the soul chains work," I added wryly. I certainly *hoped* he had. Frankly, if he allowed himself to be tricked twice, he deserved it.

Kore's lips twitched, the relief on her face unmistakable, even to me. "Come on, let's talk to some petitioners, or the line in your throne room will never get any shorter."

Our throne room, I corrected silently, turning to face the crowd.

Kore was a natural.

After the first three petitioners, it became clear that she was much more capable than I was when it came to easing someone's concerns, and most of the petitioners barely even addressed me when they got to the front of the line.

We'd been at it for hours, and for the first time in my existence, I wanted to take a break purely for the enjoyment of doing so rather than because I had some other pressing task to attend to.

Kore glanced at me nervously as she finished her conversation with a new soul whose first and second husbands from her mortal life were fighting over her now that they'd all died.

"Does it bother you that I'm doing all the talking? This is your job, I don't want to intrude."

"Please, intrude," I muttered. "They prefer speaking to you because you're kind and compassionate and better at this in every way. I'd much rather only contribute when they have questions you can't answer. Yet."

Kore gave me an exasperated look. "Orphne hopes I'll get addicted to the power and want to stay."

"Is it working?" I asked hopefully.

Kore opened her mouth before closing it again. "I don't want to answer that."

For the first time in my existence, I smiled in front of my court. She didn't want to lie. She *was* enjoying this.

Kore exhaled heavily, her eyes dropping to my mouth, a slightly dazed look coming over her face. One that I recognized.

She was attracted to me. Maybe Kore would never love me, but it seemed she loved how I made her body feel.

"You ache for me, Kore," I accused gently, leaning over the arm of my throne to speak in her ear. "Have you been thinking about the way I made you feel in your rooms? I'm finding it difficult to think about anything else."

"If you're going to bring it up, then you should at least do something about it," Kore muttered, the glow on her cheeks less noticeable when she was in her divine form.

I nodded at Keuthonymos, who handled the petitioners while I took Kore's hand and led her out of the throne room through a side door, ignoring the stares that followed us.

The moment we were alone in a quiet corridor, I pulled her body flush to mine, gently cupping the back of her neck. I wanted to kiss her more than anything, but I needed her to initiate it. Perhaps for my own ego, considering how we'd left things when we parted.

"Are you reconsidering your no coupling in the corridors rule?" Kore breathed, the faintest hint of playfulness in her voice. I laughed in surprise, the foreign noise startling me slightly.

"No, absolutely not." The idea of someone coming across Kore like that was abhorrent. I could barely stand to share her *smiles*, let alone those sweet breathy sounds she made when she came.

"Then we should probably move somewhere more private."

I pulled her into a small sitting room that the nymphs sometimes used, shutting the door behind me before pulling her against my body again, circling the soft skin at the base of her neck with my thumb. "This isn't how I expected this interaction to go, based on what happened earlier."

Had I read Kore wrong? Before I'd left her rooms, I got the impression that she wasn't in a hurry to repeat what we'd done.

"About that." Kore bit her lip for a moment, looking oddly shy considering how easily she'd expressed her opinions to me since she arrived here. "I'm sorry that I said it didn't mean anything, that was obviously a lie. I didn't expect it to feel as overwhelming as it did, and I reacted poorly."

Kore blew out a long breath, seemingly collecting her thoughts, while I tried to decide if her words were positive or not. Had she been overwhelmed in a good way or a bad way? Was it possible to be overwhelmed in a good way?

"I don't want to be a virgin anymore."

It took my mind a few seconds to catch up to what she'd said. "Excuse me?"

Kore took a step back and I let my hand fall, creating some space between us. "I don't want to be a virgin anymore. Specifically, I'd like you to be the one to make me... not a virgin. In spite of the kidnapping and your refusal to take me home, I want you. I wouldn't want to share this with anyone else."

That should have made me feel happy, shouldn't it? I wasn't sure it did. I was greedy where Kore was concerned.

"I don't want your body without your heart, Kore."

"My heart isn't on offer, you should take what you can get."

The words were delivered coolly, but her hands twisted together in front of her and she struggled to make eye contact.

I sighed, staring at the sparse room over her shoulder. "I wanted a marriage of equals, Kore. But you already have my heart, and you'll never give me yours. It *could* never have been truly equal. I should have realized that sooner."

"Good thing we're not getting married then," Kore whispered, a slight tremor in her voice. A strange ache took up residence in my chest. "I want to experience sex with you, only with you, but if it's too much to ask for, if it'll cause you pain, then forget I said anything."

"That won't be possible," I muttered. The memory of Kore asking *me* for sex would be embedded in my mind for all of eternity. And I wanted her. *Fates*, I wanted her more than anything.

But not like this.

"Not yet," I said quietly. *Time. I just needed more time.* Time to convince Kore that we were perfect for each other, that she belonged here. That sex between us could be more than just an experience ticked off her list. "Just... not yet."

"Not yet," Kore conceded softly, stepping into my space and pressing her lips against mine, taking away the constant noise in my mind for just a moment.

"I wish I could be what you want me to be," Kore murmured against my mouth.

"I've only ever wanted you to be yourself," I replied quietly, running my hands over the silk of her garment. Wanting to verify that she was real and here, and hadn't found a way to disappear yet.

Kore made a slightly pained sound, her hands balling into fists on my chest, yanking at my chiton. We should have probably stopped, but her desire called to mine, and I couldn't let her walk away from me with an ache between her thighs that I'd put there.

We stumbled toward the klinai, a tangle of lips, teeth and tongues, a desperate edge to Kore's movements that I knew was reciprocated in my own.

Maybe I wasn't ready to give her what she was asking for, but I could give her this. A taste of pleasure. A glimpse at what it could be like. How much *better* it would be if she wasn't trying to pull me close and push me away at the same time.

As I turned to face her, Kore lowered herself to the seat, leaning back slightly against it in modest invitation. No, that wouldn't do. I wanted Kore to know *passion*.

I strode briskly to where she sat, and she sucked in a breath as I leaned over, bracing my arms either side of her head. "Stop me if it's too much."

"It won't be," she breathed, chest heaving temptingly under her chiton.

I kept my eyes on hers as I roughly grabbed the back of her legs, yanking her to the edge of the seat until she fell backward onto it and pressing her knees up by her shoulders. Without any pretense, I flipped the chiton up, exposing her to me, and lowered my face to her cunt like I had in my daydreams for years.

"Hades!" Kore gasped, thighs closing reflexively, but at this angle it wasn't a problem. I slanted my mouth over her slit, licking wide strokes up the length of her to encourage her to relax. Eventually, she let me push her legs further apart, and I kept my palms firmly on the back of her thighs, pinning her in place. Spread out in front of me like a feast.

Never mind ambrosia. *This* was the food of the gods.

"Oh. Ohhhhhhhh," Kore sighed as my tongue found her clit. "That feels... By the Fates..."

Perfect. Unable to form coherent sentences was a good sign.

Kore's own hands tentatively found the back of her knees, holding herself open for me, and I rewarded her with a rapid suck of her sensitive nerves. Despite her shyness, the newness of all of this to her, she was so willing. So trusting of me to deliver her pleasure.

How could Kore not see that she was made for me? That nothing mattered more to me than her happiness?

"Hades," Kore whispered. "I'm going to..."

I groaned a noise of encouragement, and the vibrations pushed her over the edge. Reluctantly, I released her clit and moved downward, determined to drink down every drop of her release on the terrible off-chance that this was the only time I could. That she'd thank me for showing her what all the fuss was about, then go on her way.

I placed one final, gentle kiss on her entrance before I straightened, and to my intense surprise, Kore *laughed*. It was a quiet, breathy, delighted sound, and I wanted to hear it every day for the rest of eternity. Her face was glowing as she straightened, the chiton falling haphazardly into place.

"You certainly don't waste time, do you?" Kore laughed, pressing the backs of her hands to her cheeks for a moment, before gesturing at the seat. "You just... flipped me over like it was nothing."

"Did you enjoy it?"

"Oh, I very much enjoyed it," she admitted, glancing a little nervously at the tent my cock was making of my garment.

"There's no need for you to do anything," I told her, pushing the fabric aside. "But I need release perhaps more than I ever have in my entire existence, so I'm going to have to see to it."

Kore's eyes widened as I wrapped my hand around my shaft, torn between taking my time and rushing frantically to completion. I wasn't sure I *could* take my time with Kore looking at me like that.

"Can I... touch?"

A choked groan escaped me as I sat down on the klinai next to her, tipping my head back and gulping down a breath as she moved closer to my side, her soft, warm body pressing against me.

I removed my hand and Kore's took its place, her palm so much softer, her fingers so much daintier. I wrapped my own hand over hers, adding more pressure and moving her hand the way I liked it.

"Usually, I would last a lot longer than I'm going to last today," I muttered, throwing my head back. Kore leaned in closer, her other hand drifting over my thighs, my stomach, my balls, tentatively exploring me.

"I want you to let go," Kore murmured, her breath skittering over my shoulder. She leaned in, shyly, brushing a kiss at the base of my neck. That was what tipped me over the edge—not the feeling of her soft hand wrapped tightly around my cock, but the sweetness of her lips against my skin. The tenderness. The hope that accompanied it.

Kore sucked in a breath as I spilled my seed over our joined hands. Perhaps it would have been more polite to pull away, but the territorial part of me wanted to mark her, just a little bit.

"There's so much," Kore laughed lightly, extracting her hand and examining it. Her tongue darted out, swiping over her lower lip. "I want to taste it."

"Then taste it," I replied hoarsely.

Kore gave me a coy smile. "Does this count as food of the underworld? I don't want to get trapped here for eternity because I licked your seed off my fingers."

It was only my love for Kore that allowed me to capture her wrist, drawing her hand toward me so I could clean my spend off her fingers with the fabric of my chiton. If I loved her less, I might have encouraged her to try it anyway, in the hopes she'd never be able to leave.

"Maybe next time," Kore laughed, flexing her fingers. Her face was flushed with pleasure, eyes brighter than usual, and her body more relaxed than I'd seen her since she arrived in the underworld. "In the meantime, you should probably change before someone comes in and finds you like this," she said, giving my chiton a pointed look.

"I should," I agreed, maintaining my hold on her wrist. Would it ever get easier to let her go? I couldn't see how that was possible.

Kore softened, her satisfied smile tinged with sadness.

"Every time I walk away from you, I wonder if it'll be the last time I ever see you."

I hadn't meant to confess that to her. I didn't want Kore to see me as weak, and judging by the suddenly pained look in her eyes, that was exactly how she would see me now.

Kore cupped my jaw for a moment before releasing me and moving back. Reluctantly, I dropped her wrist.

"I promise I won't leave without saying goodbye."

CHAPTER 18

After Hades reluctantly left to clean himself up, I ducked out of the abandoned-looking sitting room we'd been in and down a few quiet corridors until I came out on a balcony, needing to catch my breath. The balcony must have been at the other end of the palace from where I'd been staying, and it had the most magnificent view over the Stygian Marshlands toward the Elysian Fields.

There were more flowers there than anywhere else I'd seen in the underworld, but that wasn't saying much. I mentally made a list of all the flowers I would fill it with if I could, anything to distract myself from what Hades and I had just done.

Not that I wanted to *forget* about it—it was one of the best moments of my existence. But Hades had said he didn't want to go any further yet, and I needed to calm myself down before I marched back through the palace and threw myself at him.

How was it always better than I imagined?

How was I going to give this up?

Even the thought of staying made a sharp ache take up residence in my chest. I'd been trapped there, but it was still my home. And now I was trapped *here* and growing too attached to this place too.

We'd spent hours in the throne room, side-by-side, addressing petitioners. I could feel the weight off Hades' shoulders when someone cried in front of us and I responded on his behalf. Every lesson I'd learned at my mother's knee—the things I liked about her rule and the things I didn't—had come in useful.

For the first time in my existence, I'd felt confident. Powerful. *Valuable.*

Images of the lush greenery in my mother's gardens, golden wheat fields, bright flowers swaying in the breeze as Zephyros blew through floated through my mind, reminding me of everything I stood to lose.

My hands were clenched into such tight fists that my nails dug sharply into my palms. I wanted both, and I couldn't have both. Hades wanted everything from me. Neither he, nor Mother, would ever agree to compromise. Neither would willingly give me up.

As much as I adored them both, in different ways, neither had a great record of listening to what *I* wanted.

The pain in my palms grew warm, almost unbearably so, and I opened my hands expecting to see golden ichor running down my wrists.

Instead, I found something much more startling.

In each hand was a small, slightly crushed narcissus, the petals flexing as though they were struggling to grow. Realizing that was my job, I focused my attention back on my palms, channeling my emotional turmoil into the tiny flowers I was holding. *Life,* I marveled as they began to grow. It was more than just restoring life, like I'd done for Sisyphus. I'd *created* life.

In the realm of the dead.

I placed the two full size blooms on the marble railing that surrounded the balcony before immediately repeating the process, sinking to the ground as I got lost in my task. For hours, I kneeled on the unforgiving floor, filling the entire open space with bright yellow blooms. There was no sunlight here to maintain them, but I had seen my mother revive plants with just a touch countless times.

I could just create more.

I allowed myself one unrestrained laugh of pure joy at the thought.

More! No matter where I went, I would never be without flowers again.

Well, without yellow narcissus at least, since I hadn't managed to create anything else. Still, they were beautiful. They reminded me of the sun.

Had I always been capable of this? Was this what my mother had been denying me by insisting I keep my powers to myself? It was the same gift she possessed, and it was *beautiful.* There was no possible way I'd be able to repress it again, not knowing how incredible it felt.

There was a disturbance from the direction of the balcony railing, and I squinted toward the edge, trying to figure out what was going on without stopping what I was doing.

Silence.

I'd probably imagined whatever it was.

I looked down at my palms, focusing on making more flowers, when a head with black curly hair poked over the balcony floor, deep purple eyes peering at me through a gap in the thick marble balustrade.

"Don't scream!" Mnemosyne said hastily, clambering up and perching over the railing, observing the yellow flowers with mild interest. "I'm going to be in enough trouble with the King of the Underworld as it is. The last thing I need is to be frightening his wife."

"I'm not his wife," I replied automatically, clenching my fists. "And forget the King of the Underworld, you're in trouble with *me.*"

"Oh come now, what's a little memory borrowing between friends?"

"We're not friends."

Mnemosyne had the gall to look upset. "Why not? I think we should be friends. It would be very beneficial to me to have a friend who's also a ruler of the underworld."

"I'm sure," I replied wryly. "Did you want something? I'm a little busy."

"I can see that. Pretty flowers."

I blinked at her, channeling the blank, impassive face Hades did when he felt like whatever had been said didn't deserve a response.

"My, my, aren't you feeling regal today?" Mnemosyne cackled. "I just came to let you know that the Pool of Memory is a great success. I've been lounging around watching—my favorites are the ones who get their memories back and immediately run screaming toward the Lethe to forget the terrible things they did all over again."

"Did you want to say anything about *stealing my memory*?" I asked, giving her a pointed look.

"*Borrowed*. I borrowed your memory, just until the moment when you needed it. Don't take offense, future Queen of the Underworld—you've got all the poise and power of a queen, but you needed a little more dramatic flair. The Fates know your husband hasn't got any," she added under her breath.

"He's not my husband," I reiterated, growing increasingly irate. "Swear you won't tinker with my memories again."

"Swear that we're friends," Mnemosyne countered.

"You're impossible," I sighed, absentmindedly channeling the magic in my palms as I spoke. I looked down in surprise to find a misshapen fig in my hand. *Success!* Something that wasn't a narcissus. I extended the fig towards Mnemosyne in offering. "Fine, we're friends."

Mnemosyne recoiled, staring wide eyed at the fruit. Admittedly, it was fairly ugly as far as figs went, but I'd sort of expected my gift to be better received than that.

"That's very kind of you, but I'm going to have to pass on the food, *friend*. I like being able to go topside when it suits me."

Food?

I'd *created* food of the underworld?

Realizing with horror that I'd nearly damned Mnemosyne to an eternity in the underworld with my thoughtlessness, I quickly concentrated on drawing the life I'd sent into the fruit back into my own body, watching the fig wither and die before my eyes.

"Well, that was eerie. Anyway, I promise never to tinker with your memories again. Unless you ask me to, of course. As much as I'd love to stay and braid flowers in your hair, I'm staying out of Hades' way until he's relaxed slightly about me not explicitly explaining the Pool of Memory to him."

Mnemosyne disappeared back off the balcony as quickly as she appeared, and I vaguely wondered how she was getting up and down here, but the moment I returned my attention to my flowers, I forgot all about it.

"Kore?" Orphne called from the corridor after who knew how many hours. Perhaps even all night? With the strange sky that only shifted ever so slightly in color, it was hard to tell. "Are you out here?"

"I am," I responded absently.

"Oh, thank the Fates. I've been looking everywhere, I thought you might have— Oh!" Her words cut off on a gasp as she stepped onto the balcony to find me sitting in a field of flowers. "Oh, Kore, they are exquisite."

"Aren't they?" I replied, rising to my feet. Flowers tumbled off my chiton in a yellow wave, and I carefully stepped over my creations as I approached Orphne. I held out my hand in front of her, forming a particularly beautiful narcissus with a long stem. Lesson learned, no more fruit.

"A thank you gift," I said, holding it out for her. "And a completely inadequate one, for everything you've done for me."

"It's not inadequate," Orphne said, reverently bowing her head as she accepted the flower. "It's perfect. I will treasure it always. The symbol of the god Hades made by the goddess Kore."

I turned to stare at the pile of flowers as Orphne admired the bloom in her hand.

The symbol of the god Hades.

I'd created *Hades'* flower. Of course I had. Even my gift was trying to tell me something about my relationship with the King of the Underworld.

And of course, he chose that exact moment to show up.

CHAPTER 19

Kore had truly found her gift.

I could feel it through the marble walls of the palace. More than just unleashing her divine form, this felt bright, strong, and lush. Less rigid than Demeter's magic, from what I remembered of it, though perhaps that was because it was new. I hoped Kore kept that wildness. That *hunger* that she insisted on locking up tight inside her, instead of embracing.

The polite thing to do would be to give her time to get accustomed to her new abilities. I *had* given her time.

I needed to see for myself.

I'd intended to compliment Kore. To congratulate her on embracing the power she'd always had inside herself, but had been discouraged from using. But the moment I stepped onto the balcony, words failed me.

Flowers. She'd grown hundreds of flowers.

My flowers.

"Excuse me," Orphne mumbled, quickly making her escape.

She had turned the marble floor into a sea of yellow, nearly glowing compared to the stark landscape in the distance. The Elysian Fields in the background, where heroes went to rest, was the most beautiful part of this realm, and it looked dark and dreary next to the paradise Kore had created.

What was I doing?

If there was ever a sign from the Fates of how foolish I was, how impossible the dream I was chasing was, it was this. Seeing the goddess I loved in a vibrant field of her own creation against a backdrop of darkness and despair.

Kore didn't belong here.

She'd been trying to tell me that all along.

"They're beautiful." I nodded at the flowers that covered the floor like a blanket. They were too perfect to have grown in nature, each petal precisely formed, the color so flawless it looked painted.

"I—, um, thank you." She was flustered again. I liked when Kore was flustered, liked that I had that effect on her.

I didn't like that she seemed to get flustered because she was so unused to receiving compliments, but time would change that. If she'd have let me, I would have complimented her every day for the rest of eternity, and never the same thing twice.

But she wouldn't let me. She'd never let me.

All of this had been for nothing.

No, not nothing. Kore found her gift. She had been free to explore, to grow and realize her potential for herself, and she'd found it.

If Kore left here—*when* Kore left here—it would be with more than she'd arrived with. I'd given her that. Perhaps she would remember me fondly for it someday.

And then that was that *other* request she'd made of me. I could give her that too. Hopefully, it would also inspire fond memories.

"You don't seem very happy," Kore pointed out mildly, summoning another narcissus and extending her palm towards me. "I thought you would."

I plucked the bloom from her hand, my fingers brushing against her skin, and held it up to examine. "I'm happy for you, Kore. You're brilliant and powerful. You deserve to be worshipped as devotedly as any goddess."

"Can I visit the Elysian Fields? I think it could do with some more flowers," Kore said with surprising determination, turning away from me to look out over the marshlands.

The question had me frozen in place. She *wanted* to fill the Fields with flowers? Did that mean... Was she considering staying? Carving out a niche for herself here?

"Of course," I agreed carefully. "You can grow flowers wherever you wish."

Kore shot me a beaming smile over her shoulder. "I'd like to grow more than just narcissus, but I seem to be stuck on those right now, as far as flowers go, at least. Maybe because I'm in your realm? Oh well, we could do worse than fields of bright yellow flowers. How do I get over there?" she rambled nervously, nodding toward Elysian.

I snorted before I could stop myself. "You're not in a rush to borrow the chariot again? Phlegethon said you looked on the verge of losing consciousness when you flew south to The Restless Dead."

"Gossiping river gods," Kore muttered, her posture relaxing slightly.

"They are that," I agreed. "Come on, I'll take you there."

I took Kore's arm and guided her to the edge of the balcony. I moved behind her, settling my hands on her waist and lifting her to perch on the railing, smiling at the alarmed squeak she made.

"What are you—" Her words cut off as I climbed over the rail, whistling for my chariot as I did. "Hades!"

Perhaps it would have been polite to explain my actions, but I was enjoying the way Kore watched and waited and *trusted*. She trusted me. She wanted to make the underworld a little more her own.

Hope was making me giddy. There was a warning whinny as the steeds approached, and I looped an arm around Kore's waist as I dropped toward the ground, trusting the chariot to catch us.

Kore's shriek was so loud that I vaguely wondered if I'd ever hear in that ear again. Her arms wrapped tightly around my neck, legs around my hips, clinging on as my feet hit the chariot floor with a thud, and I snagged the reins with one hand to keep us anchored.

"Hades!" Kore yelled, all four limbs still wrapped around me. "Have you lost your mind?!"

"You do know we're immortal, don't you? Even if we fell to the ground, we wouldn't die."

"This might be a strange concept for you, but I'm averse to the idea of pain," Kore snapped, slipping down my body as she straightened her legs. Her arms stayed in place around my neck, and I pulled her in close, sighing with pleasure as she buried her face against my chest.

"I hate flying," she mumbled, trembling slightly in my embrace. "Though I hate it somewhat less with you."

"I love you too."

"That is absolutely not what I said," Kore gasped, snapping her head back and looking at me with alarm.

"I know, but it distracted you. We're landing now."

"Oh," she breathed, glancing down before shoving her face into my chiton. If only it was a longer flight.

The chariot landed smoothly among the asphodel flowers that always grew in the underworld. Unlike the Meadows, very few souls made it to the Elysian Fields. The ones that did set up homes of their own, scattered across wide distances. I rarely saw any of them.

"It's so peaceful here," Kore sighed, quickly dismounting the chariot on shaky legs. I followed her, leaving the horses to graze as we walked among the low-lying vegetation.

"It is," I agreed, letting Kore lead as she explored the area. Before I'd discovered the small window to Lake Pergusa in the Forest of Kore, these fields had been where I'd come to get away from the palace.

Kore sat on the hard ground without any hesitation, sinking her fingers into the dirt and breathing out a sigh of relief as she closed her eyes. My gifts were all tied to the running of the realm, but even in the two brief trips I'd taken away from here, I'd felt a sense of completion when I was back in my element. I wondered if Kore was feeling that way too, or if the earth here was filled with too much death for her life-giving power.

A patch of narcissus sprouted beneath her hands, and I hoped it meant my fears were unfounded. Kore opened her eyes, staring down at the sudden bed of flowers she was sitting in, before looking up at me with a beaming smile on her face that entirely took my breath away.

She was *radiant*.

"Now if I just need some flowers that *don't* symbolize you," she laughed. Actually laughed. How much of a burden had suppressing her gift been? I'd never seen Kore so free with her smiles in all my years of watching her.

There were a thousand other things I should have been doing, but I didn't do any of them. I sat on the ground and watched Kore grow flowers, smiling along with her when a vibrant patch of purple crocuses bloomed among the yellow narcissus.

I would have stayed there for days, watched her experiment with her gift over every inch of these extensive fields, but a disturbance in the air broke my peace.

"Everything okay?" Kore asked, frowning at me. Considering the authority I'd conferred on her, she should have been able to feel it too, but perhaps she wasn't in tune with the realm yet.

"I felt something at the gate," I told her as I stood. "I best go check in case Kerberos has left his post again. You can stay here if you want to continue what you're doing, no one will disturb you."

"That would be nice," Kore said with a dreamy smile, plucking a purple bloom out of the ground and handing it to me. I tucked it into my belt with the narcissus, turning to head back to the chariot before quickly striding back to Kore and dropping a kiss on her forehead.

"I'll come back for you."

"Okay," she breathed, suddenly shy. How was it that throwing her down on the furniture and flipping up her chiton to devour her cunt had made her less bashful than a simple kiss on the forehead?

There was some other unwritten rule I was undoubtedly missing here.

I mounted the chariot and watched Kore's form shrink as we climbed into the sky, heading southwest toward the Port of Charon. As I grew closer, the sheer force of the presence made it clear who had come to visit.

It had always been a matter of time.

If Zeus hadn't told Demeter where Kore was, Ares almost certainly had. He was one of Zeus' least intelligent children, but surely even he would have worked out that there was a beautiful goddess missing in the upperworld and he'd encountered a mysterious one down here.

For a few brief moments, I'd been happy. Kore had allowed herself to use her gift without inhibition. She was as glorious and clever as I always knew she was, and she was finally, *finally* realizing her potential.

As I knew she would.

I loved her, but bringing her to the underworld had always been about helping her flourish because the odds of her loving me back were almost impossible. It was working—Kore was growing into her power and potential, and she'd show anyone who doubted her what a formidable goddess she truly was.

The chariot swooped downward, landing smoothly behind a furious Kerberos, who'd shifted to his larger, more terrifying form. He was nearly as tall as the walls of the palace at this height, and his fangs could crush most beasts in existence. His serpent tail hissed wildly, joining the three growling heads whose attention was trained solely on the King of the Gods.

"Zeus," I said flatly, patting Kerberos' flank as I passed him. "Welcome to the underworld."

"Hades," Zeus sighed, inclining his head. At least he didn't look any happier to be here than I was to have him here. "This is quite the welcome," he added, eyes darting warily to Kerberos.

"Kerberos, calm," I instructed, glancing up at him. I was going to be annoyed if he drooled on me. I returned my attention to Zeus. "Usually, he lets immortals through. He's feeling a little protective right now."

"Ah, perhaps he knows why I'm here. I didn't give you my blessing to take her, Hades."

"Nor did you tell me not to."

Zeus grimaced, tipping his chin in concession. He should have been more explicit in his instructions. "Demeter is... unhappy."

He was looking at me like he expected an answer, and I blinked at him in response. Demeter's unhappiness was a given. Zeus sighed.

"I have to take Kore back."

"Absolutely not," I replied. "I suggest you remember who reigns supreme in this realm before you start giving orders."

Zeus' jaw clenched in irritation at the reminder. There was a reason why he never visited me or traveled to see Poseidon in his realm.

"I can't demand that you hand her over, but there are other ways I could convince you."

"I love Kore. I intend to marry her. Kore will be my queen and equal in every way, and live a fulfilling life where she's treated as more than a beautiful doll, hidden away on a shelf. Demeter should be thanking me."

If Kore wanted to stay. We'd been making progress, we just needed a little more time.

Zeus stroked his beard contemplatively. "That does sound like a good deal for Kore. It's better prospects than she would have had if she'd accepted

Hermes or Apollo's proposals." The sky above us darkened and swirled with my rage at the reminder, and I made no attempt to stop it.

Who were they to propose to *my* Kore? She'd always been mine. The Fates had destined her for me, I knew that in my soul.

"I'm sympathetic, Hades. I am. It's clear that you care for Kore, and that you'd give her a good life here, but she must return either way. Demeter has sworn that nothing will grow until Kore is back. The earth is barren, and mortals are dying in droves." He gestured vaguely past the gate, toward the line of souls that he couldn't see over the great stone wall. "That can't be news to you."

The unfairness of it all was infuriating.

"You have *everything*," I muttered. "Every lover you've ever wanted, you've taken, consequences be damned."

Zeus rubbed the back of his neck. "Yes, well, their mothers weren't as formidable as Demeter. I'm sure we could find you another goddess—"

"No," I interjected, appalled at the thought. "If I can't have Kore, then I'll have no one. She's not just a goddess. She's not replaceable, not to me."

Zeus groaned as though I was making his life particularly difficult. I probably was, but that was his problem to deal with.

"Kore has to go back, *but* perhaps if she could make her mother understand that she wanted to be here, that she would willingly marry you, that would solve everyone's problems."

Ah. Zeus had assumed that my feelings for Kore were reciprocated. Were they? There was *something* there, but were those feelings strong enough for Kore to commit to a life here?

"Demeter isn't entirely unreasonable," he continued under his breath. "It might take some convincing, but if she genuinely believed Kore was happy, then maybe she'd be willing to let her daughter go without killing off the entire mortal population in the process."

She wouldn't.

The realization was instant and troubling. Demeter would never willingly let Kore go. Especially not to me, which I could admit was at least in part due to my own actions in taking Kore in the first place. But even if I hadn't, Demeter had always prioritized what *she* wanted for Kore over what Kore wanted for herself.

"Yes," Zeus said decisively, nodding to himself. "I'll give you a day to talk it over, Hermes can collect Kore tomorrow. Kore will convince Demeter that she'd like to take you up on your marriage proposal, and all will be well."

"And if I refuse to allow Hermes to take her?" I asked thickly, a crushing sense of hopelessness bearing down me.

Zeus' eyes flashed, a glimpse of his power rippling beneath his skin. "I'm sympathetic, Hades, but I can't ignore a direct challenge to my authority. You have no allies in this. If I were to gather the other gods and use our combined gifts to create a new underworld with a new king, cutting you off completely in this realm with no souls to sustain you, not a single one of them would oppose me. Think of the life you'd be condemning Kore to then, in an empty and decaying underworld prison. If you love her as much as you claim, you'd grant her freedom."

He turned away, stepping up onto his gleaming white chariot and taking the reins. "You have until tomorrow. I'm confident you'll make the right decision, Hades. Hermes will bring Sisyphus with him. He's doing his best to outrun Thanatos again, but no mortal is any match for an Olympian."

I watched him go, clenching my jaw so tightly that it hurt. The *right* decision, as though I had options. Kore could never become the goddess she was truly meant to be if she was trapped in a realm cut off from any source of power. I'd never wanted Kore *truly* imprisoned here.

With a heavy sigh, I mounted my chariot, directing the steeds back to the Elysian Fields, my gaze catching on the Forest of Kore as we passed. I'd promised Kore that I wouldn't watch her any longer if she returned to the upperworld, never really thinking that day would come.

But it had.

Kore had to leave.

I had to let her go.

CHAPTER 20

I hadn't meant to stay in the fields as long as I had. I'd been having so much fun playing with my magic that I'd briefly forgotten how long the line of petitioners at the palace was, and it wasn't fair for me to just sit here and enjoy myself when I could be helping.

The Elysian Fields looked *so* much better with a little color on them, though. In addition to narcissus and crocuses, I'd also grown lilies, violets, and finally, poppies—the sacred flower of Demeter. Seeing the bright red petals that were such a fixture at Henna had almost made me cry, but the homesickness had a slightly more muted feel to it now. It hadn't gone away, but the acuteness of the pain had dulled.

Flowers had been one of the things I'd been missing, and now I had them. It helped more than I expected.

Sighing happily at the progress I'd made, I picked my way through the fields toward the marshlands, hoping if I asked nicely, the waters would transport me across like they'd done when I was with Orphne. Before I had a chance, Hades' golden chariot swooped down from the sky, one of his hands capturing mine and snatching me into the air.

Not unlike how he'd snatched me from the upperworld, except everything felt different this time. My scream was more startled than terrified, and I pressed myself willingly against his body, not minding in the least when one arm banded around my waist to keep me in place.

"Is everything okay?" I asked, noticing that while Hades' embrace was as solid as always, there was a new tension to his posture.

For a long, terrible moment, I thought he was going to lie to me, and I was surprised by how much that hurt. "The deadline you gave Sisyphus has passed. He hasn't returned."

Had it? I'd been so busy with my gift that I hadn't been paying attention.

"That lying little weasel," I muttered, outraged that I'd been deceived. It was an *insult*, a blatant disrespect to me.

"He will be punished," Hades assured me, his fingers flexing against my waist. I narrowed my eyes at the stiffness of his tone. Maybe he hadn't lied, but there was something he wasn't telling me, and the chariot was already beginning its descent in front of the palace steps. "Hermes will return Sisyphus himself tomorrow. When he comes to collect you."

The hooves landed on the ground with a clatter, and we were suddenly surrounded by people, all clamoring for Hades' attention, probably because I'd kept him away for so long.

With heartbreaking care, Hades lifted me off the chariot, setting me down at his side before stepping away to answer Keuthonymos' litany of questions. The moment his arms were gone, I was cold and bereft.

He'd *left* me cold and bereft, a mask of blank emotion coming over his face. Like it was nothing to watch me leave, like what we shared had come to its natural end and that was that.

Hermes was coming to collect me.

This should have been everything I wanted. It had been everything I'd told *Hades* I wanted. No wonder he looked so resigned about it.

He'd accepted it. I was the one who hadn't.

The crowd swept him away toward the throne room, and he let them. He just *let* them.

"Looks like he's grown bored with you already," Minthe said, planting herself in front of me, a cruel smile on her face. She was with her usual cohort of nymphs, who all shifted uncomfortably at the clear confrontation in Minthe's voice.

Fates, I was so not in the mood for this.

"That's what he does. He fixates on things until he loses interest in them. You were a novelty in the upperworld where he couldn't touch you, but now you're just an imposition. Sisyphus escaped again because of you. You're an embarrassment to the underworld."

I hated to admit even to myself that some of her harsh blows landed. He'd walked away from me so easily. I *had* let Sisyphus go.

"I understood at first why he'd entertain the idea of taking the daughter of two Olympians as his bride, even if I thought it was idiotic. But now he realizes that no one could be a better Queen of the Underworld than one who already lives here and knows how it works. Why would Hades want you when he's had *me*?"

Fates, she was a talker.

"That really seems like a question you should be asking yourself," I replied flatly, begrudgingly appreciative of her unearned confidence. What kind of fearsome goddess could I be if only I were a little more shameless?

A few of the courtiers sniggered, and Minthe's mouth pressed into a tight line. I probably should have smoothed over the situation, rather than embarrassing her more. I could see that now, watching Minthe's anger ramp up as she absorbed the blow to her pride.

Mortal or immortal, no one liked to be embarrassed.

Unfortunately, I wasn't in the mood to be mollifying.

"Minthe," Daeira—the nymph I'd seen with Thanatos—whispered, stepping forward and tugging at Minthe's arm. Daeira, at least, had the good sense to look uncomfortable. Only an idiot spoke ill of a goddess with such astounding confidence. "Kore is an immortal, one step removed from Olympus. Hades will not take kindly to your loudly disparaging his choice of bride."

Kore did not take kindly to it, I thought bitterly. Though Daeira could live for having a modicum of common sense. Minthe, I was less forgiving of. The palms of my hands tingled, my gift rising to the surface to defend my honor.

"I don't care that you're one step away from Olympus," Minthe replied, staring at me. "The Queen of the Seas is a nymph. Why not the Queen of the Underworld?"

Because Amphitrite is discreet and dignified, and you are insufferable, I thought. Not that I cared. I was leaving, wasn't I? Hermes was coming to get me. Let Hades marry the loud mouth gossip of a woman. What business of it was mine if the Queen of the Underworld was obnoxious? None. It was exactly what Hades deserved for involving himself with her in the first place and kidnapping a goddess who didn't want him.

I hadn't even spoken the words aloud, yet I could taste the lie.

I did want him. I wanted Hades all to myself, I wanted to keep the devoted love and care that he offered me so freely.

But I couldn't take it. Not if it meant never seeing my family again, or the realm I loved so much. Hades seemed happy here in this eternal darkness, never venturing to the upperworld, but I knew I couldn't be. If I stayed, I'd be making us both miserable eventually.

Logically, I knew that. Logically, I understood that whatever connection there was between us, however strong it felt, we couldn't make each other happy.

But I was still a goddess, and still imbued with perhaps too much pride and not enough self-control.

Perhaps I couldn't keep Hades for myself, but it would be a bright, sunny day in the underworld before Minthe did.

The glow around my form flared brighter, and flowers fell unconsciously from my hands, a splash of color against the stark white marble floor.

Maybe I truly was my mother's daughter, because the sudden panic in their eyes made me feel powerful, and I *liked* it.

"I don't need Hades to fight my battles for me. Whether I'm queen or not, I am perfectly capable of handling pests like you on my own."

I turned my palm up to face me, directing my magic toward creating an impressively ominous black rose, spiked with thorns as sharp as blades. Idly, I imagined sending those spiky thorns into Minthe's eyeballs, and perhaps she realized where my thoughts had gone because she deliberated in front of my eyes, deciding which angle to take. I was confident that Minthe *knew* the wisest course of action was to fall to her knees, to humble herself and ask for my forgiveness, but Minthe had the pride of an Olympian.

She'd been speaking badly about me since the moment I arrived, this was just the first time she'd bothered saying anything to my face.

"I'm in a generous mood," I lied. "I suggest you take advantage of this moment of grace and forgiveness I'm extending you, and apologize."

"I don't take orders from you, Kore. You're not the Queen of the Underworld, despite whatever proclamations Hades made about you," Minthe sneered, holding her ground. Daeira backed away slowly, horrified gaze trained on the back of Minthe's head.

"Neither are you," I replied sagely. "But I *am* more powerful than you. And you've insulted me and derided me to anyone who'd listen to you since the moment I arrived, so I'd say I have just cause to exact revenge. Plus, I don't like the way you've been undermining Hades' authority behind his back. So, unless you're willing to apologize to both myself and your king..."

I shrugged as though I didn't much care either way, but I did.

I *wanted* her to refuse. I wanted to punish her. I wanted every being in this realm to take Hades' rule seriously, to not feel as though they could insult his decisions behind his back.

"I will never apologize to you—"

My magic coiled out like a whip before she'd even finished speaking, lashing viciously at the center of her chest.

Minthe's mouth opened on a silent scream, and I watched impassively as her pale green skin darkened and became more textured, and her emerald green hair shrunk into her skull. Everything shrunk. Leaves sprouted where skin had been, feet became roots, cracking the marble beneath her as they reached for soil. Minthe's face, that had been so often twisted in disdain, became the top of the plant I'd turned her into. Finally, there was no more thrashing and flailing, just sweet-scented leaves blowing in the breeze.

Daeira gaped at me, as did the rest of the crowd who'd stood by, silently watching Minthe's metamorphosis. I surveyed them blankly, wondering if any of them were going to take up her mantle. I supposed I could always come up with more plants if need be, it wasn't as though the underworld couldn't do with the splash of color.

Hades appeared at that moment, one of the nymphs who I'd seen often around Minthe gesturing frantically for him to follow her. His eyes trained unwaveringly on me. His muscles were bunched with tension, making him seem even bigger and more imposing, his face the picture of fury.

I straightened my shoulders, setting my own expression into a hardened glare. If he wanted to fight me on this, he could fight me. I wasn't about to apologize for my actions.

"Kore," he rumbled, making me shiver.

No, no more shivering. He'd walked away from me like it was nothing. Abandoned me among these vipers. He hadn't even taken my virginity when I'd asked him to, not that it stopped me from wanting him. He'd made me feel comfortable enough to express myself and use my gift and grow into the goddess I was always meant to be, and then he'd *walked away.*

And Fates, I wanted him more than ever. I wanted to know what those muscles would feel like beneath my palms, pressing against my body, bearing down on me. I wanted to be surrounded by him, his strength, his desire for me. I wanted to know what it felt like to have a man between my thighs, whether it was as good as I imagined it was, or whether my mother was right and I wouldn't really be missing anything.

And I was leaving and he was letting me go, and I hated him for making me wonder. I hated myself for hating him, when after all the times I'd told Hades I wanted to leave, he'd finally believed me.

"I turned Minthe into a plant."

He spared the briefest of glances at the aromatic shrub before returning his attention to me. "Did she deserve it?"

Did anyone really deserve to be turned into a plant? A philosophical question for another day.

"Yes."

"Good. We won't be seeing any more petitioners today," he announced, glancing at Keuthonymos, who bowed in acknowledgment before rushing toward the throne room.

Infuriatingly, all that bold confidence combined with his easy acceptance of my actions made me want him even more.

"Are you happy?" I asked quietly, aware of the eyes of the court on us as we walked side-by-side into the palace, turning towards our wing.

"No."

"Because of Minthe?" I asked cautiously. He must have had some affection for her once. Enough to take her to his bed.

He frowned at me. "What about Minthe?"

"Me turning her into a plant? Is that distressing to you?"

Hades snorted. I guessed that was a no.

"Because I'm leaving?" I asked, swallowing thickly.

Suddenly I was pressed up against the wall, but the wall was moving, and I sucked in a breath as I grabbed on to Hades' shoulders to steady myself while he pushed me through the hidden entrance into the Whispers. I supposed I shouldn't have been surprised that he would know every entrance to it—it was his palace. He'd probably seen me in here multiple times while I'd thought I was being so discreet.

My back hit the cold stone wall, Hades looming over me, hips pressed confidently against mine like he had every right to be in my space, touching me so intimately.

"Of course because you are leaving. You are leaving me forever, with *Hermes*, no less. Hermes, who has already expressed an interest in marrying you," Hades murmured, his lips brushing the shell of my ear. It was seductive, but there was a tightness to his voice too. *Jealousy.* It made the ache between my thighs grow sharper. "What if he tries to touch you like this? Will you let him? Or will you admit to yourself that only I truly satisfy you? That no one else will ever come close to making you feel what I make you feel?"

He was probably right, but it hurt too much to say those words out loud. Before I could answer, his lips were on mine, kissing me roughly, greedily. Hades' hands found mine, and he lifted them up over my head, pressing them to the wall either side of me and pinning me in place.

I didn't feel trapped.

If I asked, he'd let me go. If I asked, there probably wasn't much Hades would deny me. It was a heady feeling.

"Only you make me feel like this," he growled in my ear, sounding almost furious about it. "Wherever you are, whoever you end up with, I will never want anyone but you."

He shifted positions slightly, moving one thick, muscular thigh between my legs and I gasped loudly at the sudden sensation, rocking my hips eagerly, seeking it out before I'd even contemplated what his actions meant.

"That's it," he encouraged in a low, silky voice. "Use *me* for your pleasure. Remind me who it was you asked to take your maidenhood."

My heart hurt and I knew that this was a slope that could only descend into anguish, but I did it anyway. It felt too good, too right to stop.

My release was building, building, building, but I couldn't quite reach that peak, no matter how much I tried, how vigorously I pressed my body down on his solid thigh.

"Tell me no," Hades murmured, releasing my hand to slide his into the gap at the side of my chiton, to brush against my thigh. "You're leaving. Tell me no."

"Yes," I breathed, my legs falling further open as he moved his thigh back to accommodate his hand. My eyes fluttered shut at the first light touch of his fingers at my entrance, gently exploring me, coating his fingers in my arousal before moving them up to circle that glorious source of sensation.

"Hades," I whispered, head falling back, my entire body languid and open to him.

"Do you still want me to take your virginity, Kore? To send you away from me with an ache between your thighs and a world of options at your feet?" One thick finger pushed into my entrance, the heel of his hand stimulating my nerves. "Tell me, Kore, who will you marry when there's no oath of virginity to hold you back? Hermes? Apollo?"

He rewarded me—or perhaps punished me—by adding a second finger, and I sucked in a breath at the fullness, wanting more. *Needing* more. Needing to feel him inside of me.

"They'll fumble crudely at your cunt like the selfish bastards they are before they leave you alone to tend to their other lovers. Is that what you want for your future?"

He was mad at me and I was mad at me—a little at him too—but the repetitive grind of his palm against my sensitive nerves eventually tipped me over the edge in spite of my rage, and I came apart with a quiet cry.

I shoved Hades off me, and his look of anger morphed into one of quiet surprise as I snatched his hand and began tugging him through the narrow corridors of the Whispers toward where I believed our wing of the palace was. Perhaps I would eventually be embarrassed at how quickly and forcefully I was dragging him to bed, when my desire wasn't overruling my better judgment.

Or perhaps not. Perhaps it would be worth it.

It *would* be worth it. I'd remember this moment every day for the rest of eternity, and I didn't want to remember it as a 'what if.'

"Kore—"

"Enough," I snapped. "I'm sick of hearing about other gods and all the terrible ways they'd treat me. I want *you*. You're the only one I've ever wanted, the only one I *will* ever want."

I stomped along, outraged and filled with pent up desire in equal measure.

"Maybe I'll never marry. My mother never did. Virgin or not, I'm more than just an available bride."

Hades made a strangled sound before suddenly tugging me back, pulling me through a panel in the wall I hadn't seen as we passed. We stumbled out into the hallway right before the entrance to our rooms, where Orphne must have been on her way to. She blinked at us for a moment, before bowing and quickly backing away, leaving us in privacy.

"Well, that's humiliating," I muttered, shoving open my door. Hades laughed quietly behind me, some of the angry tension between us muted, and Fates, I was going to miss that sound. That rare, delicious noise that he seemed to make only for me.

Before we'd even made it through the sitting area to the bedchamber, I had unpinned the brooch at my shoulder and untied the belt around my waist, letting my chiton slide off my body as I walked, leaving me bare. Hades groaned from behind me, closing the gap between us and all but throwing me onto the bed on my back.

For a long enough moment to make me self-conscious, he just stared. Stared as though he was memorizing me, his hands flexing at his sides like he was aching to memorize my shape with those too.

"You're leaving," he gritted out, chest heaving. "You're—"

"Don't we both want this?" I interrupted sharply, the rejection clawing painfully at my chest. "If you don't, then by all means, walk away, I'd never force you. But if you *do* want me and are denying this anyway, then you're just as willing to disregard my wishes as everyone else in my life. So much for me being your equal."

Hades' eyes darkened ominously at the low blow. "Equals? I'm giving you *everything*, Kore. I'm letting you go. There is nothing equal about it."

Despite his words, Hades held eye contact with me as he slowly removed his himation and chiton, letting the fabric pool at his feet.

By the Fates... If I hadn't known he was a god before, there would be no doubt after seeing his naked form. He was *exquisite*. He looked like he'd been carved by the Muses, a perfect example of masculine strength and virility.

"Every time I remember you telling me you never wanted me, I'm going to remember the way you're looking at me right now too. Perhaps it will lessen the pain."

I clamped my mouth shut, wondering when I'd opened it. I wasn't sure what to do with this intensity, with the slow and purposeful way he was moving. I thought this would be a rushed affair, like when he'd roughly thrown my legs in the air and pleasured me with his mouth like he couldn't stand to wait a moment longer.

All these longing looks gave me too much time to think. To think and to hurt and to wonder.

Hades climbed over my body with quiet confidence, holding his weight off me as he dipped his head, his lips meeting mine in a slow, sensual kiss. My desire coated my inner thighs, and there was no question in my mind that I wanted him, but my stomach clenched nervously in anticipation nonetheless.

"Are you afraid?" he asked, lips moving against mine.

"Only that it will hurt."

"I would take every bit of your pain if I could," he murmured, staring down at me with undisguised adoration. "Until the world stops turning."

And then his cock was pressing at my entrance, pushing forward slowly and feeling *impossibly* large.

You are an immortal goddess. You will not be bested by a cock, I reminded myself in irritation, inhaling deeply and exhaling slowly, encouraging my body to relax. Encouraging my mind to quiet, and my heart to stop pounding like it was trying to escape my chest and press against his.

"Kore," Hades breathed, his voice so laced with both pain and ecstasy, I couldn't tell which emotion was winning. "How am I supposed to let you go?"

Don't.

I bit down the damning word before it could escape me, wrapping my arms and legs around Hades' body and rocking my hips, encouraging him to move. I wanted to feel the physical, and forget the emotional.

Hades braced his forearms either side of my head, finally meeting my movements, each roll of his hips deliberate and almost punishing. I sucked in a breath, arching my back and he immediately dipped his head, teeth scraping over my breast before capturing my nipple, his tongue swirling teasingly.

Oh, this was a terrible idea. There was no getting him out of my head, getting this craving out of my body. If anything, he seemed to be imprinting himself on me—*in* me—and I'd be stuck thinking about him and the way he felt for the rest of eternity.

"My Kore," he groaned.

Suddenly it was too much. Being surrounded by him was too good, *too* comforting, too everything. With a gentle push, I encouraged him to roll over, and with impressive coordination, he gripped my hips as he did, keeping us joined as I abruptly found myself on top of him, bracing my hands on his chest.

I wasn't sure this was any better. I felt slightly less vulnerable, but significantly more powerful. Hades stared up at me like I was the most magnificent creature he'd ever seen, and the walls I was fighting to keep up crumbled a little further.

"Beautiful," he murmured, his fingers flexing at my hips. "Use me, my Kore. Take what you want from me."

My nails dug into his chest as I began to experimentally roll my hips, lifting my weight a little off him before dropping back down and making us both groan. He was talking about more than this, and I refused to hear it.

"That's it," he growled, shifting his hand to my center and brushing my sensitive nerves. My stomach muscles clenched immediately, a gasp escaping me at the sensation. Looking far more smug than I would have liked, Hades rubbed teasing circles with his thumb, increasing the pace as my own movements grew more urgent and erratic.

I forgot to be self-conscious. It was hard to remember *anything* when Hades was acting like I was a revelation.

My body curled over his as I found my release, my nails clawing so desperately at his skin that small rivulets of ichor ran down his chest, staining the sheets. *I hope they scar*, I thought vaguely before giving up on logical thought and allowing myself to feel.

Hades was murmuring words of encouragement, and I found myself flat on my back again as he thrust into me with renewed vigor, arm muscles flexing temptingly next to my head as he found his own peak, his movements suddenly stilling.

I sucked in a quiet breath at the feeling of his hot release filling me, acutely aware of the risk of pregnancy in a way that I had never been in my life. Surely the Fates wouldn't be so unkind as to give me a child now, in the midst of all this uncertainty?

"Kore," Hades mumbled, face pressed into my hair, one hand stroking over the curve of my waist, my hip, and up to my breast again. "My Kore."

The tenderness of his touch made me want to cry.

"I hope that was everything you wanted it to be," Hades said with a sigh, withdrawing only to lie down next to me and pull me into him. I hid my face against his chest, feeling the dampness of his ichor against my skin. "Selfishly, I hope that when you leave and you remember your time here in the underworld, that this memory will haunt you. That no matter who you end up with or what you decide, that you'll never forget how I made you feel."

"For someone who refused to take me back all this time, you're suddenly very committed to the idea of me leaving," I replied sharply, hating the reminder while I was feeling so vulnerable. I blinked away the sudden wetness in my eyes, glad he couldn't see me.

"Zeus himself gave the order."

"Zeus isn't king here. Zeus can't give you orders."

Hades was silent for a moment, probably wondering why I was fighting this when it was everything I'd claimed to want. I was wondering that myself. I pulled back slightly so I could look at him, and his brow creased in concern at the evidence of impending tears in my eyes.

"The Judges have been busy recently. We've seen an influx of souls that we usually only see during war or plague."

I stared at him, waiting for him to continue. In all the fraught conversations we'd had, this was the most uncomfortable I'd ever seen him. Hades swallowed thickly, one hand cupping my jaw, stroking my cheek with his thumb.

"They are dying of famine, Kore. Demeter is starving them."

"She wouldn't," I replied, remembering Erysichthon and the insatiable hunger she'd cursed him with. She'd been angry that day, though...

"She *has*. Nothing has grown since your disappearance, Kore. The earth is barren, the animals are dead. Zeus originally claimed he wouldn't get involved, but he can't overlook the mass death of mortals."

I got the feeling that there was more to it, but I knew in my bones that whatever he was leaving out was to protect me. Probably some horrible threat from Zeus against Hades himself, if he didn't return me. Some burden that Hades didn't want to land me with.

"So that's it?"

Hades gave me a long look. "Would you stay, knowing the cost?"

They call you Bringer of Destruction.

So many had died because of me, and while I no longer saw death as the enemy like I once had, I didn't want to be the cause of it. I couldn't let anyone starve in my name.

But that meant leaving. Leaving and appeasing my mother's will so that she stopped this madness. I'd spent my entire time daydreaming of sunshine and flowers and my family that I hadn't noticed myself slowly coming to care for this place too.

To care for Hades.

Perhaps even to *love* him.

For all his awkward questions and stilted conversation, he was somehow charming. For all his rules and routines, he was still a compassionate ruler.

For all his kidnapping and refusal to help me get home, he still cared for me. Everything he'd done had been in service of that.

Hades extricated himself from my grip, picking up his chiton from the ground and quickly redressing.

"You're leaving?" I asked, sitting up and pulling a blanket over my nudity. "We do... that, and you drop that news on me, and now you're *leaving*?"

This time when Hades looked at me, there was none of the confusion that often appeared when he was struggling with my words. He just seemed tired. Tired and resigned.

"I've tried to give you everything, Kore, and I've failed at every stage. Now I need to take one thing for myself."

"What is that?"

"Distance. Or I'll never be able to let you go."

Without a look back, he strode out of the bedchamber, through the sitting room, and I listened as the door that led out to the corridor closed quietly.

The moment I was alone, I burst into tears.

HADES

CHAPTER 21

Agony.

It was agony.

I had one night left with Kore, and I was spending it away from her because I didn't know what I'd do if I was near her. Beg her to marry me, probably. Humiliate myself more than I already had.

Kore wasn't going to stay no matter what I said or did. She was returning to the upperworld like she'd always wanted, without the virginity she'd always resented. What possible reason could I give her to stay?

I had to make my peace with it.

I stormed down the front steps of the palace, my expression enough to deter anyone from approaching me. For a moment, I considered calling for my chariot, but it would be a long time before I could ride in it without thinking of Kore's soft body clinging to mine for safety.

Instead, I marched toward the western pool, the one I'd yet to visit since Mnemosyne had claimed the waters. The few souls that were there scattered as I approached, and the goddess who'd taken up residence in the pool attempted to do the same.

"Stop, Mnemosyne," I commanded, standing at the edge of the water and crossing my arms.

She flopped back into the middle of the pool, floating there petulantly. "Have you come to tell me off? It's hardly *my* fault that you never asked me to bless these waters."

"You could have volunteered," I muttered. "But it's Kore's memory that I'm truly angry about."

"I told her I wouldn't do it again. Did you know we're best friends now, Kore and me?"

I blinked at her, trying to determine whether or not that statement was true. It didn't sound like a lie, but Mnemosyne wasn't so much a liar as prone to prattling on about nothing.

"We are," Mnemosyne said, nodding her head vigorously, perhaps sensing my doubt. "She swore it. Well, she swore we were friends, but she doesn't really have any other friends here, does she? So that would imply that I'm her *best* friend."

"Orphne is Kore's friend," I replied instantly, annoyed with myself for getting dragged into this nonsensical conversation. "So your logic is flawed. And Kore is leaving anyway. She has friends in the upperworld."

"She's *leaving*?" Mnemosyne righted herself with a splash, standing in the waist-high water and glaring at me. "Why is she leaving? What have you done?"

"What have *I* done?" I repeated, affronted.

"Yes, *you*. You're the one meant to be marrying her, you've obviously done something idiotic and ruined it for all of us. Now my best friend is leaving, and it's all your fault."

How had I ended up on the receiving end of this? I'd come here to rage at her for stealing Kore's memory and not mentioning this empty pool earlier.

"Kore *wants* to leave. She's always wanted to leave. Leaving will make her happy. If you were truly her friend, you'd want that for her."

Mnemosyne frowned thoughtfully for a moment. "No, I don't think I do. I want her to stay here. Shall I remove any memories she has about wanting to leave?"

"Fates, *no*. I thought you said you wouldn't tamper with her memories again?"

"These are extreme circumstances! I'll return them after you're married."

Maybe it was for the best that Kore was leaving if these were the kinds of friends she attracted in the underworld.

"Don't touch her memories," I warned. "Don't try to force her to stay. That is an order as King of the Underworld."

For one brief moment, the infuriatingly smug look on Mnemosyne's face faded, leaving something sad and honest in its place that I understood all too well.

"You're a very hardworking king, Hades. You attack every problem with single-minded focus, even when perhaps you would benefit from taking a less rigid approach."

"Like with this pool?"

Mnemosyne shrugged. "I would have been happy to help if you'd met me halfway. Maybe Kore needs you to meet her halfway too."

I sat down at the edge of the pool to wait out the clock, knowing Mnemosyne was wrong. Knowing *Zeus* was wrong.

Demeter had let scores of humans die to get her daughter back. Even if Kore professed her love for me for all of Olympus to hear, Demeter would never consent to letting her stay. It would be too much like admitting defeat. There was no halfway.

I thought back to the now empty dungeons, free of souls who'd been chained there to overcome their addiction to the Lethe. That had been Kore's doing. She'd found a solution where I thought there was none.

Maybe there was no halfway point for our relationship, but Mnemosyne was right. Perhaps my approach to ruling the underworld *was* too rigid. Kore hadn't decided in her mind what a solution would be, then implemented it. She'd talked to Mnemosyne and worked it out from there.

The underworld was going to be a better place after Kore left here, not just because of the actions she'd taken, but because of the lessons she'd taught me.

"Where are you going?" Mnemosyne asked as I stood, smoothing out the creases in my chiton. "Are you going to win her back? Chain her in the dungeon? That's it! Chain her in the dungeon and I'll tamper with the memory of whoever comes to collect her—"

"You stay here in this pool and do your job," I cut in. "Kore is leaving, but her legacy remains, and I'm going to see it through."

Rather than flying, I walked to the bank of the Phlegethon, planning what I was going to say the entire time. The flames parted for me, leaving me space to cross, and I nodded my thanks to the river god as I crossed. The heartache at knowing I was losing Kore hadn't lessened, but I was filled with a sense of purpose that I hadn't experienced since I'd arrived in the underworld, overwhelmed with the task of making it my own.

The moment I stepped onto the opposite bank, entering Asphodel Meadows, the mood of the souls shifted like they sensed my sudden determination too. When was the last time I'd come here *not* filled with impatience and frustration? I couldn't recall.

A crowd formed behind me as I walked deeper into the heart of the Meadows, through the winding dirt roads lined by gray asphodel flowers, past the simple structures that had been built here by the souls to divide up the space and provide some semblance of privacy. Eventually, I arrived at the hills in the center, the neutral ground between territories. I climbed to the top, crossing my arms and waiting while word of my visit spread. No faction leader would stay away if they thought the others would appear, so I wasn't surprised when all six showed up, standing in a ring around me at the base of the hill, the souls under their protection gathered at their backs.

"Alexios, Paramonos, Heron, Timaios, Zotikos, and Eupraxia," I called. "Join me."

The six of them stepped forward at the same time, all eyeing each other warily, probably wondering who was going to be thrown into Tartarus today. I didn't *want* to send souls away—it gave me no pleasure to do so. Aside from the fact that I derived my own power from the souls who resided here, I saw them as under my protection, and each one I had to banish to Tartarus was an indictment on my own ability to rule.

"Hades," they murmured, bowing low as they assembled in front of me, keeping a healthy distance between each other.

"I'm sick of coming here to punish you," I announced. The six of them straightened, while the souls in the crowd at the bottom of the hill looked up at me in alarm. "It serves me well to let you rule amongst yourselves, but clearly leaving the division of power in your hands without oversight is untenable."

The leaders shifted uneasily, waiting for me to continue. Probably expecting me to strip them of power completely and start over. That's what I would have done, before Kore. Blamed the leaders for the failure of a system that wasn't working, then find myself surprised when the next set of leaders didn't solve the problem.

"That is why the six leaders of the factions—whoever they are at the time, that is still for you to decide—will have a place within my court. We will meet regularly, the seven of us, to discuss territory disputes, to ensure that the souls under your care are being well treated, and that you're not abusing the power you've been given."

I surveyed them all, letting my gaze pause on each one so they knew I was serious about this. "Should you still wish to fight amongst yourselves, that's your decision to make, but it happens *after* a rational attempt at conversation and mediation has been made."

"That sounds very reasonable, o wise Hades," Paramonos said, bowing low. He'd always been the most obsequious of the current crop of faction leaders. A trait I generally disliked, but it set the other five off in a rush of agreement, all eager to be seen as cooperative, so this time it didn't bother me quite so much.

"Prepare your lists of complaints, I've no doubt they're long," I noted dryly. They were experts at finding things to complain about. "Keuthonymos will send for you tomorrow for our first discussion. In the meantime, I intend to walk around the Meadows and observe the territories for myself. I'll be speaking to the souls as I go, and I strongly suggest you not interfere."

The idea of talking to souls who *hadn't* explicitly come to see me, to have discussions with them *voluntarily*, was slightly abhorrent. But Kore would have done it. Orphne had told me about how compassionate she'd been with the soul in The Restless Dead, how she'd taken time to listen to her and think about what kind of future the girl deserved.

I'd brought Kore here to grow into her own potential, and she had. And whether she'd intended to or not, she'd helped me grow into mine.

I walked nearly the perimeter of the Meadows throughout the night, talking to the souls I encountered about their existence here. What they liked, what they struggled with. The things they missed about the upperworld.

Those conversations were almost the hardest ones—hearing odes to the very things Kore had lamented missing. The things she would soon return to. The very hardest conversations were the ones *about* her. Even in the farthest reaches of the Meadows, word had spread about the beautiful goddess who smelled of lavender and sunshine, who'd been brought to the underworld to become queen. Who'd founded a Pool of Memory, and cured the souls who were afflicted by the Lethe's madness.

I couldn't bring myself to tell them that Kore was leaving. That I'd failed to keep her.

Eventually, Kerberos came to fetch me, butting his heads impatiently against my shoulders.

"Hermes is here?"

Kerberos let out a long whine.

"I don't want her to leave either, but I can't force her to stay."

He huffed in irritation, and I stood back as he grew to his full, most impressive form, frightening away the souls who'd been hovering nearby to speak to me. I didn't make a habit of riding him—it was vastly less comfortable than the chariot—but the walk to the palace from this far south would take hours.

Kerberos lowered himself to the ground, and I climbed onto his back, digging my hands into the thick fur at the base of his neck as he stood, towering over the structures of the Meadows and bounding north toward the Phlegethon. He moved carefully around the outskirts of the small communities, so as not to squash them underneath his enormous paws, and the Phlegethon parted once more to let us back through.

I'd never been less excited to see the palace in all my time here.

Kerberos dropped me at the front steps before returning to the gate, and I made my way into the palace, past the plant that had once been Minthe, following Keuthonymos' direction toward the balcony where Hermes was waiting. The mood was somber, and I had no doubt that, by now, word had spread about Kore's imminent departure.

Was she already there? Eagerly awaiting Hermes' arrival so she could finally put all of this behind her? Maybe Keuthonymos had been right when he'd told me to command Kore into marriage when she'd first arrived. At least that way, I would have had some claim on her.

"Hermes," I clipped, stepping out onto the flower-covered balcony, the doors closing behind me at my will. He stood at the railing with his back to me, looking out over the Elysian Fields in the distance, the small patch of color Kore had created visible even from here.

"Hades," he said with a sigh, blonde curls glinting in the light as he turned to face me. He was lean and tanned, a popular lover amongst both mortals and immortals alike, and so Olympian it made me feel ill. Would he propose again? Would Demeter consider it, now that the oath of virginity was no longer an option?

"These are pretty," he said lightly, twirling a long-stemmed narcissus in between his fingers and giving me an assessing look. Unusually serious for the normally obnoxious, mischievous Protector of Thieves. "Colorful."

"Kore's doing," I replied, gesturing at the blooms.

"It really livens the place up." He hesitated for a moment, and I said nothing, unsure what to do with this version of Hermes who wasn't trying to trick me into his usual word games. "Until recently, I was one of the few gods aside from Demeter that had even *seen* Kore in person."

Frost crept up the pillars around the balcony at the reminder, and Hermes flashed me an apologetic grin before continuing. "It was very brief—her younger brothers caused a distraction, and she snuck away. I'm sure you know I made an offer of marriage for Kore to Demeter—calm down, she didn't entertain it. The point I'm trying to make is, I never envisioned *that* Kore, the one sitting on a cushion docilely at her mother's feet, could be capable of this." He twirled the flower between his fingers again. "When Ares claimed that he'd seen her in the throne room, advising petitioners on your behalf, I struggled to believe him. *Too meek,* I thought. Too fragile, because of Demeter's overprotectiveness."

"Kore is none of those things. She was—*is*—meant for more than a life of silent obedience at Demeter's heel. Kore's feigned meekness came from a place of love and respect for her mother."

"She wants to please Demeter," Hermes mused. "Right now, we all do, before we run out of mortals. They're such fragile things, they can't survive without food. You should see how quickly they perish with no water, it's astounding. Is Kore ready to return?"

"Does it matter?" I muttered. "You're taking her, regardless."

"You seem more distraught than I expected about that." His eyes dropped to the two flowers I'd tucked in my belt, somewhat squashed now after how hurriedly I'd thrown my chiton on the floor in my rush to undress for Kore.

There wasn't a question in his words, so I didn't bother with an answer.

"What did you expect to happen?" Hermes pressed, looking genuinely curious. I crossed my arms over my chest, partly so I didn't lash out and hit him. Zeus would not take kindly to me attacking his messenger. "Even if Kore begs to stay, she's outranked by Demeter."

I really should have made Kore marry me. Even if she'd never forgiven me for it, a queen had more power to make decisions about her own life than a mere daughter of a goddess did.

"You care for her." Hermes tilted his head to the side. "How unexpected."

Was it? Those in the upperworld and Olympus had formed their opinions of me eons ago, and I didn't care enough to correct them.

"I'll send for Kore," I replied, forcing the words past the tightness in my throat.

"Well, while we wait for her, you could always deal with Sisyphus?" Hermes suggested, a look too akin to pity for my liking on his face. "He's a slippery one, I'll give him that, but I was able to drag him down here with me. I believe Thanatos is taking a moment to exact his revenge on him first."

Undoubtedly. I flexed my fingers, itching to take out my anger and frustration on *something*, and I couldn't think of a more perfect target than Sisyphus. It wouldn't assuage the pain of losing Kore, but then again, nothing would.

I spared Hermes a curt nod, leading him off the balcony and toward the room Thanatos was undoubtedly holding Sisyphus in, Hermes trailing behind me in silence.

Why couldn't I have one thing to myself?

I hadn't asked to be King of the Underworld, but this was where I'd ended up. Isolated away from the other gods, landed with the most relentless of roles, and I'd never complained.

Never asked for anything except Kore.

Would she even remember me after she left this place? Or would she be too enamored with her upperworld life to think of me?

Like I'd conjured her with my mind, Kore rounded a corner, still dressed in the purple silk chiton I'd last seen her in, her hair undone, and Orphne at her side. They both looked solemn as they took in Hermes.

"Kore," he said, bowing with an obnoxious flourish. "Zeus has sent me to collect you, and return you to your mother's home in Henna."

"Right. Yes. I heard you were coming," she replied stiffly. Perhaps I was a coward, but I couldn't even look at her. It hurt too much. "Are we leaving now?"

"Hermes has also returned Sisyphus. We were going to deal with him first," I answered, looking at a column just past Kore's head.

Her form glowed a little brighter, a glimpse of the underworld goddess she was meant to be just under the surface. "Good, I'll join you."

For the very last time.

CHAPTER 22

Each step toward wherever Hades was taking us to see Sisyphus felt painfully foreboding. Final. Like we were approaching an inevitable ending, and there was nothing that could be done to prevent it.

But that wasn't true.

Hades had been the one to teach me that wasn't true. While I'd resigned myself to fitting into the mold Mother had prescribed for me, he'd seen bigger things for my future. He'd encouraged me to embrace the parts of myself that I'd always kept repressed.

And he thought he was going to let me just *walk away*?

Absolutely not. It was outrageous that he was even contemplating it, but fine. He'd made the effort to bring me here, and all I'd done was complain. Even when I'd fallen in love with different parts of the underworld, I'd told myself that it was either one or the other. Either my family, or stay in this realm forever. Everyone else had acted like those were my only two choices too, but they weren't.

From the moment Orphne had taken me to meet Akeron and told me how they cherished their time together because of the time they spent apart, I'd wondered if maybe there was an option we hadn't been seeing.

And there was, but it wasn't an easy one. Not when my mother was effectively holding the Olympians hostage by starving the mortals—they'd never go against her. She'd never listen to Hades. She usually didn't listen to me.

If I wanted to go over Mother's head, I'd have to go *way* over her head.

If I wanted to stay, I'd have to trap myself.

The three of us entered an antechamber, the sounds of Thanatos' fists smacking against Sisyphus' flesh already echoing loudly off the walls as the mortal groaned and pleaded for mercy. He would find none here.

Sisyphus had humiliated Thanatos, and gods did not take well to their pride being wounded. I could admit I was no better in that respect. Sisyphus had disrespected my word, and I wanted to see him suffer.

"Enough, Thanatos," Hades called in a bored voice.

"But I'm just getting started," Thanatos whined petulantly, landing another wet-sounding hit on Sisyphus' mouth.

Hades was preparing himself to argue, and I could already see the judgment in Hermes' eyes that Hades was so lenient with the gods under his charge. While I wished Thanatos would have feigned compliance in front of an Olympian, I liked that Hades didn't treat those who lived in his palace like servants.

I let my gifts rise to the surface, relishing the delicious feeling of being able to use the power I had inherited, and opened my palms to release thick vines along the floor that snaked to where Thanatos had Sisyphus pinned. I directed them with my mind to wrap around Sisyphus' ankles, tugging him sharply out from under Thanatos until Sisyphus came to a sudden stop at Hades' feet, and I shot the God of Death my most imperious look as he lay sprawled out on the ground.

Thanatos snorted, climbing to his feet. "Fine, fine. I'll find something else to play with."

"You do that," I agreed, feeling Hermes' eyes burning into the side of my head while Hades fairly radiated concern. He wasn't like my mother—he wouldn't expect me to suppress my gifts in front of other gods, to make myself seem weaker—but he'd be worried about the ramifications of my using it just the same. Already contemplating what it would mean for the life he envisioned me returning to in the upperworld.

It didn't chafe the way Mother's paranoia had—the difference was that Hades trusted my judgment, I supposed. The notion made my throat feel tight.

"If you are content to drag him, Kore, then we shall be on our way," Hades clipped. "Though once we come to the entrance of Tartarus, I will continue alone."

I almost snorted. I would absolutely accompany him, no matter how hard he tried to avoid me.

Hermes shuddered dramatically. "I'm not going down there. Perhaps I'll find a friendly nymph in your court who'd be willing to help me waste some time."

"I'm sure they'll be most accommodating," Hades replied dryly as Hermes strutted away, chatting merrily with Thanatos, and leaving Hades and me mostly alone. I sent another vine out to wrap around Sisyphus' ears and mouth, muffling his voice and giving us some illusion of privacy.

Not that it seemed we needed it, since Hades was doing his best to ignore my presence completely.

A sharp pain sliced through my chest. Perhaps I'd gotten too complacent. He'd spent so long chasing me while I held him at a distance, I'd never contemplated what it would be like to have the tables turned. To *be* the one needing to chase, needing to close the gap.

I'd never thought about how disheartening it would be on the other side.

"Hades—" I began softly, but his quiet noise of discontent cut me off.

"After."

My vines tightened around Sisyphus instinctively, making him squeak in discomfort. *Fine, after,* I conceded silently, bitterness rising in my throat like bile. He'd brought me here. He'd insisted I use my gifts and given me the purpose and responsibility I hadn't known I'd craved.

He'd made me fall in love with him.

And now he was giving me the cold shoulder? Crumbling at the first hint of a challenge to our relationship?

I think not.

The strained silence continued down through the palace as the marble walls became old stone, and the temperature dropped to a painfully frigid cold. We arrived at the obsidian archway I'd walked through once before, and I did my best to hide the shiver of fear that ran up my spine at the sight of it. Maybe I'd once been naïve about what lay beyond it, but Sisyphus certainly wasn't. He thrashed harder than ever, fighting against the vines that gave him no reprieve.

"This is where we part ways."

I stared at Hades, trying to understand the look on his face. Usually, there was some kind of tell, some kind of giveaway as to what he was thinking—even if it was just frustration that he'd misread the situation.

Now, there was nothing.

I hadn't realized how open he'd been with me until he'd closed himself off. I never wanted to see that look on his face again. I refused to.

"Be specific, Hades. I know that's your favored style of communication. What do you mean by 'part ways?'"

My question seemed to make him squirm, and frankly, I preferred that to the cold nothingness he'd been showing me.

"Well, I will take Sisyphus from here," he said slowly.

"And? Where do you expect me to be?"

His eyes flashed dangerously, words coated in bitterness. "I have the least *expectations* of your whereabouts of anyone in your life."

Had he forgotten that the only reason I was here in the first place was because he'd unilaterally decided I was better off in the underworld?

How short his memory seemed to be on that front.

The problem was, he was right. I *was* better off here.

Was I willing to give up my family and my life in the upperworld? No, not entirely. But I knew with more surety than I knew anything that I wasn't giving Hades up.

"Sisyphus' punishment is mine to dole out. The slight was against me, and I want my revenge."

"Fine," Hades conceded, gesturing stiffly for me to go through the archway. I stepped through, dragging a still shrieking Sisyphus behind me, and pausing on the stone platform in the darkness with Hades at my side. I peered down into the abyss, the same faint feeling of nausea arising that I'd experienced last time. It was just so... endless.

"Tartarus," Hades called, not bothering to raise his voice. It was so dark, I could only faintly make out Hades' profile from the light struggling to penetrate the invisible barrier behind us, and uncaring of what it made me look like, I stepped closer to his side, pressing my arm against his, the solidness of him instantly putting me at ease.

Until a deafening whoosh from below announced Tartarus' presence. Then all my unease came back in full force.

The air around us shifted, and while I couldn't *see* Tartarus, there was no doubt he was there somehow. Perhaps hovering a few feet away? Or maybe his form was shapeless, and he was everywhere, within the air itself. Sisyphus' shrieking turned to muffled whimpers as he cowered on the floor, attempting to worm his way closer to where Hades and I stood like he could cower beneath our protection.

"You summoned me, God of the Dead?" Tartarus deadpanned, his voice seeming to come from everywhere and nowhere all at once.

"I did." Hades' voice was stronger and clearer than I'd ever heard it, and without thinking, I slid my hand into his, tangling our fingers together. Before I could snatch it back out of sheer humiliation, his grip tightened around me, holding me in place. If anything, there was an almost desperation to it, like he needed this support as much as I did. "This is Sisyphus, son of Aeolus. He has given us much grief, cheating death three times now. Such disrespect to the gods cannot go unpunished."

There was another roaring whoosh and Sisyphus cried out against the vines, the chill coming from behind us now where the mortal laid on the ground. It sounded like Tartarus was... sniffing him? Like an oversized, invisible beast inspecting its meal.

"Sisyphus, son of Aeolus. You smell of deceit. What a life of trickery you've led. What a trail of misery that has followed in your wake." Tartarus moved again, possibly materializing in front of us. "He will make a fine addition to Tartarus, Hades, King of the Underworld. Where would you have him?"

"Somewhere with an exit." Hades' words seemed to shock all three of us into silence. An exit? For the man who'd successfully evaded his time in the underworld no less than three times?

"As you say," Tartarus conceded, sounding faintly amused. The roaring sound grew so loud it was maddening. It felt like all four wind gods had taken up residence in my head, battling for dominance. As quickly as it began, it was over. We were standing in a dark cave at the base of a hill so steep it could almost be considered a cliff, the faintest sliver of light at the top, miles in the distance, illuminating the darkness.

"Kore, if you would be so good as to release him," Hades requested blandly, still holding my hand. I nodded silently, withdrawing the vines and letting them recede.

Tartarus was undoubtedly still present—I doubted he would ever leave us unsupervised in his realm—but he seemed content to stay quiet and invisible, and let Hades lead.

Sisyphus scrambled to his feet in an ungainly fashion, beady eyes fixed on that tiny specter of light. He wasn't bothering to disguise the gleam of cunning there, that wicked, ambitious streak that had served him so well in his mortal life.

"As you can see, at the top of that narrow path lies an entry to the upperworld," Hades said. "Kore, as a goddess of life, why don't you decide what Sisyphus' reward will be if he reaches it?"

Hoping that Hades had thought this through, I contemplated what Sisyphus would want the most. "You can resume your mortal life, with all your riches and glory, but as a young man. You will live to a ripe old age, and fulfilled by all you have accomplished, you will embrace Death when it comes for you again."

"All you have to do is reach the top," Hades added. Gesturing lazily, the stone pathway *curling* in front of our eyes, the rock twisting tightly together, growing larger like a snowball as it slowly rolled toward the base of the slope where Sisyphus stood. It came to a halt in front of him—an enormous boulder, taller than Sisyphus and so wide that it almost brushed against the now deep walls of the path.

Sisyphus stared at it shrewdly, all evidence of the whimpering, crying man gone as though it was never there. The stone walls and the boulder itself were so impossibly smooth, so clearly carved from divine magic, that there was no way he could climb around it. It was push the boulder or nothing.

"Wait," I commanded as Sisyphus took a step forward. "I have one more option for you to consider."

Hades' hand tightened around mine, while Sisyphus turned that cunning gaze on me. "And what is that?"

"An eternity in paradise. A home in the Elysian Fields. You can go there right now, no questions asked, no further conditions, so long as you don't touch the rock."

If my offer alarmed Hades, he didn't show it. He didn't need to—I was confident that he knew as well as I did that Sisyphus wouldn't take it. He didn't want to give up the power and wealth he'd known as a mortal, refused to see any other option for his future than somehow cheating death to get back to the comfort he'd known.

His stubbornness, his inflexibility, and his *greed* would be his downfall.

Sisyphus wasted no time, flattening his palms on the surface of the boulder and heaving. To my dismay, it actually moved. What was the point of setting the obstacle if it was so easy to overcome?

"You needn't worry," Hades murmured, watching Sisyphus heave the rock up the slope. "The boulder is enchanted. No matter how close he comes to the top, it will always push him back down to the bottom again. The boulder isn't his punishment. The eternal temptation of success just out of reach is."

A small rush went through me at the calm, quiet way he wielded his power. There were no theatrics, no demands for pleas of mercy. I doubted Hades would bother to check on Sisyphus again, whether he would spare him even a second of thought after we left this place.

He may be the God of the Dead, but Hades was the least callous deity I knew of.

"If you'd be so good as to return us to the underworld," Hades said calmly, turning his head back to perhaps where Tartarus was waiting. How did he know? Could Hades see him?

"Of course." That was all the warning Tartarus gave before nearly deafening us again. Without the need to hold Sisyphus' leash, I pressed myself against Hades' chest, grabbing a fistful of his chiton as the world dematerialized around us, reforming with us standing on the platform in front of the archway.

"Until next time," Tartarus called, vanishing into the darkness, taking some of the biting cold with him. I blinked for a moment, realizing I was still clinging to an uncomfortably stiff Hades. With a sigh, I released him, striding back through the archway to the palace. Evidently, he had resigned himself to the idea that I was leaving.

He was so confident that he hadn't even bothered to *ask* me about it.

Perhaps the polite thing to do would be to ease his mind now, but frankly, his ability to give up on me, on us, had annoyed me. Not only that, it had taken a full night of planning with Orphne to come up with the solution on how to stay, and I already knew he wouldn't like it, so I wasn't in any particular rush to share it with him.

He'd just have to be surprised, like I was when he'd snatched me away from the upperworld. I was due to make an unexpected grand gesture of my own.

CHAPTER 23

Kore was furious.

I did not understand women.

For weeks, all she had asked for was to go back to the upperworld. Shouldn't she be happy? This was what she *wanted*. I thought I'd given her everything she wanted.

Maybe she didn't like that she'd been *summoned* home. Kore's fierce independent streak had grown more pronounced in the time she'd spent here. She wouldn't return to sitting obediently at her mother's feet in silence, smiling blandly like she wasn't a fearsome goddess in her own right, that much I was certain of.

Except I couldn't even *watch* her anymore, since I'd foolishly agreed not to. My own hubris in thinking I could convince Kore to love me had come back to haunt me.

Kore's chiton swished around her ankles with each impatient step as *she* led *me* up from Tartarus, stopping in the entryway between the throne room and the front steps and surveying the space equally. Souls and courtiers alike bowed low, and while they'd do it anyway because I was here, I couldn't help but think that the gesture was more for her.

"Where is Hermes?" Kore asked Keuthonymos, her voice regal and icy.

"I'll fetch him," Keuthonymos said immediately, jumping to attention at the command in her tone.

"Tell him to meet us at the Port of Charon," Kore responded, inclining her head in thanks before giving me a sweeping imperious look that clearly said *follow*. As if I could be anywhere else. As if I wouldn't have watched from a distance until the very last moment, when she was gone from my realm and I was left here alone.

My heart, the one I didn't know existed until Kore had brought it to life, ached more than I could fathom. I wasn't used to feeling helpless. I wasn't prone to indecision. I didn't lose control.

No, that wasn't true. I'd lost control when I'd taken Kore in the first place. This was the natural consequence of my impulsivity.

I whistled for the chariot, wondering if Kore would let me hold her one last time. Wondering if I could stand it if she did, and if it would be worse if she didn't.

Even the horses seemed more subdued as the chariot landed, and I gestured for Kore to climb on before carefully stepping up next to her, leaving an inch of space between us as I picked up the reins.

"You cannot be serious," Kore said flatly, glaring at me. "I thought you loved me."

"Of course I love you," I replied instantly, horrified she would ever think otherwise.

"Then you will *hold me* like you love me, or we will walk to the ferry. You know I don't like flying," she snapped, lifting my elbow and stepping beneath my arm, squeezing between my body and the front of the chariot.

"My apologies," I murmured, wrapping an arm around her waist and inhaling her sweet scent, committing it to memory. I flicked the reins, directing the beasts to the port. Back the way we'd come when I first brought Kore to the underworld.

Kore closed her eyes, tipping her head back against my shoulder and folding both her arms atop mine. It was a position of complete trust, and I felt honored that I'd earned it.

If only I knew what to say. How to say goodbye. Nothing felt sufficient.

We landed far too soon, a cheerful Hermes fluttering down on winged sandals, looking entirely too relaxed. He'd probably found a willing nymph.

Kerberos, on the other hand, was slumped on the ground, heads resting morosely on his paws. A few other courtiers were slowly coming to join us to see Kore off, traveling along the river by boat.

Even those who'd originally shared Minthe's concerns about Kore's suitability to rule had mostly changed their minds while she'd talked to the petitioners. They'd seen the potential in her to be a good and fair queen, a position that had been left empty too long.

That would continue to be left empty, because there was no one else I wanted at my side. I'd rather rule alone for eternity. It was Kore or no one.

Even Charon dipped his skeletal head low, standing at the edge of the port and leaning on his oar with his eyes downcast. Grieving. The smile dropped from Hermes' face as he took in the somber expressions and silent support of my court.

"You've made quite the impression here," Hermes remarked, astounded.

"That's because I'm one of them," Kore replied simply. "I belong here. But I belong up there too."

The only wife I'd ever wanted, the only queen I'd ever considered, turned to face me, her golden eyes shining with a look I struggled to place. Perhaps it was determination? A determination to finally go home, to see the family she loved so much. I cupped her jaw, stroking my hand over her delicate cheekbone, struggling to accept this would be the last time I touched her.

"I love you," I murmured, not caring who heard. Let every one of my subjects, let the gods themselves hear how I cared for Kore. I hoped the terrible reputation I had in the upperworld preceded me. I hoped everyone lived in constant fear of my retaliation for taking Kore away from me.

"As I love you."

I stared at her for a long moment. "What did you say?"

She gave me a catlike grin, leaning in and pressing her hands to my chest. Mine found her hips instinctively, pulling her in close, relishing the feel of her body against mine.

"Hades," Kore purred, her voice rich with the power she'd come into since she'd been here. Her seductive confidence gave me pause. I hadn't expected her to weep or anything at our parting, but I hadn't expected *this* either. "Of course I love you. And you love me. We're equals, aren't we?"

"Until the world stops turning," I agreed immediately, searching her face, willing her to believe me. "Even if you're no longer here, even if we're not married, you'll always be my queen and my equal."

Kore took a step back and grabbed my hand with both of hers, raising it to her lips to brush a kiss over my knuckles, her eyes never leaving mine. Heat traveled up my fingers first, settling in my palms, the telltale tingle of Kore's magic embedding in my skin, feeling as vibrant as life itself.

Within moments, I felt something solid and smooth forming under my palm. Kore smiled at me, pressing the item up into my hand. I flipped it over, admiring the lustrous red pomegranate before lifting my gaze back to Kore.

It was made here. Grown here. It was food of the underworld.

"My mother will never *let* me stay," Kore said quietly, for my ears only. "Even if we were married, she'd wage a war against this realm until the other gods intervened again. But this... It's the Fates who ruled that anyone who eats the food of the underworld has to return there. No one can fight fate."

"You're sure about this, Kore? This will tie you to this realm for all of eternity."

"Take me as your wife."

I blinked at her. "Of course. It would be my greatest honor to take you, Kore, as my wife."

Hermes looked on in alarm, a witness to this rather sparse marriage ceremony on the banks of the Styx.

"And it would be my greatest honor to take you, Hades, as my husband. Now, feed me," she commanded softly, no trace of fear in her face. I held her stare as I ripped the fruit in two, the sticky juice running down my wrists and dropping on the gray stone floor. The entire area had grown still, even the River Styx itself was quieter than usual.

I pulled a jewel-like seed free, watching Kore's face for any sign of hesitation and finding none. Her lips parted, and I pushed the tiny seed that would seal her fate into her mouth. Her tongue curled around my finger before she nipped it mischievously with her teeth. My eyes tracked the movement of her throat as she swallowed, tethering herself further to me, to the underworld.

"More," she whispered, for my ears only. "I need to feel the sun on my face, grass under my feet, the wind on my skin. I can't give you all of my days, but I'd never walk away from you. Not permanently."

Meet her halfway, Mnemosyne had said. This was halfway, I realized as I picked another seed out of the fleshy fruit. This was the compromise I'd never considered, not believing it possible that I'd be able to share Kore's time with both Zeus and Demeter demanding her return.

But even the Olympians answered to the Fates.

"Kore," Hermes said nervously, a mixture of awe and alarm in his voice as I pressed two more seeds between her lips.

"Not here," she replied without turning. "I'll always be Kore the Maiden in the upperworld, but here I'm Persephone, Queen of the Underworld."

Persephone. The name meant Bringer of Destruction, and she'd embraced it.

I fed her another three. Six seeds. Six months of each year.

"And I am yours, Hades," she added, just loud enough for me to hear. "Until the world stops turning."

She leaned forward and pressed her lips against mine, tasting of the tart berries and the promise of an eternal future. All too soon, she was pulling away, giving me a small smile as she walked backward toward where Hermes was waiting.

I nearly snarled at him when I realized he was going to *carry* her to the upperworld. Why couldn't he use a chariot like everyone else? I didn't want his arms around my wife.

"Don't fret, my love," my Kore—my *Persephone*—told me, coming to a stop next to Hermes. "I'll return as soon as I can. I'll always return to you."

I nodded thickly, fighting the urge to snatch her back into my arms, but knowing that this was the best way. The only way. Persephone was mine—body, heart and soul—and it was more than I ever thought I'd have, even if I had to share her time.

Hermes wrapped his arms around her as respectfully as possible, shooting me an apologetic look before launching them both into the air on winged feet.

I didn't move, didn't dare to blink or breathe, as they flew over the River Styx and toward the upperworld. *Only temporary,* I reminded myself. Demeter could rage all she wanted, but eating the food of the underworld gave this realm a claim over Persephone that no one and nothing could fight.

I pressed the sides of the split pomegranate together so that the seeds faced outward and turned the fruit to solid bronze in my hands.

"Hades," Keuthonymos said with a bow as I summoned him.

"I want this on a plinth between the thrones."

"Of course," he replied, a small smile playing around his mouth. The queen had truly left a lasting impression on her subjects today.

I couldn't wait to see what she'd do next when she returned to me.

Queen Persephone.

CHAPTER 24

I expected the journey back to the upperworld to be tense, considering what Hermes had just witnessed, but he whistled gleefully nearly the entire way. Perhaps I shouldn't have been surprised—he was the God of Cunning after all, and that had been a rather cunning move, if I said so myself. I'd navigated a path around Hades' obstinacy, my mother's heartbreak, and Zeus' commands, and I'd forged a place for myself, where I belonged, on the way.

Well done, me.

I had no doubt that my solution wouldn't be pleasing to everyone—perhaps not to *anyone*—but I couldn't find it in myself to regret it. I just hoped that in time, everyone would come to terms with the arrangement.

Or not.

Let them think what they wanted about it, it was done now.

Hermes guided us to an opening in the earth that was possibly natural, or perhaps he'd created it as the Messenger of the Gods, able to move easily between realms. Something I'd have to learn undoubtedly, if I was to split my time between domains.

A small smile played around my mouth at the thought, but my mother's anguished cry quickly squashed it.

"In case it wasn't clear from the long queues of dead people, she hasn't handled your absence well," Hermes muttered under his breath. He pulled in his divine form a moment before we entered the mortal realm, and I promptly did the same as Hermes flew us out of the giant gaping hole in the earth with a flourish.

Mother snatched me away from Hermes with surprising strength and speed, dragging me to the ground with her arms banded around my waist, sobbing loudly into my hair.

"Kore, my Kore. You're finally home."

I sniffled, all the bravado that came with being Persephone, Queen of the Underworld, gone in the face of my mother's pain. Carefully, I extracted my arms from her grip to wrap them around her shoulder, squeezing her tight.

"I missed you so much," I whispered, stroking her head like she had done so often to soothe me. "Don't cry, Mother. Please don't cry."

"I thought he'd never let you go. I thought I'd never see you again." She sniffed loudly, and I tensed as I felt a ripple of icy rage flow over me, my mother's magic at her most dangerous. "Look at you! What are you *wearing*? I will never forgive him for what he has done. I will never let Hades rest for this."

"Mother..."

"Demeter," Hermes interrupted, arcing gracefully before landing next to us. "Persephone has eaten the food of the underworld. As per the Fates' decree, she must return to that realm. Six months of each year for each pomegranate seed consumed."

"No," Mother whispered, eyes wide with horror. "Kore—her name is *Kore*. Darling, tell me you didn't."

It was easy when I was curled up in her arms to be *that* Kore again. To be meek and quiet, to pretend that I didn't have goals and wants of my own. But I wouldn't disrespect myself and the progress I'd made by shying away now.

With all the courage I possessed, I pulled away from the mother who'd given me everything, given *up* everything for me, and climbed to my feet, reaching my hand down to help her up. With a wary expression, she slid her palm into mine, pushing up to stand and gripping my hand tightly in both of hers.

"Kore. Tell me honestly, darling. Whatever you've done, we can fix it. Just tell us what it is." Mother gestured toward a woman who was waiting nearby, one I didn't recognize. She had dark brown skin, inked almost completely with long scrawling lines of script, her black hair twisted into tight coils and piled high on her head. She was certainly striking and looked nothing like the nymphs my mother usually spent time with. "This is Hecate, Goddess of Magic, among other things. She has been instrumental in finding you, I could never have done it without her. We searched every corner of the world for you. We can fix this."

"I don't need you to fix anything, Mother," I told her softly. "I willingly ate those seeds. I grew the pomegranate with my own hands. You want me to be Kore here and I'm happy to be Kore. But I'm also Persephone, Queen of the Underworld. I *will* spend time there, not because I'm a prisoner, but because I have a role there. Responsibilities. And my love, my *husband*, he's there too."

"No—"

"*Yes*. I know you're angry at Hades, but I hope you can look past that for my sake, Mother. For the sake of any children—" I pushed on, ignoring the noise of horror she made at that. "—we might have. I love him, Mother, and he loves me."

"It's too late for you to swear the oath?" she asked, a little desperately.

"Far too late for that," I agreed, thankful that the option was no longer on the table. Mother let out a slightly anguished sound. "It wasn't... Mother, it was like you and Iasion. I wanted it. I wanted him."

"I witnessed their marriage, and their love for each other myself, Demeter," Hermes volunteered. "And whether you believe that they care for each other or not, the fact remains that Kore will need to spend half the year there, regardless."

"Who's to say he'll let her leave?" Mother snapped, glaring at Hermes as though this was all his fault somehow.

"Hades doesn't *let* me do anything," I replied primly. "We're equals."

Mother scoffed.

"I will deliver Kore to and from the underworld personally," Hermes said smoothly. "At least until we can all trust that Hades is true to his word."

I shot the messenger god a withering look, and he shrugged unapologetically in response before shooting back into the air. "I need to update Zeus, but I'm sure he'll be very pleased with this outcome. See you in six months, Kore."

Mother was still shaking her head in denial, and I knew that this argument wouldn't be resolved overnight. Only time, repeated trips between realms where she saw me come and go freely, would convince her that Hades' intentions were honorable. As frustrating as it would be for me to hear Hades' integrity questioned, it was inevitable. He had kidnapped me, after all.

"Hecate," Mother pleaded, her grip tightening on me nearly to the point of pain. "Surely there is some dark magic you know that can fix this."

Hecate gave my mother a sympathetic look. "You would need to talk to the Fates, Demeter. It's their rule. Though I've been looking for a permanent home and I imagine I could find a comfortable spot in the underworld, should the queen be good enough to accommodate me."

I blinked at her. I supposed that would be within my power as queen.

"I won't have you in my realm to spy on me," I replied instantly, even as the empty expanse of The Restless Dead came to mind. It seemed like the kind of place that *needed* leadership, and a few more deities in the underworld would be useful if they were actually willing to work.

Hecate's lips twitched. "I would merely watch over you as a friend of your mother's, and perhaps one day, yours."

"I'm sure we can come to an agreement, so long as your loyalties are to the underworld."

To my surprise, my mother burst out laughing, though it was a slightly hysterical sound. "Oh my, Kore, how *regal* you sound."

It was a patronizing compliment, and I nearly fell back into my usual habit of letting her comments slide, knowing that they usually came from a place of love and concern. But that was the old Kore. I'd come too far in my journey to return to being *that* Kore now.

"I *am* regal. With or without your approval, I am the Queen of the Underworld. I know you despise Hades, and perhaps you always will, but you won't disrespect him, the underworld, or my place within it if you wish to have a relationship with your daughter."

Mother gaped at me while Hecate grinned rather maniacally. *She'd probably get along with Mnemosyne*, I thought to myself. They both had that slightly deranged look in their eyes.

"I'd like to spend my six months of each year in the upperworld with you, Mother. I missed you, and I adore you. I love my siblings, and I don't want to be parted from them. But I'm a goddess in my own right now. If I'm not welcome in your home as I am, I'll visit Olympus myself and request a home there from Zeus instead."

"No," Mother said quickly, looking on the verge of tears. "No, I don't want that, Kore. I don't want to lose you any more than I've already lost you."

"You *haven't* lost me. I'll always be your daughter. I can't imagine how difficult it is to send your children out into the world, knowing the dangers that exist there, but there comes a point where it's crueler to hide them away than to let them find their own path in life."

My voice wavered slightly, despite my attempts at sounding sure of myself. Standing up to my mother was still one of the hardest things I'd ever had to do.

"How wise you've become," Mother murmured, gently stroking my cheek. I leaned into the gesture, since those words sounded genuine. "I wouldn't have chosen this life for you, and I can't say that I'm happy with it, but I'm not willing to risk spending even *less* time with you."

It wasn't quite the glowing approval that I couldn't help but hope for, but it was something. It was progress.

"Come, let's go home," Mother said, pulling on my hand. "Despoina has been distraught since you left, and the twins have caused nothing but chaos. We were lost without you, Kore. It's so good to have you home."

THREE MONTHS LATER

I walked arm-in-arm with Despoina along the edge of the new sanctuary at Eleusis, a wild explosion of narcissus flowers blooming in my wake, filling the place with color.

"You have your own temple," Despoina teased, nudging me as we passed a relief depicting both Mother and me, either side of a young boy. Mother was providing him with wheat, while I had my hand on his shoulder, offering my blessing.

"It's not really for me," I pointed out. It was for... us. Mother and me. My return had brought with it renewal, growth, *food*. Mortals were very grateful for food.

They'd even come up with a name for it. They called me the *Goddess of Spring*. Demeter had made it known to anyone who'd listen that she would mourn every second of my absence, that little would grow in her despair, but the ever optimistic mortals had chosen not to focus on that. They spoke of renewal, and growth, and rebirth.

"It makes it easier to return here," I told Despoina. "Knowing that my presence actually heralds something good."

She glanced at me in surprise. "I didn't realize it was a hardship. You miss the underworld that much?"

"I do." I smiled softly, looking at the brilliant yellow flowers of Hades I'd planted everywhere. "I love my husband, I miss him every single day. I miss my life there, my friends, my role. But when I was there, I missed you all too."

Despoina rested her head against my shoulder for a moment. "I'm not sure that I care much for marriage, but I'm definitely never going to marry for anything less than the love you have for Hades."

"*Good*," I said firmly. "I'm glad Mother didn't force you to marry, in the end."

"She would have if you hadn't disappeared," Despoina laughed. "It was fortunate for me that finding you captured all of her attention."

"You'll never be forced to marry," I told her decisively. While I'd done my best to be respectful of my mother's authority since my return, I'd also let her know in no uncertain terms that Despoina would be welcome in the underworld if her wishes weren't being respected here.

"I'm grateful for you," Despoina replied, giving my arm a quick squeeze. "I don't think Mother would have actually gone through with it, or sent you away to Artemis' temple either. She panicked that night and reacted poorly."

I hummed noncommittally, tipping my face upward and relishing the warmth of sunshine on my skin. Despoina had found her place here at Eleusis, a key figure in the worship that occurred here. It gave her the sense of importance she'd always craved, and her relationship with Mother had improved accordingly. *Of the two of us, now I was the less pliable one,* I thought wryly.

"Come on, let's go find the twins," I suggested. "By the time I return after my next trip to the underworld, they'll be fully grown and off living their own lives. I don't want to miss out on any more memories with all of you than I have to."

CHAPTER 25

THREE MONTHS LATER

"Today's session is complete," Keuthonymos called, dispersing the petitioners. "You can line up again tomorrow if you wish to speak with the King of the Underworld. Remember that while the Queen is in residence, session times may be shorter."

I nodded at him in thanks, striding out of the throne room and down the palace steps. While the months immediately after Persephone's departure had been busier than usual with all the dead we still had to contend with, I'd worked with Keuthonymos recently to better structure my time, in order to devote more of it to Persephone when she was in the underworld.

I wanted my nights free. I wanted to spend them in her bed. I never wanted to miss a single one while she was here.

I whistled for the chariot to take me to the Port of Charon, close to smiling at my courtiers out of pure joy. Today was the day she was returning home, if all went to plan.

True to my word, I hadn't watched her through the lake at all during her absence. A glimpse of her face would have meant everything, but maybe she'd been right to tell me not to. Otherwise, I might have stood in the Forest of Persephone all day, waiting for the briefest flash of her smile.

Usually, to an immortal, six months would pass in the blink of an eye. In the span of *eons*, it was such a short space of time that it was hardly worth mentioning. But six months without Persephone felt like centuries, and I expected that six months *with* her would pass in mere moments.

The chariot took me to the port, the horses more excited than usual, though they were nothing compared to Kerberos, who was darting back and forth like a pup, skidding to a stop at the end of the ferry before running excitedly back again.

"Calm, Kerberos," I muttered, smoothing my palms down the front of my chiton, secured by a golden pomegranate brooch. "You're going to frighten her."

Kerberos huffed what sounded like a laugh, apparently confident in himself that he wouldn't frighten Persephone. He was probably right—she'd never been afraid of him. That should have been the first sign that she'd grow to love the underworld.

We both looked out over the horizon, the faintest glimpse of Hermes appearing in the distance. As much as I still hated that he had his arms around Persephone, apparently this travel arrangement made Demeter feel better. It wasn't a battle worth fighting for now. So long as I had Persephone to myself while she was here, the Olympians could make whatever edicts they liked between them. It was all a farce, a way of making them feel more in control over a situation that had been completely out of their control.

Hermes deposited Kore on the bank in front of me, immediately turning around and flying back across the Styx. Persephone's expression lit up the moment she saw me, a beaming smile taking over her entire face, and a knot of tension I didn't know I'd been carrying loosened.

Perhaps I'd been more worried than I was willing to admit that she might have changed her mind about me in the time she was away.

"Husband," she breathed, throwing herself into my arms the moment she was within reach. "I've missed you."

I gathered her up against me, hauling her off the ground and burying my face in her shoulder. "My life is meaningless without you."

Persephone burst into tears.

I held her tighter, a little bewildered. That hadn't been the response I was going for at all.

"I was worried you'd get sick of waiting for me and change your mind," Persephone sniffed.

"Never," I replied vehemently. "You know if it were my choice, I'd never let you go, but I'm grateful for the time with you I have. I will *always* count down the days until you return, Persephone."

I sealed my mouth to hers, uncaring of who was watching as my tongue swept against hers, groaning at the sweet taste of her. Persephone's hands tangled in my hair, yanking at my head roughly as she kissed me back with all the passion I felt for her, her thighs coming up to wrap around my hips, squeezing me tightly.

It had been so long. *So* long. It took everything in me not to shove both our chitons to the side and enter her hot, welcoming body right here in front of my court.

"I love you," she gasped, breaking away, her chest rising and falling heavily.

"I love you. I'd like to show you how much, ideally in bed," I replied, pulling her body more tightly against me.

Persephone laughed, leaning back and wiping her eyes. "Hold on, we have a guest coming first. Hermes will be back with her in a moment."

I barely suppressed my groan of irritation. I didn't want a guest, I wanted Persephone.

If it was Demeter, I was going to leave her at the gate with Kerberos and take Persephone back to the palace anyway.

While it had been a long time since I'd seen Demeter, I knew the goddess Hermes deposited on the banks of the Styx before taking off again wasn't her. This goddess was dark energy and a general contempt for the world. There was no fear in her eyes as she looked at me, just pure disdain.

It wasn't like I was excited to meet her either.

Persephone unwrapped her legs from my waist and wriggled down my front, reminding my body again of just how long it had been since I'd felt her flesh beneath my hands. She rested her palms on my chest, looking up at me with slightly apologetic watery eyes.

"This is Hecate, daughter of Perses and Asteria." A daughter of Titans. Interesting.

"The Goddess of Magic, Witchcraft, Ghosts, Necromancy, among other things," Hecate added while she looked around the place, pressing into one of the many runes on her arm before brushing her fingers over another on her neck. Two familiars materialized at her side—a polecat who immediately scampered up her body to perch on Hecate's shoulder, and an enormous black dog which sat obediently at her feet.

Kerberos' three heads sniffed the air, examining the newcomer lazily, before deciding that it was apparently no threat and turning his attention to nuzzling Persephone's back.

"Hecate would like to make a home here, in the underworld," Persephone explained, reaching behind her to scratch one of Kerberos' chins. "Partly to be a companion to me, though also to watch over me as a friend of Demeter's. We've grown close over the past few months, and I believe she is here for my interests, rather than my mother's."

There was a slight edge of warning to my queen's voice that had Hecate's mouth twitching in amusement. "You can rest assured that my loyalties are with you."

"Well, we can always send you back if they're not," Persephone replied mildly. "Perhaps Keuthonymos would be so good as to find Hecate somewhere suitable to stay. I was thinking The Restless Dead could use a divine presence to center them, and there's plenty of space there to build a home."

That was a very good idea from a very brilliant queen. Keuthonymos stepped forward, with a beaming smile I'd never seen before in the centuries we'd worked together, to introduce himself to Hecate.

Persephone was already dragging me back toward the chariot. "Let's go. I am *long* overdue to spend some time with my husband."

The chariot deposited us on the palace steps, and we ran through the corridors holding hands like errant juveniles, Persephone laughing the entire way, as did the courtiers who saw us.

There'd been no joy within these walls since Persephone had gone. Her presence here may have brought destruction to the upperworld, but she brought nothing but peace.

I'd already warned Orphne to stay *far* away from Persephone's rooms until we were ready to emerge. The moment I shut the door to the corridor behind me, I had Persephone pushed up against it, my mouth all but devouring hers as she whimpered softly against me, her hands running over every inch of me she could reach.

"I've missed you so much," she panted, deftly unclasping my brooch and undoing my belt to pull my chiton off. I did the same, noting the thin fabric of the garment compared to the heavier woolen chiton she'd been wearing the first time she'd come to the underworld.

"Did your cunt miss me?" I asked, dropping to my knees and throwing her leg over my shoulder, not giving her a moment to respond before burying my head between her thighs. So sweet. So perfect. So mine.

"Yes," Persephone breathed, her shoulders pressed against the door while she arched her back, thrusting her hips into my face. "So much. Every night, I rode my own fingers in bed, craving your cock."

I growled in frustration. "I was going to make you come first, but if you tell me you've been craving my cock, then you're getting my cock."

Within moments, I was standing, Persephone's leg hitched over my hip as I drove forward, impaling her in one thrust. My eyes rolled back, and I nearly came then and there at the feeling of her warm, wet heat gripping my cock.

It felt so overwhelmingly good, that it took me a moment to realize Persephone *did* come. That the tight clasp of her walls around me was actually her finding her release, her nails scratching vicious lines into my skin as her pleasure consumed her.

My hips were moving without conscious thought, drawing out the sensation, my hands gripping her hips hard enough to leave marks. "This was meant to happen on the bed. I was going to take my time with you."

"Take your time with me after," Persephone gasped. "I want to feel you come. I need it."

I really had intended to take my time, and I swore silently that I'd make it up to her afterward as my movements stuttered and I came harder than I ever had in all of my existence.

Persephone tugged my head down to her shoulder, holding me in place and running her fingers through my hair while my mind slowly returned to my body. My cock didn't soften in the slightest, and the moment sensation came back to my limbs, I grabbed her backside and lifted her, carrying her into her bedchamber while we were still joined.

"Oh," Persephone sighed, wrapping her arms around my shoulders. "That feels amazing. I didn't even realize that this would feel amazing. Now I'm going to want you to carry me everywhere like this."

I laughed, pressing my lips to her shoulder. "Don't tempt me, my love. We still have a kingdom to rule, and only I get to see my wife like this."

"Your wife," Persephone sighed dreamily, the sound morphing into a moan of pleasure as I lowered her to the bed, pressing my weight against her as I rolled my hips, ready to see how many times I could make her come before she begged me to stop. "Have I ever told you how grateful I am that you kidnapped me?"

CHAPTER 26

"You are looking very large," Hecate observed, staring at my stomach somewhat distastefully. She wasn't a virgin goddess, but she had absolutely no interest in bearing children.

"I'm feeling very large," I sighed, reclining on the klinai in the sitting room of her palace, located at the fork of the rivers Akeron and Kokytos, at the edge of The Restless Dead. She'd taken charge of them, as I'd known she would, giving them a sense of direction. Even if that sense of direction was using her necromancer gifts to temporarily bring those souls back to the upperworld for ritual haunting purposes.

It made their hundred year wait pass faster, at least.

"You're sure you don't want to hold on a little longer?" she pressed. "Your mother is a fertility goddess. Surely you want her present for the birth of your child."

I shook my head, wondering what Hades was doing outside while he waited for me to reemerge. He and Hecate had a strange sort of friendship. One that flourished when they didn't spend too much time together.

"My daughter," I told Hecate. "I was shown her in a dream. When she's young, she'll travel between realms with me, but once she's grown, she will find her place here in the underworld. She'll look to you for guidance."

Hecate looked both surprised and flattered as I clambered to my feet and linked our arms together, leading her outside.

"Where are we going?" she asked.

"It's time. I had a vision that she would be born at the Kokytos, and that the river god would watch over her alongside you. A true child of the underworld."

Hecate swallowed thickly, gripping me tightly as we descended the steps to the mouth of the river where Hades was waiting, staring up at me in awe. I was a goddess of life, but not of fertility. Mother, in her capacity as a fertility goddess, had assured me that we'd have at least one child, but she couldn't see any beyond that.

Both Hades and I had watched every moment of my pregnancy obsessively, committing it to memory. I'd never been so grateful that immortals grew babies faster than mortals did, so he could witness all of it during my time in the underworld, but taking the baby away from him when she was so young would be agony.

"It's time?" he asked, reading the look on my face. I nodded silently, and he took my other elbow, helping me into the water. I sat on the rocks, the river god present but silent, ready to receive the child he'd sworn to watch over.

Hades sat behind me, his front pressed against my back, and pressed a kiss to my shoulder. "I've already shooed Mnemosyne away three times. Orphne and Akeron are now keeping her imprisoned in his river until the baby is born."

Despite the solemnity of the moment, I laughed, squeezing Hades' forearm in gratitude and leaning my head against his shoulder, letting my eyes fall shut. There was no pain, no discomfort, just the gift of life amongst the realm of death as little Melinoe joined our family. I cradled her in my arms as Hades undid the top of my chiton, baring my breast for her to feed, one of his arms under mine, supporting us both.

"You are a gift," Hades murmured over my shoulder, staring down at our daughter. "You both are. I will never stop being grateful for you, until the world stops turning."

THANK YOU,
READER

If you got this far, let me just say how grateful I am to you for taking a chance on this book. Dead of Spring was a real passion project for me, slightly outside my wheelhouse, and I'm so thankful that you took the time to try it out. Unlike most of my books, which start of as half an idea at best, Dead of Spring was almost fully formed in my mind before I started writing. I wanted to do a fairly true-to-the-myth retelling (with some creative license, of course) and I hope I've pulled it off, and that you enjoyed reading it.

This book wouldn't have happened without the support of some amazing people in my life—firstly, my husband and daughter for their patience with me, especially during the editing process. To my beta team—Rachel, Lucy, and Bridgette—thank you for your understanding while I wrote and rewrote, and constantly changed things around. Your feedback was so helpful in writing this book. My dev editor—Steph from Rawls Reads Author Services, you are a rockstar and I love you, thank you for taking this on so last minute. Jennifer from Bookends Editing, you were such a joy to work with. TS and Rory, thanks for putting up with me and my panic spirals, I'd be lost with you both. To my ARC team and reader group, thank you so much for your support.

I also owe a big thank you to Melissa, who encouraged me to take the leap and write this book in the first place.

For the latest news and teasers, join the Colette Rhodes Facebook Group or subscribe to my newsletter.

Colette x

Also by Colette

SHADES OF SIN

(MF - monster romance)

Luxuria

Suberbia

STATE OF GRACE:

Run Riot

Silver Bullet

Wild Game

Dare Not

State of Grace #5

THREE BEARS DUET:

Gilded Mess

Golden Chaos

LITTLE RED DUET:

Scarlet Disaster

Seeing Red

KNOTTY BY NATURE:

(RH omegaverse with T.S. Snow)

Allure Part 1

Allure Part 2

EMPATH FOUND:

The Terrible Gift

The Unwanted Challenge

The Reluctant Keeper

DEADLY DRAGONS:

The (Not) Cursed Dragon

The (Not) Satisfied Dragon

STANDALONE:

Dead of Spring (MF)

Blood Nor Money (RH)

Fire & Gasoline (MF)

Colette Rhodes

ROMANCE AUTHOR

www.ingramcontent.com/pod-product-compliance
Lightning Source LLC
Chambersburg PA
CBHW051138190726
48290CB00006B/1892